MARGOT

OTHER BOOKS BY

WENDELL STEAVENSON

Paris Metro: A Novel

Circling the Square: Stories from the Egyptian Revolution

*The Weight of a Mustard Seed: The Intimate Story of an Iraqi General
and His Family During Thirty Years of Tyranny*

Stories I Stole

MARGOT

A NOVEL

WENDELL STEAVENSON

W. W. NORTON & COMPANY
Celebrating a Century of Independent Publishing

This is a work of historical fiction. Apart from the well-known actual people, events, and locales that figure in the narrative, all names, characters, places, and incidents are the products of the author's imagination or are used fictitiously. Any resemblance to current events or locales, or to living persons, is entirely coincidental.

Copyright © 2023 by Wendell Steavenson

All rights reserved
Printed in the United States of America
First Edition

For information about permission to reproduce selections from this book, write to Permissions, W. W. Norton & Company, Inc., 500 Fifth Avenue, New York, NY 10110

For information about special discounts for bulk purchases, please contact W. W. Norton Special Sales at specialsales@wwnorton.com or 800-233-4830

Manufacturing by Lake Book Manufacturing
Book design by Barbara M. Bachman
Production manager: Anna Oler

ISBN 978-1-324-02084-4

W. W. Norton & Company, Inc., 500 Fifth Avenue, New York, N.Y. 10110
www.wwnorton.com

W. W. Norton & Company Ltd., 15 Carlisle Street, London W1D 3BS

1 2 3 4 5 6 7 8 9 0

For my brothers, Misha and Xander.
A sister could ask for none better.

CONTENTS

PART

ONE

—

BEGINNING

1

MARGOT PULLED HERSELF UP. THE RUNGS OF THE ROPE ladder sagged under her Mary Janes. Don't look down! Below, the mossy planks of the old treehouse; above the blue sky, laced with leaves. Stevie said there was a nest with three blue eggs inside. The trunk of the oak was crumpled up and hollowed with squirrel hidey-holes. Catkins, dangling yellow and powdery, splotched her hands like finger paint. The leaves made whispering sounds like the seashore. Some of the leaves had ragged edges, Margot saw a fat caterpillar with green stripes eating them. She reached out to touch his soft bristles. A gust of wind blew up. The rope ladder swayed and banged against the trunk, her knuckles scraped on the bark and Margot let go—felt herself fall. Heard a loud CRACK, right inside her head.

Her first thought was: Perhaps I am dead now and Mother will be mad at me for gallivanting. But then Margot realized her thoughts were still thinking, so she must be alive. She began to count to ten for when the pain came, but by the time she got to six, her vision blacked out.

Assessing this development, Margot wondered if she could stand. Her mother would be furious if she had gone blind and had to miss Trip Merryweather's birthday party. She tried to sit up, but felt seasick. If she threw up, her mother would say she had done it on purpose because she didn't want to go to the party. She spread out her palms to steady herself. The stone path was cold to touch. She put one hand up to her face, it was warm and sticky. "Help!" Tried again to shout, more urgently, "HELP!" But the Big House was on the other side of the hill, it was unlikely anyone could hear. She decided to try and crawl.

Her fingers grubbed between the flagstones of the old path, knotted roots, mulchy leaves, dirt. Shuffled slowly on all fours, grazing her knees on twigs and acorn caps. The very dark behind her eyelids began to lighten reddish, then dissolved into a blur as her vision cleared. The sky fizzed.

She managed to limp back and push open the great big front door. Her mother was standing in the hall, sorting the pile of mail on the silver salver. A diamond flashed on her finger, the hardest of all minerals; her carmine lipstick drew a thin red line, her hair was lacquered into a Trojan helmet. She turned and stopped.

"*Margot*! Oh for heaven's *sake*!"

Margot looked down and saw that her new dress was ruined with mud and blood. She felt the fear-tears gathering and pressed her lips together tightly to stop them from falling.

"Don't make that *face* at me, young lady!" Her mother encircled her neck with her hand and tilted her head backwards to inspect the damage.

"Nanny Hastings!"

Nanny Hastings appeared in all haste.

"Look at the state of the *child*! Her dress is a write-off and her hair looks like she's been dragged backwards through a *hedge*."

Her mother's fingernails pinched like clothespins. Margot felt her nose fill up, stinging, briny.

"Margot, I have told you before about your *selfish* behavior. You are eight years old. Old enough to know better! And Nanny Hastings, I have made it very clear she is not to go running off like some kind of feral *goat*."

"But Mrs. Thornsen, children need fresh air and—"

Margot watched her mother's nostrils flare.

She said, "It was my fault, Mama, I wasn't thinking."

"You never think! You never think of anyone but *yourself*!"

Nanny Hastings opened her mouth but no sound came out.

"Take the child upstairs and clean her up." Her mother looked at her watch. "I've told James to bring the car around at ten to three *sharp*."

Margot put her quivering hand in Nanny's. Her shoes squeaked on the marble hall where she was not allowed to play hopscotch on the multicolored squares, past the bronze Nubian, through the swinging door into the servants' wing.

"Am I in trouble?"

"Don't worry you," said Nanny Hastings. "We'll get you ship-shape in a toddle." She laid a cool palm against Margot's forehead. "That's quite a bump. If you're lucky, you'll have a proper black-and-blue shiner to show off to those hooligan Merryweathers."

AS MUCH AS MARGOT loved exploring, as much as she was brave when it came to climbing trees or balancing atop stone walls, she was as wobbly as Jell-O in society. Lots of people in a room all together made her hang back, hug pillars, hide behind curtains, want to disappear. She could never think of the right thing to say, her words mumble-stumbled, her voice dropped to a hesitant whisper. Grown-ups patted her head distractedly, yes-yes and went back to talking about Russkies and Reds. The other kids didn't reply to the questions she had so carefully prepared—What are your top five books? Who is your favorite explorer of all time? Where would you go if you could go anywhere in the world?—but only snorted, snotted, stuck their tongues out, pulled her hair, ran around in circles playing games she didn't understand.

Trip was the youngest of the four Merryweather brothers who lived at Sage Hill, the estate next door. Firstborn were the twins, Runny and Dick. Trip had named his brother Runny when he was

a baby because he couldn't say Rutherford properly and now everyone called him that. Margot was disappointed that Runny and
Dick were only fraternal twins because she had never seen identical
twins. Runny was older by five minutes and, everyone agreed, the
handsome one, who had inherited the protuberant Whitney eyes
from his mother and had an asymmetrical pucker of a harelip scar.
The twins were six years older than her, and Margot didn't like
Runny because he was mean. Once he put a pinecone on her chair
at a lunch party and then laughed when she yowled and her mother
had told her off in front of everyone. Another time he made her
dress up in his mother's evening dresses and call him "my lord."
Dick was nicer but he was always up in his room reading. Margot
liked reading too and one time she asked him, "What are your top
five books?" but he only said, "Oh, they are all sci-fi and you won't
have heard of them."

Hal came next but everyone called him weirdo or oddball or goo-
fus. He tried to suck up to Runny, but Runny mocked his big head
and big cow eyes and sent him on impossible "missions." Whatever
was broken—which was many things with four boys tearing about
that big old house full of porcelain tchotchkes—Hal got blamed
and was made to take his punishment without complaint, according
to the rule of "fagging," which Runny had picked up reading *Tom
Brown's School Days.*

Terrence Romney Merryweather, Trip, was the spoiled tow-
haired baby of the family, angel-imp, dimpled, always smiling,
never chastised. Even as a small child he had the natural confidence of the adored one who could do no wrong. Margot wanted
to be his friend, but he was friends with everyone. Sometimes, if
she was lucky, she found herself alone with him. These felt like
warmly spotlit moments. With so many brothers and cousins
around all the time, they were few. Once they sat in the conserva-
tory and played backgammon and ate a whole box of Oreo cookies
Trip stole from the larder. Once Trip let her play pirates with his
grandfather's real cavalry sword and had just laughed when she

sliced a gash in the damask curtains. "Don't worry, we can blame Hal for it."

Once he had been the first to find her hiding in the linen closet playing sardines.

"Come and see what I've got in my trouser pocket."

She looked and saw his wormy peter nestling in his jockey shorts.

"Ew, gross."

"Don't even think about touching it," Trip told her, as if it were a great prize. "You'll give me cooties."

THE BAND-AID NANNY HASTINGS had stuck over the cut on her eyebrow pulled the skin and made her wince. James the chauffeur drove Margot and her mother down their long tree-lined driveway, a few hundred yards along Skunk's Misery Road and then back up another long tree-lined driveway.

"We don't 'do' sick," said her mother. "I am sure Trip would be very disappointed if you were not there. Such a darling boy. A good catch for a mousy girl like you."

How do you catch a boy, Margot wondered, was it like softball? Was that why she had to wear special itchy gloves?

The car pulled up beside the familiar colonnade of white pillars. Margot thought Sage Hill looked as romantic as Tara from *Gone with the Wind*, her mother derided the architecture as cookie-cutter neo-Colonial. Her dress felt tight across her chest. Her head pounded. She was thirsty. Margot always dreaded birthday parties. "Stand up straight," said her mother, running a fingernail down her spine. "Run along now and join in!" Joining-in was terribly important, but Margot could not understand the mechanism of it.

"Heya Pinecone!" Trip called out, running around the lawn after Hal. The boys were roughhousing, shirttails untucked. The girls stood to one side and Margot noticed, with a familiar dismay, that none of them were wearing white gloves. She suddenly hated her

stiff-starched sailor dress; Lydia Cummings had pretty pink roses
on her skirt, and Bernie Pratt was wearing knickerbockers!

Her mother walked briskly towards the other mothers, calling
out "Hallo hallo hallo!" in her distinctive treble that could famously
carry across the acre of ballroom at the Sherry-Netherland.

"I don't know what I did to deserve such a *tomboy*! Margot fell out
of a tree and gave herself a black eye. Run along, dear"—her mother
pushed her away—"go and make nice with darling Trip," and then
turned to Dotty Merryweather, "Aren't they just adorable together!"

Margot trotted off towards the gathering knot of children. The
party entertainer, dressed up like a cowboy with a ten-gallon hat,
was dividing them into pairs. She got Hal.

"Geez Louise!" said Hal, pointing at her black eye. "Did you get
in a fight with your boyfriend Stevie?"

Margot opened her mouth to deny it, but was swept with a wave
of nausea. She doubled over and vomited all over his feet.

The mothers arrived in a clucking clutch.

"What happened?"

"Poor dear."

"Hal Merryweather! What have you done now?"

Hal was wiping his spattered shoes on the grass, laughing and
pointing.

"She came! She saw! She spewed!"

Margot looked up at her mother, who was pursing her lips in
disgust and irritation. "Now I suppose *I'll* have to take her to Dr.
Dome."

Then the sky turned white. Margot's knees buckled and, with a
soft crunch, she fainted onto the gravel.

MARGOT'S CHILDHOOD DREW A chauffeured loop between the
family estate of Farnsworth and her parents' apartment at 655 Park
Avenue. Back then, before the Long Island Expressway was built,
the grand New York families traveled to their country estates on the

North Shore, leaving the Manhattan grid via the 59th Street Bridge and following Northern Boulevard through the low-rise suburbs of Queens to the flat farmland beyond which it became the Hempstead Turnpike; turn right for the Phippses at Old Westbury, left for the Vanderbilts and the Guggenheims in their Gold Coast mansions, or continue on to the Teddy Roosevelts in Oyster Bay. Margot usually got carsick around Little Neck, where the clams came from.

In the city, Margot's bedroom window was at the back and faced a gray brick air shaft. But at the Big House in the country her bedroom had a view of the rose garden and a turquoise stripe of swimming pool.

"It's the largest private swimming pool in the world," Margot told Lydia Cummings on the first day of first grade.

"My mother says it's not polite to boast," said Lydia Cummings.

Perhaps Margot's reticence was the result of this early social trauma, perhaps it was a reaction to her mother's resounding loudness, maybe it was just natural recalcitrance. But she would not learn this word until the finals of the third-grade spelling bee. Lydia Cummings was the most popular girl at the Chapin School, surrounded by acolytes who wore their kneesocks falling down and talked endlessly about sleepovers and ponies. First grade and second grade, Margot shared a desk with Bernie Pratt; best friends according to proximity. But over this past year Bernie had shed her puppy fat, insisted on being called Bernadette, and dropped Margot like a rotten apple when she was invited to Lydia's for a tea party.

Winter was dark early mornings, clammy school corridors, do your homework, practice the piano, brush your teeth, bedtime seven-thirty. Winter was icy wind that cut like knives down the avenues, rain and splash from trucks dunking in the potholes, muggy fuggy updraft from subway vents. Her mother went through nannies like sheer stockings. A crabbity German woman who smelled of mothballs, a blowsy blonde her mother dismissed as "that floozy from Manhasset." One was Scotch, like the drink Mr. Merryweather drank, with reddish hair, so that for a long time Margot thought

Scotch was a color, not a country. Natalie from Montreal was the nicest; she took her skating in Central Park and to see the mummies at the Metropolitan Museum. (They were not real mummies; they were dead bodies preserved in formaldehyde and myrrh, which is a kind of hardened resin and one of the gifts the wise men gave the baby Jesus.) But Natalie fell in love with a dentist and moved to New Jersey. Nanny Hastings came from England, wore a brown uniform, and did not like candy, humidity, or dogs, but on the other hand she read stories at bedtime and Margot liked falling asleep to the sound of her voice.

Margot was an only child, she had no companion or comparison. She had once overheard Nanny Hastings tell Mrs. Hanna, the housekeeper at 655, "Mrs. T is too hard on the poor girl," but she had thought she was referring to the new laundry maid who had recently ruined one of her father's shirts. Her mother was implacably her mother. Peggy to her friends, Mrs. Harrison Vanderloep Thornsen to the world, a woman polished to a high gloss, who knew how to run a house, gave the most marvelous parties. "Raving perfectionist, competitive to the point of a fish fork tine," Margot overheard Mrs. Cummings saying to Dotty Merryweather once. "She judges every smudge on your silver."

It was true that her mother could spot a fingerprint on a knife blade at twenty paces. "Don't touch that, Margot!" Her mother moved through the world making as little physical contact with it as possible. When she kissed a woman hello, she kissed the air beside her cheek. When she greeted a man, she proffered her hand limply, so that he was obliged to press the ends of her fingers instead of taking her palm in his and shaking it. When Margot tried to hug her, her mother arched away and kept her on the edge of her knees; Margot was not allowed to settle in the comfortable recess of her lap. After a few minutes of perching, her mother would set her down, "That's enough."

Of her father, Harrison Thornsen, Margot knew even less. He was a father-shaped man who came in from work at six o'clock, stowed his hat in the front hall closet, stopped at the bar to pour a balloon glass of his apple brandy, went into the den, closed the door, and watched the evening news on the television. On weekends he played golf. He was a remote being, far off, like Pluto. "How's it all going in school, Margot? Are you valedictorian yet?" He tousled her hair and said, "Good night, don't let the bedbugs bite." He smelled of cologne, cigars, and wet leather. His shirts had his monogram embroidered on the pocket. He worked at Grand Old King's corporation, United Union Steel, on the forty-second floor of the Pan Am Building. Last Christmas Margot had saved up her pocket money and bought him a silk handkerchief from Brooks Brothers.

Margot's birthday was May 8. "Victory Day!" as her father liked to remind her every year. "Got the telegram right after that Hun general surrendered to Old Blood and Guts Patton, and we stood about, at ease, not even saluting. They locked him in the butcher's shop and my sergeant found a case of French brandy—and boy, did we go to town on that town—"

"Harrison! Enough war story-ing!" said her mother, cutting through with a cake slice. "We've heard it all before."

Margot couldn't imagine her father as a soldier. His military tunic was hung up inside a dry cleaner's paper sheath at the back of his closet. The wool felt thick and rough. Once, in the pocket she found a small brown glass jar, the kind that ointments came in. Margot unscrewed the lid and a trickle of sand poured out; she had to brush it around the carpet so that no one would notice.

Her parents were usually out in the evenings: cocktail parties, charity balls, galas at the Met. When they hosted dinner parties, Margot was required to come and say good night to everyone in her dressing gown and slippers. The ladies sparkled with diamonds and the mirrors twinkled reflections from the chandelier. "Do *smile*, Margot!" her mother would say, pushing her forward. Margot tried very hard to be polite and grown-up. She was careful to do as she was told. Please and no, thank-you-very-much. Shake hands and curtsy. Best behavior. Mind your manners like a young lady.

In the winter they went to the Big House in the country for Thanksgiving and Christmas and Easter. In June, when school got out, Margot and her nanny were packed off to Farnsworth for the duration of the summer. Her mother arrived for July 4th and stayed through Labor Day; her father came out on weekends. Her grandmother, Marguerite Fantasia Vanderloep, known to all as "Goody," lived at Farnsworth all year round. Margot thought Goody must be a hundred years old. Her skin was like silk stockings fallen down at the ankle. The lace edge of her blouses ruffled against the slack skin of her neck and smelled of lily of the valley. She was blind in one eye and deaf in one ear and wore a wig. When Margot kissed her, white talcum puffed into the air like a powdery halo. Everyone whispered her name behind her back, but to her face, on account of her deafness, they shouted. Margot saw that everything happened because of her grandmother, but that her grandmother did nothing. Perhaps Goody was the Wizard of Oz.

"I THINK YOUR DAUGHTER is concussed." Dr. Dome's voice was doomy-boomy, far away. "She'll need an X-ray." Margot's eyelids itched. "Ah, now she's waking up." Dr. Dome was looking at her but talking to her mother, who was sitting in the chair by the door, smoking a cigarette. Margot's head was hammers and daggers, her arms heavy lead pipes. Worse, she realized, mortified and goose-flesh, she was completely naked under a gaping paper gown.

"Where are my clothes?" she asked.

"Don't whine," said her mother, and Margot stifled her sob.

Dr. Dome loomed above, shadowed by the penlight that he beamed right into her eyeballs. "Lie back now and I'll put the stitches in. Don't move or you'll make me jolt and you'll get a scar." Margot gripped the edge of the vinyl gurney and crossed her legs for privacy. "Lie flat," Dr. Dome insisted. The needle stung like the bejesus, as Mrs. Hanna would have said. Margot bit her lip, tears rolling down the sides of her temples and collecting in her ears.

Afterwards, in the waiting room, waiting to have the X-ray, shivery, exposed, forehead throbbing, her mother gone to berate the nurse for the delay, Margot picked up a newspaper and read that Watson and Crick had discovered the shape of DNA.

She didn't understand the words: *deoxyribonucleic, defraction,* or *double helix*; it was the diagram accompanying the article that caught her eye because it looked like the twisted-up rope ladder she had fallen off. She traced the elegant ellipses with her fingertip, headache receding, counting-climbing the looping rungs, turning around the turns in her mind as they wheeled her through to the X-ray room, where the technician told her to close her eyes and count to ten, counting-climbing, still looking for the blue eggs laid by a bluebird that flew upside down in a blue sky—

"WHY IS THE SKY blue?"

"Because it reflects the sea," said her mother without looking up from her breakfast.

"Why is the sea blue?"

Her mother put down her knife with a clatter, "Oh Margot, stop asking *questions*." Margot reached up and felt the knotted threads above her eyebrow. "And stop touching your stitches. You'll make a scar."

"Like Daddy," said Margot. Her father's scar was on his thigh, a pink plastic crater near the tan line of his bathing trunks.

"Scars can give a man character, but they are *ruinous* for a woman's looks," said her mother. Margot scraped the cold, hard butter against her scratchy toast. "The sky is blue because of the earth's atmosphere," said her mother after a pause.

"Is that so, dear?" said her father, squinting at his wife over the top of his *Wall Street Journal*. "I just thought it was one of those unanswerable questions. Like the chicken and the egg."

"What about the egg?" asked Margot.

"It's nothing to do with any egg," said her mother.

"Well, I could do with an egg," said her father, looking down at his empty plate.

Margot knew there weren't any eggs because it was Saturday and Mrs. Ambrose's day off. On Saturday at Farnsworth, there was only cornflakes and toast.

"What is the earth's atmosphere?" asked Margot.

"Margot, do *stop*! You would try the patience of a *saint*."

"Here's one for you, Margot," said her father, trying to lighten the tone. "Why did the chicken cross the road?"

Margot knitted her brows together to think, but frowning made her stitches pull.

"To look for the egg?" The egg was somehow important.

"Ha-ha!" Her father ruffled her hair.

"To get to the other side," answered her mother wearily.

Margot did not risk asking again "Why?" even though it seemed odd for a chicken to want to cross a road. Later, Stevie told her it was a joke, but she still didn't really get it.

She didn't get, either, why the sky was blue if it reflected the sea. Because sometimes the sky was gray and the sea was greenish, and sometimes the sky was baby blue and the sea was navy blue. And when you took a bottle of seawater, it was just as see-through as tap water, which was just as see-through as air.

Mrs. Ambrose told her: "And while you're chewing this notion of yours like a cow on cud, don't be forgetting the Red Sea which is red and the Black Sea which is black and the Dead Sea which is all white and encrusted with salt."

"It depends which way you're looking at," James the chauffeur explained gravely, as if he was measuring out a larger truth. "Blue is like beauty, everyone sees it their own way."

None of their answers made sense. In the bath Margot pulled her head under the surface and opened her eyes and saw a pale blue blur. She put her eye just at the water level and saw the blue diminish— or turn gray? she couldn't be sure. From above, the water made her pink legs look alien and greenish. Colors, Margot divined, were not like rainbow crayons, they were more complicated than they appeared, like adults, changeable, possibly untrustworthy.

LIGHT DID NOT PENETRATE the Big House; the curtains were kept drawn against the sun. The east wing had long been shuttered, its furniture draped in dustcovers. Time had collected drifts of spiderwebs in unused corners, mold bloomed in clouds across the ceilings, carpets were rolled up against the walls. The tang of Borax sprinkled over the floor against mice made Margot's nose wrinkle. Margot pulled to unstick warped drawers that rattled with treasure: a silver dollar, a fountain pen with a rusted nib, a single sapphire earring.

Nanny Hastings had been given her notice, but it was proving difficult to find a replacement. James let Margot help him wash the old Rolls-Royce that had running boards like Al Capone's. Mademoiselle Mathilde, Goody's ladies' maid, showed her how to powder her nose but the swan's-down puff made her sneeze. Mrs. Ambrose, who had cooked at the Big House since the days of Old King Vanderloep, slapped her knuckles with a dishcloth when she caught her stealing sugar lumps, but let her listen to the coronation of Queen Elizabeth the Second on her radio in the pantry.

Her mother took her to the hair house and instructed that bangs be cut to hide her new pink scar. Now she was allowed outside to play again, "But no running, no climbing, and no tomfoolery with that disgusting boy Stevie!"

Liberated from nannying and invalided out of birthday party duty, Margot had the free swoop of the woods, the estate's overgrown hunting trails, the gardens and the lawns down to the beach, where she looked for toenail shells and tried to rescue washed-up jellyfish. She stole cherry tomatoes from the kitchen garden, bounced balls on the cracked asphalt tennis court, counted snails in the nasturtium patch by the servants' door. She pulled off cylinders of birch bark to see the beetles beetling underneath. She found a glob of tadpoles in the pond and visited them every day to watch them grow legs and lose their tails and take their first steps out of the water, hop-hop onto the green grass and feel it strange and plop back into the water again. Discoverings gave her a bubbling-up feeling in her chest.

One afternoon Stevie tried to get her to climb down the rusted iron ladder set in the concrete jetty to prize mussels off the rocks below, but Margot got stuck halfway. Her insides twisted up, her mind went blank, she couldn't-wouldn't, never mind how much Stevie yelled lily-livered chicken. Another afternoon, alone, she wanted to pick the high-up apples but she couldn't make herself stand on top of the split-log fence to reach them, even though she had a dozen times before, never thinking twice about it.

"I didn't notice at first," Margot confided to Mrs. Ambrose, piping swirls of sour cream onto the jellied surface of madrilène soups, "but the fall has taken away my heart, like the Lion lost his courage."

"It's part of growing up," Mrs. Ambrose told her, "learning the consequence of things. Anyways, there's a bowl of fruit right there, if you want an apple."

Margot bit into a shiny Red Delicious, but it was mealy and dry.

Maybe this was what Nanny Hastings had meant when she said, "Think before you act." But thinking about the bad thing that could happen—the *con-sequence*—took all the fun out of doing it.

ONCE A MONTH, THE swimming pool, built before the days of filter systems, was drained and scrubbed out with brooms. It was so large it took a whole day to refill. Margot liked to sit cross-legged on the concrete bottom and splash in the gushing pipe and make a game of the rising water level that covered her toes and then her knees and then her belly button until her whole body was lifted up. People are mostly made of water, that's why they float.

One day, when she was swimming, Stevie cannonballed her, and her mother found out.

"If you can't be trusted, I'll have to send you to summer camp," said her mother.

Margot bent her head and prayed to the gods concealed in the carpet knots, Please don't send me away to the mercies of other children.

"I'll be good, I promise."

"Not good enough," said her mother, unmoved by remorse. "I've told Noreen that Stevie is not allowed anywhere near the house or the swimming pool." Her mother pointed with her long, crimson-lacquered nail. "Go to your room and think about how to be a better girl."

Margot crouched on her bed and cried hot tears, hugging her chest to her knees. *Not good enough*, be better. *Not good enough*, be better.

Shame that burned and brined her face was soothed by the ether of sleep. But in sleep, it settled into her tummy, squatted like a toad there, heavy, leaching its heaviness deeper. This new thinking-before-acting didn't seem to stop her from getting into trouble. She still got yelled at for digging with the gardeners, getting under the feet of mean old Jean Craft the cleaning lady, or for watching cartoons on TV with Stevie in his parents' apartment above the stables. Stevie's mother, Nice Noreen, let them even though she wasn't supposed to. Sometimes, when Mother was out playing tennis or bridge at the club, Nice Noreen made hot dogs with melted Velveeta and left them all alone while she went to do the ironing at the Big House.

One overcast afternoon, Stevie filched a set of keys from his father's office and they set off to investigate the haunted corridor on the third floor. Farnsworth was castle, museum, blind doors, dumbwaiters, rooms no one had slept in for forty years. Stevie said there were skeletons in cupboards locked up in the attic, but Margot was pretty sure he was just fooling. They tried the locks of three doors until one opened into a blue sitting room with a grand piano under a cloth covering. On the wall was a portrait of a young blond woman wearing a straw boater and holding a white rose on her lap.

"That must be Long-Gone Sarah," said Stevie.

"My mother's sister," said Margot, testing the words "my aunt" out loud.

"She was the one who fell in love with a cobbling Jewboy," said Stevie, all-knowing. "And Old King was so mad he cut off her head without a penny."

"My mother says family matters are not for public consumption," said Margot primly.

"Jean Craft says Old King was a tough old bustard who never let anyone cross him. Jean Craft says Sarah had two daughters and they are kept out of sight in a walk-up!"

Margot had no idea what a walk-up was; she imagined a high platform, like the high diving board at the Piping Rock pool, it sounded outlandish.

"Jean Craft is an old busybody and my mother says not to believe a word she says."

Margot had heard of these shadowy cousins in the dipped cadences of grown-up conversations, a distant fairy tale, babes lost in dark woods, a faint shh! on the lips of adults. Now that Stevie had blustered them into real life, she felt somehow guilty, as if she were the unwitting changeling in their place. Stevie ran his finger across the piano keys, clunking thunder notes. Margot juddered, suddenly chilled in the shadow of the wolf.

"Let's blow this pop stand," she said as nonchalantly as she could muster.

"You scared?"

"I'm not scared."

"Are."

"Am not."

"You are too scared! Ever since you banged your head. Like it knocked all the fun out of you."

OCCASIONALLY MARGOT WAS INVITED to tea with Goody. For this honor, she was obliged to put on a smocked party dress. Goody

liked to have tea in the solarium with the mosaic floor that Old
King Vanderloep had copied from a villa in Pompeii. Goody's hand
shook as she poured the tea from a teapot with porcelain butterflies
perched on the lid. Her teacup rattled precariously in its saucer.
Margot held her handle very carefully between thumb and forefinger and watched a painted butterfly appear at the bottom of the cup
as she drank.

Goody said, "When I was a girl, the streets were dirt and there
was no hot water except at the bathhouse. I carried an ivory-handled
pistol against outlaws. The sheriff strung them all up like Thanksgiving turkeys under the hanging tree. Nowadays nothing like
that ever happens and everything is very boring." Margot nodded
in agreement. "Except on the television," continued Goody, "they
seem to have a high old time laughing on the television, although
I don't know what's so funny. Mathilde says the laughter is kept in
a can."

"I'm not allowed to watch television except on weekends," said
Margot.

Goody did not reply. Her head fell back against the lace antimacassar, dislodging her yellow wig so that it hung askew. Her eyes
were closed. Perhaps she had fallen asleep, but she was so still that
is was also possible she had quietly died.

Presently a snore rasped gently. The snore purred and caught on
a snort and stopped. Margot leaned forward in suspense. She summoned the courage to ask, as loudly as she dared, "Goody, are you
alive?"

A blue gleam appeared between ruffled folds of eyelid.

"Yes, I am still alive," said Goody, "no matter my daughter
wishes me not."

Some further moments passed in silence. Goody raised a gold
lorgnette to a bleary cataract eye and peered at the plate of finger
sandwiches.

"I can't abide salmon." She picked up a small silver bell and jingled it. The butler appeared.

"Has Mrs. Ambrose made salmon sandwiches again?" Goody asked him. "I have talked to her about this impertinence before."

"No, they are ham, ma'am, with no mustard."

"Well, that's a mercy. I don't like sneezing."

The butler withdrew.

"Why don't you like sneezing, Goody?"

"Because someone has been stealing my handkerchiefs."

The tapestry seat cushion chafed her bare legs. Margot was mindful that she must not upset her grandmother. Goody alternated between nonsense and naps. While she was still awake Margot risked asking:

"Where did Sarah go?"

Goody sank back into the recesses of her padded chair, her eyes unmoored, adrift.

"It wasn't my fault!" she said, and let out a wail like a low foghorn and began to talk very rapidly in her olden-times voice. "There was blood on my hands because I was wringing the necks of the chickens."

Margot was alarmed. "Goody, are you talking about when you lived back in the Old West? Before civilization?"

"My old pa went to Duluth looking for gold, but all he found was a giant panic. He used to sell china dolls out of an old perambulator by the Stage Tavern but he never gave me one. And then he went and froze to death in the Great Blizzard!"

She looked at Margot tenderly. "Do you like dolls, dear heart? I'll buy you twenty now that I'm as rich as Croesus."

"I like books," said Margot.

"Just like my poor brother Ike," said Goody. "Well, no good ever came of book reading, I'll tell you that for free. Ike had the only microscope in Duluth and he kept his eye over the eyepiece as if it was glued to it."

Goody's voice took on a sinister burr. "It's all in the substrata! Hematite, hematite hematite! But don't tell your precious King! He'd chop off our heads for it! Poor old Ike, he bled out like a stuck pig, but I never believed who the townsfolk whispered whodunit."

"And Sarah?" Margot ventured.

Goody nodded emphatically. "Oh yes, King did for Sarah too!"

OLD KING VANDERLOEP'S LIBRARY in the Big House was enormous, but Margot wasn't allowed to touch the books because she would leave marks with her sticky fingers.

The shelves went up and up in leather-bound volumes stamped with gold lettering. Margot let the books fall, as if by magnetism, into her hand. The pages were thick and full of marvels: unfolding maps, bills of sale from Victorian booksellers, engraved nameplates, pencil marks of forgotten marginalia. She borrowed one at a time; as long as the books were rearranged not to show a gap, no one noticed. *The Decline and Fall of the Roman Empire*, *The Wealth of Nations*, *On the Origin of Species by Means of Natural Selection*, heavy weights that made her wrists ache to hold them up and made her brain ache untangling sentences knitted with subclauses that went back and sideways with Latin in italics, *ibid.*, *ad infinitum*, *et cetera*. But every so often, if she concentrated hard enough, Margot felt an understanding unfurl and flutter out, like a butterfly emerging from a chrysalis, and she smiled to herself at this private reward.

The library had been Old King Vanderloep's special preserve, and the tables were covered in his collection of curios: lumps of shiny geological samples, ores and quartz crystals, a scrimshaw shark tooth, a stuffed puffin with orange wax feet, a narwhal tusk mounted on a silver plinth.

"What a lot of dust-collecting gewgaws," said mean Jean Craft, roaring the vacuum with such violence that she butted the nozzle over Margot's feet. Her hair was scrunched up in curlers under a shower cap, a hand-rolled cigarette stuck to her lower lip.

"In the old days," she continued, "there were fourteen of us maids and we lived in those partition rooms up in the attic—oh! the Old King kept us polishing everything shiny for his swing-dings, never mind all the polishing in the world was never going to unblack the tarnish—"

"DID GOODY GROW UP on a farm?" Margot asked her mother.

"It was different back then."

"Was Ike murdered?" Margot was reading the Agatha Christie novels Nanny Hastings had left behind.

"Your grandmother's stories are all made up."

"Goody says Grandfather King did for Sarah the same as he did for Ike."

"Don't listen to Goody. Her medicine makes her confused."

"Is it true Old King cut her off without a penny?"

"Who told you such things?" Her mother stared into her eyes looking for the culprit.

Margot directed her gaze at the carpet, where there was a pattern of a heron with a fish in its long beak. She felt exactly like the fish. Tried to wriggle back to open water with a bold dart, "How did Sarah die?"

Her mother's mouth slackened, she said softly, almost sadly, "Something exploded in her brain."

Could a brain explode like a grenade?

"Sarah," her mother continued, "did exactly as she pleased. Sheer willfulness. She would not be told. That is why I wear myself out telling you the right way to behave. I don't want you to end up like her—and bring nothing but unhappiness to everyone around you."

Could bad, naughty thoughts make her brain to explode? Margot pulled her arms into her sides, the better to make herself meek and sleek to disappear down the pink swallowing gullet of the heron.

Her mother went out of the room.

Margot followed her and stood outside the bathroom door. She pressed her palms together in a plea . . . heard her mother making a strange unknown sound on the other side of the door, like she was sniffing or finding it hard to breathe.

"Mama—are you OK?"

Her mother came to the door but opened it only an inch. "I'm perfectly fine. Run along."

The door closed and Margot heard the key turn in the lock. She stood there for a long while, not daring to leave, lest her footsteps give her away.

GOODY REIGNED AS DOWAGER of the house, infirm and flighty, and yet as permanent a fixture as the foundations she had watched poured as a young woman in the year nineteen hundred and seventeen. They couldn't go to Europe that summer on account of the war and the liners being taken over for troopships, so King had declared he would build a vacation cottage right here goddamnit! on the North Shore. Granite Merryweather sold him a pretty price for the adjacent sea-view plot, and in revenge King made sure Farnsworth was built twice as grand as Sage Hill.

Kingsland Garrison Hungerford Vanderloep died in 1947. Feared titan, the last of the tycoons, he had buried all his rivals. The stock price of United Union Steel remained buoyed by a surfeit of war profit; his obituaries ran as hagiographic as any puff piece he might once have paid for. No mention was made of his relationships with the Bolsheviks or the National Socialist Party in Germany or J. Edgar Hoover, Lucky Luciano, or Benito Mussolini, nor of the rumors that shadowed the origin of his name, his fortune, his wife's early career as a vaudeville dancer, his domination of Wall Street before the Great Crash and, curiously, *after* it. The *New York Times* wrote that he was "the embodiment of the American Dream, a man of humble, even obscure birth, who rose to join the highest ranks of the great capitalists and founded one of the largest corporations in America."

After Old King's death, an intransigence had fallen upon the Big House. Things were done because they had always been done that way.

Once a month Mr. Penny from Bankers Trust arrived by appointment. Goody received Mr. Penny, who did not age or smile, in King's old office off the solarium, which was lined in soundproof shagreen. After he left, she always complained that signing checks was the most tiring business in the world, and called for a brandy-and-molasses "sharpener."

"If Mrs. T had her name on the bank accounts, you can be sure she would be stamping her mark on the place, instead of letting it rot away," Margot heard mean old Jean Craft telling Nice Noreen one day. "When she was a girl, I remember, she wanted blinds *and* curtains, she wanted *hot* milk in her cereal, not cold, she wanted a *gray* pony, not *brown* like the other girls. And she knew just how to ask her father too: straight out, as clear-demanding as he was, and Old King laughed to see himself in his daughter, so he let her have her own way. Poor Sarah never got a look-in." Margot pressed her ear close to the doorjamb. "Make no mistake: if Mrs. T. was mistress of this house, she would go about installing all the latest fads, shower baths and electric air-conditioning and rolls of florally wallpaper. But she can't do anything while her mother controls the purse strings. It's all according to the trust. It's as if Old King is still signing checks from his grave."

UP THE HILL, THROUGH the spreading chestnut trees, their leaves tired and dusty dark green, the end of summer days. Stevie ran ahead through the woods, past the plankings of the treehouse Margo's mother had ordered torn down. Along the long wall that bordered the property, to an old green door with a busted lock. Margot caught up, panting, stopped.

"James says it's called 'Sarah's door,'" said Stevie, "because that's where she escaped."

He pushed it open. The bottom edge scraped a rut in the black soil.

"They'll know we were here," worried Margot.

"Aw, quit your scaredy-cat routine. No one ever comes up here."

Stevie pushed the door against the turf just enough to open a gap they could squeeze through. On the other side were more woods. Margot stood, hung between the right thing to do and the wrong thing to do. Her mother's voice in her head said, *Come back here, young lady*, but another voice, more immediate, called, "Come on!" Margot was tired out with all this back-and-forth thinking pros and cons. She worried that what happened to Sarah would happen to her. But she worried about being called a priss too. "Come on!" called Stevie again, urgent, irritated. So she went.

Over a rise the trees thinned, a squirrel scuttled up an oak, a crow cocked its head and looked straight at them and cawed.

"Shh! Get down!" Stevie hissed, ducking into a crouch.

An expanse of green lawn fell away from the woods. To the right Margot saw the redbrick and white columns of Sage Hill.

Stevie said "Looky!" and pointed at a dormer window under the roof. A boy stood behind it, naked from the waist up. He raised one hand, without waving, and pressed it against the pane.

"Hal!" Margot called out, too far for him to hear.

"Shh!" repeated Stevie. "They shoot trespassers."

"But we're not trespassers," said Margot. "I know them."

Still, she didn't move from their hiding place. On the greensward below, the Merryweather brothers and cousins were chasing each other, shooting off cap guns. Margot watched Hal watch them, tilting his big round head to follow the chase around the hydrangea bushes. His second hand came up to join the first so that both hands were pressed against the window, then his forehead, the squashed tip of his nose, a flattened cheek. His open mouth made an O of breathy condensation. For a moment he looked like a pressed wildflower, trapped in the frame. Then his hands turned into fists and began pounding on the glass. Startled, Margot stood up. Her movement drew his attention and for a split second their eyes met. Hal began to shout something but no sound carried and in alarm Margot ran ran ran away.

2

MARGOT GREW UP AND UP. SHE WAS SIX FEET TALL BY
the summer she turned twelve. She hoped the vacation would bring
respite from the daily slings and arrows of school, but this year her
mother had insisted on enrolling her in the Junior Sports program
at the Piping Rock Club.

"You cannot go around with your miserable long-nose face stuck
in a book. There won't always be school for you to be good at. What
are you going to do for the rest of your life if you can't play tennis?"

Margot shrugged, a gesture that never failed to irritate her
mother. "I don't like sports."

"We all have to do things in life we do not like."

"Why?"

"Because." Her mother rifled through her pocketbook as if she
was searching for a better answer, but only came up with her com-
pact. She balanced it in one palm and peered into the mirror to fix
her lipstick. One perfect delineated crimson curve above another;
satisfied, she pressed her lips together. "You must introduce your
cousins. How would it look if they were there and you were not?"

Over the past couple of years, there had been a minor thaw in
family relations. The origins were obscure; Margot only caught parts
of it overheard in telephone conversations. Her mother's voice, sigh-
ing, as if much put-upon, talking to Dotty Merryweather, "Well, I

do what I can, for the sake of those girls—growing up above a drug-store! We have offered him the garage maisonette at Farnsworth, but he won't take it! That man would cut off his nose to spite his face—" After the school Christmas carol concert, she was standing next to her mother when Mrs. Cummings had asked, in that rosy-thorny way she had, snagging her words on a high-trilled laugh, why they never saw Margot's cousins at children's parties? Her mother answered like a pair of scissors, snip-snip, "Ask their father."

"The man who works at Bay Shoes? He always looks so ghastly gray and sad."

Her mother had invited her cousins, Fay and Phyllis, to her tenth birthday party. "If we can have a détente with the Russians, I guess I should try to make an effort with my sister's husband."

Fay was a year older than Margot, and Phyllis was a year younger. They were both pretty, but in different ways. Fay was a Rita Hay-worth type, Phyllis was more like Doris Day. Margot was careful not to say anything when they arrived wearing nylon party dresses with shiny sateen bows. Their father kissed her twice, once on each cheek, but it didn't feel quite right to call him "Uncle." Her mother referred to him as "that Jew," but he didn't have curly-wurly fore-locks like the druggist on 72nd Street. He looked perfectly normal really, with a receding hairline and tortoiseshell spectacles. He wore a heavy tweed jacket like a university professor, but he was actually a shoe salesman in Oyster Bay. He didn't own a car, the Sterns had taken the train.

Margot's father made a big show of pumping his brother-in-law's hand in greeting before he launched into his favorite monologue on the mismanagement of the Long Island Rail Road. David Stern nodded politely, but offered no particular comment. Her father con-tinued, warming to his theme: Suburbs were the new cities! Look at all the new highways and bridges and tunnels being built!

"Better get out of shoes and into automobiles, Dave! In the future no one is going to walk anywhere!"

Margot had asked for an insect theme for her birthday but her mother had nixed that idea, so there were *Alice in Wonderland* paper napkins and party hats. Mr. Hoppity-Happity had been engaged as entertainer, and Margot cringed because she knew all the girls thought they were too old for clowns. Fay blew a big pink bubblegum bubble. Margot whispered to her to stop chewing because her mother would go bananas, but Fay just said, "Let her! I don't care!" Then Lydia Cummings asked for a stick and Bernie Pratt, who always did everything Lydia did, asked for one, and soon all the girls were snapping pink bubbles and Margot was left out like a goody-two-shoes.

She was glad to be able to show Phyllis where the bathroom was, and to be extra polite, as her mother had asked her to be, Margot took her to her own bathroom, which was through her bedroom. Right away Phyllis noticed the small dish of bright blue copper sulfate crystals on the dresser.

"I got a chemistry set for Christmas too!"

Encouraged, Margot showed off the microscope she had gotten for her birthday. "Look! You can magnify to the power of five."

"It must be nice to have enough money to have whatever you want."

Undeterred, Margot continued, "It's good for studying butterfly wings and beetles. Spiders have six eyes!"

"Yes, I know," said Phyllis, peering into the eyepiece and turning the focus dial. "It's all blurry."

Margot bit her bottom lip, "I'm sorry, it's only a toy one."

Despite Margot's misgivings and a bowl of ice cream spilled on the carpet, her mother deemed the birthday party experiment a success. The Sterns were duly invited to the annual Christmas Eve party at Farnsworth. Nevertheless, a certain awkwardness between the two families persisted. Margot had pieced together parts of the story. She knew that Fortune had cast the two sisters apart. First in personality: Sarah was romantic and dreamy after her mother; Peggy was her father, fast and fierce, the first to declare herself the winner and never played a game she couldn't win. Secondly in love:

Sarah had run away with a poor, unsuitable man; Peggy had married her father. Thirdly in sickness and in health: Peggy had never taken to her bed a day in her life; Sarah suffered migraines all her childhood and at twenty-four years old had suddenly fallen dead of a brain aneurysm, a word Margot had stumbled on in the semifinals of the school spelling bee.

Margot had long let go of the silly notion that bad thoughts caused brain damage, but the consequences of Sarah's decision to run away were undeniable. According to the encyclopedia, an aneurysm was caused by pressure in a blood vessel; to Margot the diagram looked like a swelled-up balloon. "Pop goes the weasel," as Stevie said. It was Sarah's "*wayward* ways," her mother insisted, that had caused so much trouble. "If only she had done what I told her and waited." Her mother used the same word, *wayward*, with the same inflection of tragic exasperation when Margot tarried on the sidewalk, or was caught reading late by torchlight—

And then there was the whole money business that Margot didn't understand—codicils, provisos, the trust—except to know that she went to the Chapin School and the Piping Rock Club and her cousins went to Bayside Middle School and swam at the public beach. It was something awkward and unmentionable. She had seen, for example, her mother signing the check for the girls' enrollment in the Junior Sports League at the club, even though her mother had said several times she was sure they wouldn't fit in.

AS FAR AS MARGOT was concerned, the Junior Sports League was purgatory. She was gangly, two-left-feet, had no backhand to speak of. There was a weekly tennis tournament, and when she lost the first match she was always secretly relieved of the misery of not having to play the rest of the day. She would spend the afternoon alone, indoors, hiding in the small library room next to the pro shop and reading a biography of Marie Curie.

Trip had gold hair and gold medals from all the tournaments

he'd won. He and Lydia Cummings were partners in the mixed doubles and considered the ones to beat. Chip Reid and Larry Gerald had the best golf par of the group, Bernie Pratt puttered about on the putting green, tapping in hole-in-ones she had carefully set up and then making a spaniel yap of victory.

Phyllis and her older sister Fay were not popular at JSL either; while not exactly outcasts, they were in a separate category because they were not proper members of the club. Phyllis was good at tennis and she was teamed with Larry Gerald, who had a walloping serve and a baby paunch he fed with endless bottles of Coca-Cola. Fay wore lipstick even though she was only thirteen, and spent her time cozying up to Lydia Cummings. According to the laws of social dynamics, her cousins preferred to ingratiate themselves with the popular kids, rather than take shelter with someone as unpopular as themselves.

So Margot spent the summer glowering, hiding, scratching up her poison ivy blisters to get out of swim meets. Behind her back she heard the other kids call her "Moody Margot." Once or twice she had sat down on Lydia Cummings's table, "Hi Phyllis!" "Hi Bernie—I mean Bernadette!" But they just kept on talking about dreamboats and eyeliners, all the while inching their chairs into a tighter and tighter circle so that by the time she had finished her sandwich, she was talking to three turned backs. Trip and Chip Reid and Larry Gerald shared a table, but it was impossible to sit with boys. Too-forward Fay ate her lunch with the tennis pro.

ONE AFTERNOON MARGOT CAME back from the club (James, the chauffeur, was usually sent to pick her up) just as her mother's bridge four was breaking up. She loitered by the servants' door so she didn't have to say hello and endure the usual chorus of "My, hasn't she grown!" After the goodbyes, Mrs. Merryweather remained. She heard her mother say:

"If I were you, I would send Hal directly to military school."

"Oh! I couldn't send the poor boy away!" Mrs. Merryweather's voice wavered. Margot had often heard her mother complain, "Dotty Merryweather will worry a problem to death before she would think to *do* anything about it."

"He has to learn," Peggy insisted, "that there are *consequences* in life. You can't indulge him."

"That's what Clarence says," replied Dotty Merryweather, "but when Hal was thrown out of school, he didn't care at all. He just said, What's it to you? At least the twins have graduated—that's a mercy."

Runny had botched his SATs, but would follow three generations of Merryweather men to Yale nonetheless. Dick had bucked tradition and his father's wishes by applying to Harvard.

"Ah, dear Trip—he's quite my favorite," said Dotty Merryweather, her voice now honeydew, "even though I know a mother isn't supposed to have them."

"Yes . . . Trip," said her mother in a way that made Margot cock her ear closer. "He's turning into a fine young man."

"Now don't discount Dick!" said his mother loyally. "He may look like a grouper on a fish hook, but I bet he will surprise us all."

"Trip is Margot's age," said her mother. Margot leaned on tiptoes. "And they are *such* friends—" Margot put her hand out to stop herself from falling over, caught her thumb on a rose thorn, almost yelped.

"Well, I'm sure Margot will grow into herself, in time," said Mrs. Merryweather.

"It's a *disaster.* I don't know what to do with her ridiculous *height!*" said her mother. "You would think there would be anti-growth hormones these days, but the doctors refuse to help. There's no one tall on Harry's side nor mine; it must be a *genetic mutation.* But just look at Trip, growing fast."

"Yes . . . well . . . Peggy dear, let's not get ahead of ourselves."

"Who is to look out for them if not their mothers?" Margot heard one of her mother's theatrical sighs. "I couldn't bear it if she made the same mistake as my sister—"

"Peggy, that's hardly—"

"But you see the problem! It's the same *selfishness*. All she does is mope with her nose in a book. She is *clever*, which is terribly off-putting for men. Sometimes I say to Harry: What in heaven's name are we going to *do* about *Margot*?"

Margot turned and ran. The heels of her sandals rang as loud as bells on the flagstones.

WHAT ARE WE GOING to *do* about *Margot*? Margot repeated, herself-her-mother, monologue-dialogue, but at least, in her mind's echo chamber, a conversation in which she could reply: We shall turn you upside down and shake vigorously until every fact falls out of your head and you're as ditzy dizzy as Labrador-obsessed Bernie Pratt, who couldn't fight her way out of a paper bag. And when your head is good and empty, we shall reupholster it in chintz. I am too tall and there is nothing she can do about it! Margot allowed a small smile of consolation in her mother's recent defeat: an orthopedic surgeon had flatly refused to shorten her shinbones.

She walked away from the house, hardly knowing where she was going, not caring, with only the idea to get away. The glory of the unfurled summer whispered in the colonnade of elm trees swishing along the driveway. Gravel pricked her toes and skittered under her sandals. Soft moss on the verges, pity the plain old buttercups yearning to grow up as beautiful and frilly as their ranunculus cousins. What are we going to *do* about *Margot*? The question pinched hard, the way a stitch hurt when she ran. Past the mailboxes for the gardeners' cottages. Margot swiped a copy of the L.L.Bean catalog and swished it along the split-rail fence. Keep walking.

It was not her fault, Margot rationalized. Being tall wasn't anything to do with anything she did. It had nothing to do with her *behavior*, it wasn't because she stayed up reading late, or had forgotten to brush her teeth or been rude or not said hello-how-lovely-to-see-you-all with the right enthusiastic syrup. Her height was not her fault. It was not fair of her mother to blame her for being too tall.

Margot unspooled the familiar litany of her deficiencies:

She was not pretty, like Fay; instead she was clever, like Phyllis, which was of no practical or social use, as her mother kept reminding her. Yes, she could do differential equations, she had memorized all the parts of the eye—cornea, pupil, aqueous humor, iris—she did not flinch like Lydia and her giggling pony club acolytes when they dissected a frog in biology. She understood how electrons were simultaneously repelled and attracted to protons; the principles of kinetic and potential energy were as primary and obvious to her as blue and yellow makes green.

"Always with your nose in a book. Stop daydreaming!" Margot understood she was being compared to silly Sarah, who had read romance novels even when she was told not to.

Still she couldn't help it. Books were her favorite places, her favorite people. Walking alone sometimes, she gave future interviews to herself, full of the benefit of hindsight, "Well, of course growing up I was considered the oddity, but now, after all my great success, I have so many friends—"

Margot read fast, whatever she could lay her hands on in Grand Old Vanderloep's collection or at the public library on 71st Street. Burial rites of the ancient Egyptians, Russian folk stories, biographies of Ben Franklin, Louis Pasteur, Edward Jenner, Albert Einstein. She wanted to be great like them, but how? They were men and she was only a girl. Maybe she could proceed one step after another, like the tortoise that wins the race against the boastful hare, counting-climbing. Next year, boarding school, valedictorian, college, summa cum laude, postgrad, research— but wait—what about her debutante season? When would that fit in? A parallel schedule unrolled: coming-out ball, engagement, wedding, wedding night—Margot suppressed a giggle. She had recently succumbed to the thrill of Nancy Drew kissing Ned Nickerson: Would anyone ever want to kiss her? What would it would be like if Trip looked at her the way Clark Gable looked at Scarlett O'Hara? Margot wondered romantically, but wondered too if it might be possible one day to fire people on a rocket to the moon like in Jules Verne or look down a microscope and see an atom spinning electrons. Her secret fantasy was walking up the red-carpeted steps to meet the King of Sweden, who would hang a Nobel medal around her neck. At the ball afterwards she would dance with the Prince of England.

Margot sighed at the great distance of the far-off impossible. Her intelligence only irritated people. When she climbed onto the stage to receive her prize for outstanding academic achievement at Chapin for the fourth year in a row, the headmistress Miss Scrivener said to her, in a sarcastic aside, "What a surprise! You again."

She had thought getting good grades was what teachers wanted, but if she put her hand up too many times in class, Miss Scrivener got annoyed, "It's not polite to hog the limelight, Margot!" She had spent the whole of April growing radishes from seeds for her sixth-grade nature project, measuring the shoots, documenting their progress on a graph, drawing careful diagrams of their leaves, hypocotyl, root, taproot, secondary roots, coloring the diagrams with watercolor paints (much more accurate than waxy childish crayons!). It was by far the best project (even better than Bernie Pratt's forty pages on Every Aspect of Labradors), but Miss Scrivener had only riffled through her pages and pronounced: "You have clearly had help with this, Margot Thornsen, and I expressly said that this project was to be by your hand only." She gave Margot a B. It was as if no one wanted her to be clever. Because clever was somehow connected to "loner," and according to her mother, a "loner" was the very worst thing you could grow up to be. Margot stopped asking questions that called attention to herself, she did not say her thoughts out loud, she got used to being quiet instead of speaking up. Especially in front of Trip. If she mentioned a book to Trip, he called her a "brainiac," which sounded uncomfortably close to "maniac."

She came to the end of the driveway with the two eagles on top of the gateposts, one with wings outstretched, one with a rabbit in its talons, "one taking flight, one taking luncheon," Mr. Merryweather had quipped once. She wanted to keep walking, walking, working out the problem of *what to do about Margot*, but there was nowhere else to go.

She hugged the warm brick of the gatepost; gateway. Her feet hovered between the gravel drive and the blacktop of Skunk's Misery Road. It felt like an important moment, but at the same time it was an entirely ordinary minute that ticked though its seconds to the next.

A truck went by in a whoosh. Margot retreated a step. No, she wouldn't go any further. Why not?

"Dunno," she said out loud, loathing the cowardice that held her back. "Just won't."

3

THE FOLLOWING FALL HER MOTHER SIGNED HER UP FOR Miss Waverly's dancing lessons, held every Thursday afternoon at the Park Avenue Armory. Miss Waverly wore flowing chiffon skirts like Cyd Charisse in *Silk Stockings* and scraped her hair into a high bun. She liked to call her group of twenty beginners, drawn from the eighth grade of the Chapin, Brearley, Spence, and Dalton schools, her "young personages." At the beginning of the first lesson she walked among them, looking each up and down, taking the measure of an ungainly shoulder slump, the potential of an arched neck, appraising the ducklings that might turn into swans. She tutted at ink-stained fingers and untucked shirts.

"You! Stop running your hands through your hair like that greaseball Mr. Elvis Presley! Stand up like a gentleman! You! Put your hands together like a lady, please. No chewing gum. You will be partners. Introduce yourselves politely."

"Lawrence Gerald the Third," said the boy, putting his hand out.

"Lydia Cummings," said Lydia, appalled that she had been given Fat Larry.

Margot was paired with Trip. He had grown over the summer. No longer blond beanpole, she could see biceps in his shirtsleeves. His face was larger, his cheekbones sharper. Swimming-pool eyes. He looked like Montgomery Clift in CinemaScope.

Trip put one arm around her shoulder. His other hand rested on the small of her back, mildly electric. Trip looked down at his feet. Margot looked down at her feet. The music started. There was no piano in the cavernous gym at the Armory, so Miss Waverly brought an old Victrola to play the music. It was hard to hear the beat over the rumble of the subway, and to compensate Miss Waverly tapped time with a baseball bat, bang-bang against the varnished hardwood floor.

"One two-two, one two-two."

Trip stepped forward—too far, Margot hopped backwards. Together they shuffled awkwardly, counting out loud. The Blue Danube flowed towards the inevitable, bom-bom bom-bom.

Trip said, "Hey, what happened to you at our Labor Day barbecue?"

"We had to leave before the fireworks. Dad can't stand the bangs." She did not tell him about the argument between her parents, the slammed door splintered at the hinge, the rumpled coverlet in the guest room the next morning. She tucked these things, like her ears and her dreams, under a pillow.

"Oh, you missed a doozy! Hal got into the liquor cabinet and climbed out onto the roof as high as a kite. Father yelled at him to come down. And do you know what he did?"

Margot shook her head; mention of Hal always made her feel squirmy for a reason she couldn't quite place.

"He stood right on the top of the triangle thing—"

"The pediment."

"OK, teacher's pet. On *the pediment*, from whence he pissed a giant arc of piss right over the heads of everyone on the terrace and into the swimming pool! Father yelled for Runny, but Runny had disappeared with one of the waitresses; I heard them at it in the pool house—so brother Dicky starts shimmying up the trellis like Spider-Man. Meanwhile dearest Mommy dodo-brain calls the fire department!"

Margot put her hand over her mouth, shocked.

"Margot Thornsen!" called Miss Waverly sharply. "Please assume the correct embrace position!" They resumed their waltzing shuffle.

"Was Hal OK?"

"He was fine," said Trip dismissively. "Got his stomach pumped out at the hospital. Hal's such a screwup. After this trick it's military school for sure."

"And smile! And glide! And smile! And glide! Look up, Margot Thornsen! Shoulders back and smile! You are having a simply marvelous time!"

Trip tipped, trod on her toe.

"Yowza!"

"Pipe down, Pine Tree."

"Don't call me Pine Tree."

"Well, it's better than giraffe." Margot almost found it in herself to laugh, but he trod on her toe again.

"Ow!"

"Oh now, don't be Piney-Whiny."

"Stop treading on me!"

"You're supposed to move out of the way."

"We are supposed to be coordinated."

"No, I lead and you follow."

"How can I follow going backwards?"

"That's the whole point. You're the girl."

TRIP COULD BE NICE when they were one-on-one, but in a group he fell in with the crowd. Margot got to tag along with the gang sometimes, grandfathered in by dint of social geography. After the last lesson before Christmas break, the whole Miss Waverly posse went to get milkshakes at the Lexington Diner, and Margot's nanny—Maureen from Iowa, whom her mother described as "bovine"—said that Margot could go if she, Maureen, would sit at the counter as chaperone. This was mortifying. No one else had a nanny who picked them up, although Sara Greenberg had a chauffeur to take her home because she lived all the way over on the Upper West Side.

At the diner, Margot tried to say something blasé about carol concerts and church and cold feet, but it fell flat; Lydia Cummings showed off her new nail polish and everyone oohed and aahed. Chip Reid said it would be a gas to swap out Miss Waverly's orchestral records with some doo-wop.

"Not that gyrating Elvis the Pelvis!"

"No, not rockabilly."

"Johnny Mathis. Something for the cheek-to-cheek of it."

"I like the Everly Brothers," said Lydia, "they're dreamy."

"Dream all you want."

"Whaddya think, Pine Cone?" Trip nudged her.

Margot tried to believe these pet names meant he liked her, because boys always teased the girls they liked. If they had been alone, she would have said, "Trip, cut it out," but she was trying to fit in so she blurted, "I like Chuck Berry." Stevie had played her a Chuck Berry forty-five; it was just the first thing she thought of that wasn't Perry Como, universally despised as a parental favorite.

Lydia looked at her askance.

"But he's black."

IN THE SPRING THEY learned to waltz.

Margot swayed on her long legs. Her knobby knees stuck out between her kneesocks and her skirt hem. Her mother said she couldn't wear stockings until she was fifteen. Slide back together, slide back together. Her patent leather dancing shoes slipped on the parquet.

"Stop shuffling! Arch your back, Miss Thornsen!" Miss Waverly cried out. Margot felt her face flush hot red.

"Arms curved now, delicate delicate, as if you were hugging a Ming vase."

"Old bat," whispered Trip.

Margot would have smiled, but she'd had metal braces fitted to her teeth the week before and she was trying to hide them.

"Oh poor Pine Tree, you look like a Cadillac!"

Trip walked her home. It was raw March. Maureen had gone back to Iowa. Margot's mother had relented and agreed not to hire a replacement. "Frankly I'm exhausted babysitting these Hicksville girls." The wind whistled down the avenue, there were tight buds on the magnolia trees. Trip was tanned from skiing in Sun Valley.

"I was going to kiss you but I won't now."

"One minute you are nice to me and the next minute you are not."

"It's my natural charm," Trip assured her. "Everyone loves it, except you because you're a nerd. Runny says the thing with girls is to keep 'em keen. He's having a high old time at Yale."

"How's Dick doing at Harvard?" Margot liked Dick. At Christmas he had said he heard she was top of her class, well done!

"Dick?" Trip's face went blank for a moment. "Oh, he's still the same boring closed-door. Except apparently he introduced himself to his new classmates as Richie. Which is perfect"—Trip eye-rolled—"because of course now he's known as Rich for short, which is what we *are* after all. Meanwhile Hal has been sent home from military school for going AWOL. So it's down to me to be the great white hope of the family."

"God help us all!" said Margot, trying to tease him back.

"You don't take me seriously," said Trip, apparently serious.

"You don't take yourself seriously."

"What's there to be serious about?"

"Seriously?"

"I don't want to turn into some Holden Caulfield taking everything too seriously."

"Or not seriously enough."

"Oh do stop being clever for a moment, Margot. It's unbearable."

"I'm sorry." Margot looked down at the granite curb. She always spoiled it somehow.

They arrived at the green awning at 655. Trip stood for a moment facing Margot, looking up at her. He rose on his tiptoes, waited there four whole heartbeats, as if he was thinking about it.

"Put your lips together."

Margot obeyed, closing her mouth, painfully aware of the metal braces scaffolding her teeth.

Trip seemed to relent. "Alright, just for practice." He leaned forward and stuck his tongue out and pushed it between her lips. Margot stood motionless. His tongue was a warm, slimy stranger inside her mouth. He twirled it around in a circle. Then he withdrew it, sank back on his heels, and said, "That's a French kiss."

Suddenly there was the doorman holding an umbrella. "Come on in, Miss M, it's starting to rain," and in an abrupt panic she bolted inside and leapt onto the elevator.

"And up we go to six, Princess Margot," said Elevator Ernie, rattling the cage door and jerking the hemisphere lever to ascend. Princess Margot was Ernie's old joke.

"You look pale; it's close to freezing out, better get some hot tea inside you."

Her mother was standing in the hall in her mink, sorting through the pile of invitations on the silver salver.

"Margot!"

But Margot pushed past her, not crying, not thinking, horrified. Horrified because a French kiss must surely need a French letter because otherwise—oh God—oh God—she could be pregnant.

4

NINTH GRADE, MARGOT WAS SENT AWAY TO THE ETHEL
Walker Boarding School for Girls, set on twenty acres on the edge
of the town of Simsbury, Connecticut. Seven bells rang every morning before 9 a.m.: reveille, dress, assemble, crocodile, breakfast, end
of breakfast, chapel. The head of school read the lesson, the headmistress announced announcements. There were four classes before
lunch and four after, except on Wednesdays and Saturdays, which
were sports afternoons. Life was regimented, communal, and cir-
cumscribed. "We have a duty of care to all the girls," wrote Miss
Wall the headmistress in the school brochure. "We are dedicated to
the academic and spiritual well-being of all our pupils." Lights-out
at 9:30 p.m.

Margot missed her New York City freedoms, stolen hours after
school—"I'll be home a little late, Mama, library duty, Miss Scrivener wants me to help with the Christmas pageant." She used to
go to the Doubleday bookstore down on 53rd and Fifth, sit on the
floor in the Science section and pull out different volumes. There
she had found an obstetrics textbook with a diagram that illustrated
insemination. She followed the double-branched ovaries down the
connective chute to the word *vagina*, which she misread at first as
Virginia, which seemed to make more sense than the idea that the
penis, drawn in outline, a flopped sausage, could be inserted into it.

How? Wouldn't it buckle and fold? Luckily the text made things a little clearer: a sperm swam to an egg and fertilized it. It was the same as pollination with anthers and stigmas, they had learned in biology. Here was the explanation in clear print. Margot felt a great flood of relief: you could not get pregnant from kissing.

AT BOARDING SCHOOL THERE was no privacy. In her first year Margot shared a dormitory with three other girls: Madeleine Clements came from Texas and told everyone on the first day that her daddy's ranch was bigger than Rhode Island; Sally Main talked about nothing but horses and told Madeleine that western saddle was not the right way to ride; and Bernie-Bernadette, who had grown an enormous bosom, and like her nemesis Lydia Cummings had followed her from Chapin, the two of them, it seemed to Margot, like a bad smell.

Within the walls of the boarding school the girls were sexless: there could be no feminine without the masculine. Which is not to say that the girls did not think about sex, talk about sex, pass around Maddy Clements's copy of *Lolita* (which seemed very unconvincing to Margot: why didn't Lolita just run away and find the nearest policeman?), discuss kissing, giggle about third base and wonder: What was second? Maddy said it was a finger, but Bernie said she didn't believe her and how would she know anyway? But boys, in any case, were theoretical. Among girls, gradations of beauty and figure were lost. No one thought of anyone as "pretty" and the girls were not allowed to wear makeup. People were rated according to their personalities: there were good eggs and rotten eggs, sporty girls, horsey girls, West Coasters and weirdos. Margot fell into none of these categories, but neither was she an outcast for her academics as she had been at Chapin. Good grades were a good thing at Ethel Walker's. A certain respect— if not popularity—was conferred on those with A's. Bernadette, always at the bottom of the class, was considered a bit of a joke.

Lydia was in the middle, but good at field hockey, so continued her reign as one of the populars. But no one made any particular connection between their grades and their futures, even though Miss Wall made it clear she hoped her students would go on to college and told Margot that she should consider herself a strong candidate for one of the Seven Sisters.

"We are going to need educated women," Miss Wall told her. Margot thought, What for?

Margot did not exactly find her feet, but she kept her head down looking at them and the straight A's continued. She liked chemistry best, biology next best, physics was frustrating because it was endless calculus: levers and loads and fulcrums. Mr. Zweig, the physics teacher and the only man on the faculty (disappointingly gray and stringy; the girls called him "mystery meat"), told her that all the interesting stuff—relativity and black holes and space and time—were not on the curriculum. The students were streamed for math and English lit. Margot was gratified to see Lydia consigned to the middling Betas; Maddy Clements, who never did any out-of-class assignments, declared she didn't care if she was in Gamma with Bernadette, "It's a stupid system anyway." At Walker's, Margot's unpopularity was no longer acute, she was just another student, subject to the same regime as everyone else. At home, her mother insisted on dressing her up; Margot, of course, never liked to stand out.

When it seemed that she had finally stopped growing, Peggy took Margot to her own seamstress and ordered a dozen day dresses and three party dresses. Margot endured the fittings in the drafty atelier, half naked, cold and stuck with pins.

"I'll have to add another foot of fabric to the skirt," said Madame, addressing her mother, who sighed at the extra expense. "But her legs are so long the proportions will not be right—let me see if I can drop the waist a few inches and even her out."

When Margot winced under the yanking tongs at the hairdresser, she was told, "You must suffer to be beautiful!" The permanent wave felt tight against her scalp. She couldn't twirl her finger through her bangs like she used to.

"Now let's see what we can do with these eyebrows," said the beautician, clicking a pair of tweezers.

Now that she teetered—perhaps a little too literally in her unaccustomed kitten heels—on the brink of "grown-up," there were more rules to adhere to. Hats were to be kept on at lunch, but not worn in the evening. Nothing that sparkled before sunset. No white shoes after Labor Day. A drink was permitted when the sun was over the yardarm at noon; the evening cocktail hour began at six. The butler passed the meat platter, maids passed the vegetables. Corn should always be served cut off the cob, butter was spread with a butter knife. Always dress for dinner and for traveling. Sit with your hands gently resting in your lap. Never light your own cigarette, wait for a man to do it for you.

In the winter breaks Margot accompanied her parents to charity balls and Christmas parties. During the summer there were junior dances at the Piping Rock Club most Saturday nights. Trip's card was usually full and Lydia Cummings tailed him like a lapdog, but sometimes Trip would ask her. "Aw c'mon, Pine-Sol, you know you want to."

Margot felt a Cinderella shiver as his fingertips pianoed down her spine, his signal for her to slouch-scoot down to his level. Once she caught him doing the "cut" on her, waving a twenty-dollar bill over her shoulder to entice someone else to cut in before the number was finished.

"Don't make a fuss, Margot string bean," said Chip Reid, seeing the tears in her eyes. "I'm sure he'll make it up to you at the party at Sage Hill tomorrow night."

"What party?"

Such was her world, the world she knew. Childhood is a room before you have seen the door. Margot did not complain. She minded that she was a late developer and had to catch up somehow. Some of the girls had beaus already. She was almost fifteen and had not even had her period. Her mother took her to be examined by her gynecologist. Margot emerged from this humiliation with her mouth clamped shut. During the consultation afterwards, she kept her eyes on his desk.

"I can see nothing particularly wrong with her," Dr. Slimeball told her mother, "but she's too thin. I suggest a regimen of high-calorie protein. Put some color into those cheeks." He took his pre-scription pad and wrote "lobster and steak" with a loopy flourish. "Come and see me again in six months."

Her mother took her to the Colony Club for lunch afterwards. When Margot got up to go to the buffet, she could still feel the icky smoosh of the Vaseline smeared on the inside of her thighs.

"There's no need to go into one of your sulks, Margot. I know it's not pleasant," said her mother. "Did you get the vichyssoise? I do think it's very good here.

"And by the way, the Geralds are giving a New Year's party at the Sherry for the whole crowd and their boy Larry and all the young, won't that be fun?"

Margot tipped the two-handled bowl away from her in the polite manner and sipped her soup from the edge of the soup spoon. She did not look up.

"I know it's not pleasant," repeated her mother, something in her tone almost soft. "It's part of being a woman."

Margot looked up from her soup bowl.

"Well, I wish I was born a man," she said simply.

"We all do," said her mother.

5

"WHAT'S YOUR NEW YEAR'S RESOLUTION, MARGOT?" HER father asked at breakfast.

"What's the point in good intentions?" said her mother, buttering her toast and pointing the blunt blade at her father at the far end of the table. "If they are as elastic as that new panty hose."

Margot answered, "My resolution is to read every *Scientific American* from cover to cover, even the parts I don't understand. Miss Marlow says that the only way to understand Shakespeare is to keep reading and reading until the verses are tattooed on your brain."

"That sounds mighty painful," said her father.

"Reading *Scientific American* is *not* a resolution, Margot," said her mother. "That's just you indulging yourself. A *resolution*," she said, pointedly looking at her husband, "means changing your behavior."

Margot's father opened his *Wall Street Journal* like a partition.

"For example, your New Year's resolution could be to be more sociable. Life is like a *mirror*, Margot, smile and people will smile back at you."

Margot wore her new dress for the New Year's Eve party. It was royal blue slubbed silk and belted with a pretty appliqué of satin cornflowers. The seamstress had padded the bust at her mother's request.

"Stop slouching, Margot, chest out!" exhorted her mother as they decanted from the limousine. "Pay attention to Trip, don't let that Lydia Cummings—as vulgar as her mother—get her claws into him."

"Trip is not the only boy in the world," said Margot, but not with any great conviction.

"Do you want to end up with Larry Gerald? He'll turn out just like his fat lush father?" Her mother ticked off her options on her fingers. "Chip Reid is as dull as *ditchwater*, his mother wears army boots, and everyone knows the money is *running out*, they sold half the old man's estate to the developers. Trip is a darling boy and there's the Whitney Trust!"

Margot's wrists itched against the seams of her evening gloves. Her kid-soled evening shoes slipped on the marble foyer. When the coat check girl took her wrap, she felt a chill across her naked shoulders.

"Chin up and smile, Margot! Dear God! Do I have to pay for smiling lessons on top of everything else?"

The reception room was already full of people. Her mother scanned Lydia Cummings in a red cocktail dress with a sweetheart neckline.

"She looks like a harlot. Just like her mother."

Her father said, "Don't, Peg, not here."

"Don't 'don't' me, Harrison."

Her father turned towards the bar; bumped against Clarence Merryweather, put his big beaming social smile back on, "I hear Nelson's going to run after all."

"He's got my vote," replied Clarence Merryweather, who occasionally played golf with Nelson.

"I don't know if the Rockefeller name is going to play with the hicks in the sticks. After all, it's not Roosevelt."

"And thank God for that, we don't need another socialist taxing us up the wazoo."

The ceiling was hung with silver stars and balloons. The decorative theme was "the future," and the centerpiece on each table was a tin robot toy holding a bouquet of roses sprayed with silver paint.

Margot hovered, minding her mother's admonition never to stand with her back against the wall. Mrs. Cummings waved a cigarette and the rising blue smoke made an umbrella. Lydia stood out like a fire engine, no wonder Trip was talking to her for so long. She watched Mr. Merryweather plunge a shrimp into a bowl of Marie Rose sauce and swing it so high that a big red glop landed on his shirtfront.

Margot stood apart, the distance between alone and belonging, between herself and parents, between childhood and adolescence, was measured in a few feet of empty parquet. She wondered if it had always been like this, parties and dinners and balls, scrolling back through the generations, skirts swelling and narrowing according to the fashion of the day; hairdos elaborately curled, then demure and plain; social mores louche and then chaste again; and all the while the same white noise of chitter-chatter, waltzes to conga lines to the flapping-arms chicken dance that everyone was suddenly mad for— was this progress? A succession of postures and poses that made up a life that was called having fun. Would it always be like this? Would she be standing in this same ballroom in twenty years' time, subjecting her own daughter to the same rituals, the same people, the same talky-talk: golf, the GOP ticket, vacations in the islands, so-and-so's engagement—

Dinner was announced. Margot was on the young people's table with Trip and Hal, Chip Reid, Larry Gerald, Lydia Cummings, one of the Rockefeller cousins. The chair next to her was empty, the name card read *Alexander Full*. Margot didn't know any Fulls.

"Everyone calls me Sandy," he said, pulling out the chair for her to sit down. He was tall, taller than she was; he was older than the rest of the table too, hair shaved close at the back of his neck, sandy-colored like his name.

"Sandy Full, I know," he said, making a joke, "full of it."

"Sandyful?"

"Not the Locust Valley Fulls, I'm afraid." His smile was wry. Margot didn't understand wry. "I'm Larry's cousin from the wrong side of the tracks," explained Sandyful. She must have looked confused because he added, "I'm the cautionary tale. It was a terrific scandal at the time: my mother married the help. I grew up in Philly."

Frilly? Was that somewhere in Connecticut?

"I'm not supposed to be here," he continued, just as mysteriously. "I had to borrow this penguin suit." He opened his hands like a magician showing off his evening jacket. "Don't worry. I'm on my best behavior. I think they want to see if a yokel can pass."

Margot did not know what a yokel was and she wasn't about to ask.

A waiter put plates in front of them. Margot looked down at the beef tournedos, prodded the tomato rose with the tines of her fork.

Sandy rescued her. "So tell me about you."

"I'm nearly fifteen. I go to Ethel Walker's School. I'm clever." So clever she sounded like a dolt. Margot was so used to everyone knowing who she was, root and branch and family tree, that now she had a queasy feeling she was squandering the chance to present herself as just, well, herself.

"I want to go to college," she added tentatively.

"Ah, an ambitious girl!"

Margot felt her cheeks redden.

"I meant it as a compliment," said Sandy.

Sandy had blue eyes. What did they see? Margot wondered. Too tall, parrot beak nose, rounded shoulders, flat bust. Another lapse in conversation. Sandy Full seemed almost as fish-out-of-water as she felt.

"I'm sorry you got stuck on the kids' table," said Margot, ever ready with an apology.

"Don't be," said Sandy. "I'm pretty relieved. Every time one of these swells hears I just graduated from West Point, they want to tell me how when they were in the Big War they took Paris single-handedly."

"Golly," said Margot, "West Point."

"About to get my first commission."

"Where are they sending you?"

"I don't know yet." He dropped his voice. "I hope it's not some peaceful backwater. I'd like to have the chance to test myself with some real action."

"I understand that," said Margot. "For me, I think going to college would be the test. Can I be clever at college or am I only school clever?"

"What's the difference?"

"At college you have to present your own ideas." She paused. "I don't know if I have any."

"Oh, don't worry about ideas," replied Sandy, reassuring. "There are plenty of good old ideas kicking about that could use a fresh coat of paint. Sometimes I think everything has already been thought up before by some ancient Greek guy staring at the stars. I mean, I can pretty much guess that all the folks in this room right now are having the same conversations as the fancy-pants did two thousand years ago in Athens: which tribune is going to win the election, how to make sharper spears to defeat the Trojans, will it be stewed quail with honey again for dinner?"

"I've never thought about it that way," said Margot, even as she realized she had, in fact, been thinking about it exactly that way.

"I mean, we have all these new technologies, but do they really change who we are?"

"Who are we?"

Face-to-face, like the sun and the moon sharing the sky at dawn, at the hour when something is about to begin. "Who do we want to be?"

"Doesn't that depend on who we are?"

"Who are we?" Sandy asked again. He was teasing her, but she liked it.

"We are what we are born, aren't we?" said Margot, feeling that this was a narrow definition, but perhaps a place to start. "We are half our mother and half our father and the place where we grow up."

"My mother got knocked up by the chauffeur's son," said Sandy cheerfully, as if this was nothing to be ashamed of. "Her father tried to ship her off to a convent like it was the Middle Ages. So she eloped with my dad."

"Gosh, that's brave."

"Her father never gave her a penny." Sandy shook his head, emphasizing a point of pride. "Not even when my dad was shipped out to the Pacific and she had to work in a factory as a regular Rosie the Riveter. My mother didn't turn into what she was born into."

Sandy half sighed, half smiled. "Anyway, my dictator of a grandfather finally kicked the bucket last year and my uncle says he wants to make amends. This trip to the Big Apple is the first step towards a family reconciliation."

"I think my grandfather was an autocrat too," said Margot quietly, a word she knew from Napoleon in history class. "My aunt ran away for a love match, and Grand Old King banished her and never let anyone see her again. I was only two when he died, so I don't remember him. But everyone says his will was law."

"Half the men in this room think their will is the law," said Sandy, "but from the other side of the tracks, you see it pretty clear: the rich make the laws. They say behind every great fortune lies a great crime."

Sandy's lips pressed together to make a hard line, and he pushed his chair back from the table. Margot followed his gaze across the room filled with tuxedoes and evening dresses. When she squinted, the people dissolved into a sparkling blur.

"Would you care for strawberry mousse?" asked the waitress, leaning between them with a bowl of pink foam.

"Oh! No. Yes. Please. Thank you." Margot felt flustered, prickled, as if she had been told off. The mousse trembled on her plate.

"You probably think we are all spoiled rich kids," she said, fishing for a reprieve.

Sandy poured strawberry sauce from a silver sauceboat over his dessert and licked a drip from his finger.

"I think you are a very thoughtful person," he said. "You are a person who listens."

"That's because I am shy," said Margot, never willing to take a compliment. "My mother always tells me I hang back too much."

"Shy is not a bad thing." Sandy tilted his head. Across the table, Larry Gerald and Chip Reid were racing glasses of champagne, and Trip and Lydia were laughing like geese.

"Was West Point very tough?" Margot asked at length.

"Four years of marches, humping packs, classwork, military codes, honor codes, codes of conduct. Sometimes I think I joined up to test myself against what my father did. They say there's always a war going on somewhere in the world. Most cadets study math or mechanical engineering, good military subjects, but I majored in literature. There were only three of us and we were pretty much known as the poetry pansies. Blame my dad because he used to make me recite Wordsworth, Whitman, Shakespeare growing up. He would tell me, no matter where you are, no matter how far or how scared, you can look up at the stars and feel wonder, and you can remember a few lines of poetry and feel comforted."

"Do you write poetry?" Margot asked boldly.

Sandy put his finger to his lips and leaned closer. "It's a secret, don't tell anyone or they'll take away my commission!"

"I can't imagine writing poetry."

"Well, the trick is to look at the world with your own eyes. To try to see it as it really is. Yourself too. Poetry can be personal and universal at the same time—like Chagall's blue floating world."

Margot suddenly longed to float in Sandy's sky blue eyes.

"I spend too much time studying," she admitted. "I am always looking down, reading or staring into a microscope."

"You're a scientist—" said Sandy, and Margot stopped breathing for a moment because no one had ever called her that before. "You are looking for the same thing as a poet."

"Really? What am I looking for?"

"The truth," said Sandy, with conviction. "You want to under-stand how things work, I want to write what is honest. One is vis-ible and one is not, that's all."

Sandy had made two small words—"that's all"—into a bridge between the seen and the unseen world, one observable, evident; the other a complete mystery.

Margot said, "You see stars and imagine an ancient Greek look-ing at the same stars. And I look up at the night sky and think: What are they doing there at all?"

"Yes," said Sandy, smiling at her with a man's look, sheepish and wolfish at the same time. Margot felt herself blush again, but this time she didn't look away.

DINNER WAS ENDING, TABLES breaking up. Margot had forgot-ten the rule about talking to the man on your left for the first course and then to the man on your right for the second. She had ignored poor Hal Merryweather. He was two sheets to the wind, tipping champagne down his throat like it was soda pop. The flute wob-bled as he set it down and reached over and took hers, tiny deli-cate bubbles streaming to the surface like swimmers coming up for air—it all depends on how you look at the world, Margot thought, whether you think you are drowning or being saved. Hal swallowed her champagne in two gulps, burped, ahh.

"Thirsty," he said, and began spooning the leftover strawberry mousse from her plate. "I'm a bottomless pit."

Hal was so thin his dress shirt flapped against the hollow space above his cummerbund. Military school had been a bust, so had Swiss boarding school and a place her mother referred to as "that dipsomaniac hospital in California where they sent Marilyn Mon-roe to dry out."

"I like your bow tie," said Margot, to say something nice. It was greenish, but now that she looked closer, it looked like pleated paper, not silk—

Hal cackled. "I folded up a hundred-dollar bill! Dad thought he could bribe me to behave myself."

"Bribery only encourages corruption," said Dick Merryweather, arriving from another table. "Come on, brother, let's get you some fresh air—"

Dick hauled him to his feet and held him up under his armpit. Hal listed to one side, stumbled through the crowd, his brother excusing him with mouthed apologies, as the backs turned and tutted.

The violins of the Lester Lanin Orchestra began to croon. A soft male tenor soothed the opening bars of "Night and Day."

"I'm sure your dance card is full—" said Sandy, standing up and pulling back her chair to help her out.

"Hey Pine Tree!" Trip appeared grinning and threw his arm around her shoulders. "First dance is mine! Let's show the whole Miss Waverly's crowd a jazzy number."

Margot was amazed to find herself the sudden object of Trip's attention. He put his hand under her elbow and push-steered her towards the ballroom.

"Poor Piney-Whiney got stuck with Larry's poor relation from nowheresville, and my brother is so useless he couldn't rescue a fly out of his soup."

"He's a West Point graduate," said Margot. "And a poet."

"Larry says he's got a chip on his shoulder the size of the Smithsonian."

They glided jauntily, two-step two-step. The funny thing about Trip was that he knew just where to hold her, one hand at the small of her back. He'd grown a bit too, she no longer towered over him like a crane, and that helped. Margot let herself be swept along.

"Isn't Lydia Cummings a gas! Is James picking you up later with the Town Car? Are your parents going on to the governor's dance? Can we get James to take us up to Smalls Paradise? I can slip him a twenty."

The tempo double-timed along with Margot's heartbeat. The

party swirled and the hi-hat sparkled; the singer swung the micro-
phone, as cool a cat as Sinatra. Her father danced with Mrs. Cummings. Mr. Gerald danced with Mrs. Gerald, a cigar in one hand
and a martini glass in the other. Trip swapped her out for Lydia
Cummings. She saw Hal stub out his funny roll-up cigarette in
a potted plant and sway across the dance floor towards her—but
Sandy found her first, "May I?"

Just one of those things, Just one of those crazy flings.

"What is gossamer anyway?" asked Sandy. He did not fit as well
as Trip. He shuffled rather than step-stepped, he didn't know which
beats to turn her on. Swung around and around, a little giddy—
Margot caught sight of her mother sheathed in black velvet, standing beside the stage, oddly alone, a marble statue—Sandy spun her
and they nearly overbalanced, and by the time she recovered she
couldn't see her mother through the throng.

Everyone stopped dancing as the drummer drumrolled the final
seconds of the year. The year counted backwards from fifty-nine
to zero, the beginning of a whole new hour of history's tick-tock.
1960! Sandy leaned over and kissed her cheek, close to the edge of
her lips.

"Oh!" said Margot.

"Oh good or oh bad?"

"Oh!" Margot repeated.

"Oh surprised, I guess," said Sandy. His eyes drooped.

Margot didn't know what to say. She was startled and her usual
knock-kneed awkwardnesses kicked in, but she felt an unaccustomed glimmer of feminine insouciance. Trip stood beside Lydia,
watching her in the company of another man. Man, not boy. Not
quite his old Pine Tree planted with the wallflowers.

Silver streamers fluttered against the walls like leaves and
branches in a moonlit forest, the snare drum crackled with distant
gunfire. Margot worried for Sandy then, bound for unknown roads,
night patrols, clouds blocking out the stars, bursts of ambush and
night attacks.

"I wish you good luck," she said.

"You have a very serious expression on your face suddenly," said Sandy. "Are you about to turn into a pumpkin?"

"Pine Tree! You coming? I've squared it with James." Trip appeared, tugging at her elbow. On seeing Sandy, he added, "A bunch of us are going to a place uptown, you're welcome to—"

Sandy put on a mock-paternal tone, "Oh, I wouldn't want to spoil your fun." He kissed Margot's forehead, "I've got to haul out at 0500, best get some shut-eye." He burred her temple with his lips, leave-taking, lost sentences, Trip pulling at her wrist, Chip Reid hollering from the door to hurry up! and his fingers slipped through hers, let go.

6

AT FIRST THE NEW DECADE LOOKED VERY MUCH LIKE THE old one, although whatever was going on in the wider blue floating world, Margot thought, the girls at Ethel Walker's School would be the last to know. They had no access to television, no nightly news, no radios, not even a daily newspaper. "Washington could get nuked before we would hear of it." It was permissible, however, to subscribe to some magazines (not the trash rags; not *Teen* or the *National Enquirer*). Everyone was desperate to be friends with Maddy to read her copy of *Vogue*. Margot was the only girl to take *Scientific American*. Sometimes she would leaf through copies of *Time* magazine and *National Geographic* on the table in the juniors' lounge.

Communists, baseball, H-bomb tests, starlets, earthquakes in Iran; Margot read about the global population explosion and saw pictures of miracle new rice plants that could produce double yields. In Arizona they were plowing cornfields in the desert. If you pour water into sand, does it become soil? Russians and summits. Margot flipped through directions on how to build an atomic shelter and worried about fallout and half-lives. "Did you hear, 'Margot-I-know,'" Lydia Cummings goaded, "radiation mutates your genes so you turn fluorescent green and grow two heads." Margot told her that was monster-from-the-black-lagoon crap, but at the same time she wondered if it was really possible—because she had read about birth defects in Hiroshima and Nagasaki—that DNA could change, could be altered. Radiation caused mutation; could it also resolve mutations? Like, maybe, she half joked to herself, the too-tall *genetic mutation of me?*

When she came across photographs of GIs, Margot always looked for Sandy among the uniforms. No letter ever came. Would he remember the name Ethel Walker's School? Would he know to look her up in the Social Register?

Every morning, for the whole winter semester, Margot checked her cubbyhole for a letter with a US Army postmark. She was sure he would send something on Valentine's Day. Lydia Cummings received a red envelope and she opened it at breakfast, signing ostentatiously, and was very put out when a bouquet of red roses arrived for Miss Madeleine Clements. When Margot went home to Park Avenue for spring break, she harbored hope of an envelope waiting for her. She opened several invitations to junior dances.

"Is there any other mail for me?" she asked Mrs. Hanna, the housekeeper.

"Is there any other mail for me?" she asked her mother.

"Were you expecting something?"

"No—I just—"

Her mother raised an eyebrow, "Just what?"

"Just, nothing."

Classes, biology dissections, essay assignments, book reports, exams. The following fall, she read *Doctor Zhivago* and it occurred to her that waiting could be a romance unto itself. At night she lay in her creaking narrow bed listening to the other girls whisper about their beaus and imagined herself Lara; despite everything, Yuri would find her.

Two years revolved clicking through a carousel slideshow, a blur of new-and-improved! The advertisements in the magazines were as aspirational as the people in the articles that ran beside them. Rock Hudson was a dreamboat. Elvis came out of the army. John Glenn went into orbit. Jacques Cousteau dove deep into the oceans in his skin-diving suit wearing a red wooly hat. *Bathyscaphe* sounded marvelous to Margot, like bath and an escape in one. Bermuda shorts, longer-lasting underarm deodorant, Kent filter cigarettes, Canadian Club ginger ale.

Maddy Clements thought Che Guevara was sexy; Lydia Cummings retorted that she only used the word "sexy" to shock everyone, and besides, Che Guevara was a Commie and he had a beard. Margot read *War and Peace* and became Natasha, pining for the wounded Prince Andrei. After all, Grace Kelly married a prince and Princess Margaret married a commoner. Bernadette wanted to be a figure skater, Maddy Clements wanted to be Sophia Loren, which was controversial because she was so *dark*. All the girls wanted to be Jackie Kennedy, because she was *so* glamorous and she had redecorated the White House *so* tastefully. (Peggy said everyone in the Long Island Bouvier clan knew Jackie had wanted to leave Jack after all his philandering, but old Joe had paid her to stay.) Margot read the *Time* magazine cover story about the new dean of Radcliffe College, Mary Bunting, who was a microbiologist. "*Girls in college have scarcely begun to use their brains.*" At the end of her junior year, she told her parents she wanted to apply to Radcliffe. Her mother said, "Are you deliberately trying to provoke me?"

BY THE SUMMER OF '63, Margot and her mother had become poles of opposite and opposition. In childhood Margot had been docile, eyes cast down, yes Mama. Now that she was older, she had begun, gingerly, to test maternal boundaries. Peggy had to acknowledge that Margot was, at eighteen, able to drive, permitted to smoke in company, to wear sheers and high heels. She had become a young lady, but in Peggy's eyes, her daughter would always be her child. Fourth of July loomed with typical argument. Margot didn't want to go to the big barbecue at Piping Rock. Her father didn't want to go either, "You know I can't stand the whizbangs, Peg," and took her part.

"Why don't we stay home this year, we could even make a little party of it," he suggested, trying to lure his wife with the temptation of playing hostess.

"Don't be ridiculous, all the good caterers have been booked up for months."

They went to Piping Rock. Margot acquiesced and wore the white sundress printed with cornflowers that her mother had picked out. As the fireworks began to pop, her father ostentatiously stuffed cotton balls in his ears and stalked off to the bar. When Chip Reid asked her to dance, Margot tried to demur, but her mother pushed her forward with a knuckle poke, "Go ahead, have a good time!" Margot danced with Chip and then Trip cut in. His breath smelled of booze and maraschino cherries, and he swept her around the dance floor like a flapping newspaper before depositing her in Larry Gerald's galumphing embrace. Lydia Cummings swept by like a Grecian goddess floating on a cloud of pleated chiffon.

Margot longed to fall in love, the way that people fell in love in the movies, desperately, against all odds. In her fantasies she played the part of a Lara/Natasha, waiting faithfully for her hero to come back from war and kiss his princess awake. The reality of boys, however, made Margot nervous. Trip made her blush when he scooped his hand under her behind, but most of the time he only had eyes for Lydia Cummings, and if Lydia wasn't around you could bet that Bernie Pratt would be standing by to take up the slack. Margot shied away from the boys she didn't know. One time she made up some excuse and overheard the boy say to Larry Gerald, "Oh, she's probably frigid." Sometimes, during dances at Piping Rock, she would disappear into the little library off the main hall (the same nook where she had once hid from tennis matches) and read a book. Trip caught her once, "Ah, here you are, Pinecone!" The tension of her mother's disappointment tightened over the course of the summer. Margot was counting down the days till school again.

One morning, filled with ennui and wishing only to indulge her loneliness with her own company, she told her mother, "I can't go the club today. I've got the curse." For once, her mother let her stay home.

Margot had slipped the leash. She kicked off her shoes, went into the kitchen, ate up the leftover bacon from breakfast, dragged her fingers through the bowl of whipped cream in the refrigerator, filched a packet of Goldfish crackers from the cupboard and roamed the Big House munching them, idly, wildly.

Came to the door of her mother's dressing room, sanctum, went inside and sat at the vanity in front of the mirror framed by Holly-wood lightbulbs. She wriggled a ruby ring from the velvet bolster inside the suede jewelry case and tried it on. Her mother said she was too young for diamonds; she must wait to wear the Vanderloep tiara at her coming-out ball. Margot wondered what it would be like to have her own ring on her ring finger, wife to a husband, mother to children, mistress of the house. Would she be the same Margot as now, giraffe-mouse, or would she be grown-up like her mother, imperative and directive. Would diamonds give her confidence?

She opened the top drawer of the vanity and took out one of her mother's Hermès scarves and tied it, Queen Elizabeth style, over her hair and under her chin. Now she definitely looked like a woman! Margot ran her fingertips over the row of lipsticks in gold cylinders and recklessly selected "Scarlet Desire." She pushed the slant of grease stick in a bowed wave over her top lip. She wasn't practiced and the color slipped over the curve of her filtrum. When she kissed her lips together, it only smeared more. In the mirror she saw a grotesque, a parody. She pulled open the second drawer of the vanity looking for a Kleenex. Inside was a chamois neck-lace pouch; probing behind it, her fingers encountered a padded silk purse. Inside was a blue envelope. For a moment her heart fluttered with an old flame, but as she pulled it out, she saw that it was not addressed to her but to Miss Jeanette Craft, Farnsworth, Locust Valley, Nassau County. Why did her mother have a letter for the mean old cleaner lady so carefully secreted?

Two pages, the first, dated in the top left-hand corner, May 12,

1945, with an address, 41 Rivington Street, Apt. 3C, written in blue-black ink, with the same cursive loops at the bottom of *t*'s as her mother's handwriting. She turned the second page and read the signature, *Sarah*.

Dearest Peggy-sister-mine,

I read the announcement in the Times yesterday, and no matter the bad blood and misunderstandings between us, I am so happy and glad! Congratulations on Margot Kingsland Thornsen!

"Me!" said Margot out loud.

Now we both have daughters! I long to share so many maternal thoughts with you, so many hopes and dreams! When my Fay was born, I never missed a sister so much. There is a Russian lady in the apartment above ours, who speaks French as perfectly as Mlle LeRoux (do you remember how she used to torture us with irregular verbs!), who was a great comfort to me in the early weeks. I want to tell you that it is only natural to be overwhelmed and exhausted at first, but this feeling of bewilderment soon passes, and when the first smiles come, rest assured, you will feel quite differently.

I have written to you many times, and I have wept every time the letters have been returned unopened. I do not know if it is you who rejects them or Father. Maybe this route, through dear kind Jeannie, will work.

Now the war against Germany has been won and the Japs will surely surrender soon—the little Princess Margot must surely be a harbinger of peace between us also. There is no use in clinging to old arguments when there is a new generation to be raised. I know that our father will never change his mind, but I do believe if anyone can defy his bullying, it is you.

I am sure he has threatened you with Pinkerton's and with

his great and ultimate weapon, the withdrawal of his money. You were always more practical than I ever was. I see that now. You called me a dreamer with my head in cloud-cuckoo-land, and I have often thought since that you were angry not against me, but for me. Because you were right that I was swept away with romantic notions and I didn't know what I was doing.

We can hardly guess the consequences of our decisions when we are young and in love. It has not been easy, as you predicted. Davie has had a devil of a time getting work because people are suspicious of his German accent. It is not easy for a proud man to struggle so, to feel so far from his home and with all the desperation of guilt and despair at his family's fate. It is not easy to be his wife either. This I grant you—olive branch, recognition, if you like—that I know you meant well, that you meant to spare me, when you tried to stop me from leaving.

I won't ask you for money—even though I would like to, even though I would like to imagine that you would (now that you may enjoy, as a married woman, a measure of financial independence) like to help me. The truth is that just as much as our father's spite and arrogance contrives our penury, my husband's pride would deny us any indebtedness. One man vengeful, the other kind and good; the result seems to be the same. Perhaps it is our lot that we women must be subject to male obstinacies.

Now is not the time to make sense of these many forces ranged against us. Let us put the matter of finances to one side, let us ignore the legal writs and lawyers and agents, those sentries that patrol our estrangement.

I have a dream that one day I will take my Fay to the swings in the park beside the bronze lions where we used to play as children, and I will see you there with your Margot and we will laugh as we push our daughters higher and higher. We will be sisters again and they will be cousins. The sun will be shining and the terrible shadow of our father will be gone.

You will say I am dreaming, but as sure as bad times come

to test us, I believe in the promise of good times that come after
them, as day follows night. I try to console Davie with my opti-
mism; it will make you smile perhaps to learn he is almost as
resistant to it as you.

Do know, dear Peggy, I would very much like to have your
love and your forgiveness. I wish you great happiness in your
new role as "mother." I know we have not had a very good exam-
ple in this regard, but forgive her too, if you can.

With my hope and love,

Margot carefully folded the letter and replaced it in its paper and
padded silk envelope. Discombobulated, washing-machined, upside
down in the rolling surf on Jones Beach. Sarah had been cast as the
bad sister, the headstrong, self-indulgent *wayward* girl, her mother
the long-suffering dutiful daughter. But the love and wisdom of this
letter upended this version. Margot could hardly keep her hands
steady to screw the cap back on the lipstick and return the diamond
ring to its pillow and make sure everything looked undisturbed.

In the corridor she heard the clank of the dumbwaiter—
Mathilde, drawing up the tray for Goody's lunch. Not wanting to
encounter her, Margot ran down the ducal staircase and took refuge
in the library.

She sat in a black leather armchair, unforgiving horsehair, stiffly
buttoned. Her hand groped the side table, searching for the silver
cigarette box. Felt the gravid incisions of the monogram, *KGHV*, in
looping whorls. The cigarette trembled in her fingers.

The tar tasted sour on her tongue. Until now Margot had been
a child, and her mother, her mother. Their roles had been fixed:
looking-up-to and looking-down-on. "You are too young to understand. You don't want to end up like my sister." But how Sarah's
words sounded as her own cries! Clarion and alive: hope, hope of
tenderness, reconciliation, understanding, a moment of being given,
of being given over to gratitude, to solace, to the comfort of hearing,
"Everything will be alright, I'll take care of you"—never mind all

those times alone, sobbing; wipe your tears and splash cold water on your face and face the world and hope it could be kinder.

"Watch it, Miss M, you'll burn a hole in the carpet with that cigarette."

Margot had not heard Jean Craft come into the room. Startled, she jerked her wrist and a droop of cigarette ash fell onto the Turkish rug. The old woman shuffled forward and bent over, creaking and huffing, to pick it up with a yellow dust cloth. Margot remained inert, caught. Jean Craft took the cigarette out of her hand and stubbed it out in the ashtray.

"You looks as if you saw a ghost."

"Sarah."

"Yes'm." Jean Craft sighed heavily. "I seen her too. I seen her oftentimes on the third floor, up in the piano room where you and that rollicker Stevie used to play. The spirits of injustice don't settle easy."

"What really happened? Why won't anyone talk about it?"

Jean Craft turned off the vacuum cleaner. Her face was wrinkly and her bulbous eyes were two blue marbles rolled into a mussed-up bedsheet. She shuffled her secrets with her carpet slippers, made a half turn, perhaps reconsidering, and lowered herself heavily into an armchair. Her nylon blue apron was incongruous against the plum velvet of the upholstery. Margot had never in her life seen Jean Craft sit down.

"You best ask your grandmother about Sarah."

"Goody can't remember. Or she remembers an episode of *Bonanza*—"

"That's what a lifetime is"—Jean Craft leaned on the handlebar of the upright vacuum cleaner—"some story so faded and torn or unraveled bare or embroidered back over itself that you can't tell truth from remembrance. Best ask your mother."

"My mother never tells me anything."

Jean Craft nodded. "Takes after her old dad. As hard and straight as his selfsame railroad ties. You can see the effort of all that standing-up-straight written all over your mother's face. She could have helped her sister, maybe she thought she did. But she did it in her way of doing, which is to pay for someone else to do it. It was me who was the go-between when Sarah was pregnant again, red face from crying her eyes out, scalded hands from washing the diapers in carbolic. The poor girl was reduced to taking in laundry. That Stern was stern, all I can say. Didn't want no charity. So Sarah let him believe it was her doing. But it was me that took the envelope from your mother to pay the rent for the apartment in Oyster Bay. It was me who risked my job when your mother dared not risk a meeting. The King had spies everywhere!"

"Why didn't anyone help Sarah after he died?" asked Margot.

"The King's will was ironclad, locked against Sarah, what I heard. Don't be asking me for ramifications. There was a lot talked about, not much anyone knew the truth of."

"The trust and the codicil." Margot had overheard her mother on the telephone to Mr. Penny from the bank.

"I daresay," Jean Craft said. "Things above my station, as I've been reminded."

"My mother says we have an obligation to my cousins."

"I sees her trying to make amends, but I sees too that stern Stern has imparted his own cankers to his daughters. No one likes to be an obligation."

"Do you think Sarah regretted running away with him?"

"I don't have the mind to stretch to another's thoughts," Jean Craft said, getting to her feet. "Maybe that's a bad thing: not to be able to dream of something different than the life you were born to. All I know is Sarah's head was always full of bookery and stories. I don't know what she thought about the world outside her father's gates, but I am pretty sure she never knew what a tenement was before she had to live in one."

Jean Craft hefted the vacuum cleaner to the door. "There was a softness in Sarah, the kind that hard people will punish 'em for. Maybe it was her dreaming that gave her kindness, maybe it was her dreaming that led her wayward. There's some of her in you, I see it," Jean Craft said in parting. "I'll bet your mother sees it too."

7

BEHIND THE SENIOR DORM BUILDING AT THE ETHEL Walker School was an oak wood. A mud lane led through the trees, girls were not permitted to "go off-track." Still, they did.

Half a mile in, if you knew how to follow the bent twigs and the shuffled undergrowth, there was a clearing with a circle of tree stumps. It was a kind of open-air clubhouse, rediscovered by successive classes and cliques. Girls in the know gathered there, sat and gassed, smoked, passed around a shampoo bottle filled with Martini Rosso and talked about beaus and kissing.

In their junior year Maddy Clements had been the ringleader of the backwoods gang. She had a mane of tumbling red curls that the teachers were always telling her to tie back. Maddy just shrugged, she didn't care how many demerits she got. She had her own confidence, as if she knew this place and time, school and society, were a temporary construct she would soon be free of. Margot was in awe of her. Maddy was fast and sharp and witty, she was good at what her mother called "repartee." But even though she was obviously the coolest girl in the school (a coterie of disciples followed her about), she always said hello-how-are-you-doing? to Margot when they ran into each other after class or at mealtimes. They both had Miss Puzio for Combined Biology-Chemistry. Maddy called her "Miss Pubis," and the nickname stuck because Miss Puzio had three wiry whiskers that grew out of a mole on her neck.

Margot had the habit of walking in the woods to be alone. She didn't want anyone to see because going off by yourself was the sort of thing sneaking *lesbians* did (although Margot had only the faintest idea of what lesbians did, so faint that it was really no idea, only the idea that it was the most shameful thing you could be accused of doing).

Now they were seniors. One Saturday afternoon in November, Margot set off with the idea to look for mushrooms. Fall falling, leaves crackled underfoot, giving her away. Birch trees striped silver bars, the sky was a pale far-off blue through the last frail, dying yellow leaves. She kept her head down, looking for the veiled oyster caps that grew in villages under white oaks and hickories. It seemed to be a myth that mushrooms appeared after rain, because Margot noticed they sprouted in dry weeks just as many. Perhaps they grew according to relative temperature, humidity levels, or barometric pressure. For two weeks there would be none, and then suddenly a great sprouting. Maybe they followed lunar cycles. Can a mushroom see the moon? Did it look up at the stars? But this would not, Margot suspected, be a suitable topic for her science project.

There, through the trees! A red peacoat she recognized immediately as Maddy Clements's. She was further into the woods than she had ventured before, all the way to the far fence, the edge of school property. Maddy was sitting in an unexpected armchair, completely incongruous, like a Narnia apparition, smoking a cigarette that unfurled a ribbon of sinuous smoke into the cold, still air.

"Come sit," said Maddy, indicating a wooden folding chair. Mad had her feet up on the legless carcass of an old pinball machine that served as a coffee table. The fence behind was rotten gray wood, there was a door in it. Ajar.

"I had no idea this was here," said Margot.

"I created it," said Maddy simply. "The door leads to the path that goes through the graveyard down into the town. A couple of the boys from the local high school helped me with this open-air setup. They were more into it when the weather was Indian summer. I snuck out on Saturday nights and we had some parties. Suburban jukebox cowboys. Nothing like real cowboys—"

Maddy sighed a wide-skied missing sigh. Her cigarette guttered and she lit another from its cherry ember.

"The dorm mothers all know about the stump circle. They let girls go there so they don't sneak into Simsbury to drink. But once you're eighteen they can't stop you really; they know they can't throw you out in your final year or parents would be up in arms and they are terrified of scandal, so they provide this phony outlet for 'rebellion.'"

Margot flinched at Maddy's cynicism.

"Sorry, Margot, I didn't mean to shock you. I'm having a bad time, that's all. You ever get stuck in a corner?"

Margot nodded. "My mother says it's the worst thing that can happen at a cocktail party, to get penned in by some bore who won't let you mingle."

Maddy hugged her knees to her chest, like a child trying to comfort itself.

"Is there something I can do to help?" Margot asked softly.

"What? Like call the abortion doctor for me?"

Margot blinked. Two days ago Maddy had abruptly run out of science class at full pelt. Miss Pubis had watched her bolt with narrowed eyes. Afterwards she said it was nothing, just period pains.

Margot hesitated, "I don't know—"

"I know, I'm sorry, I shouldn't have—"

"No, it's OK."

Maddy drew herself up. "It's not OK," she said, grim and clear. "I'm more than four months gone, and if I tell my mother she'll send me to some clinic in Idaho where I will endure the unendurable, give birth and then be made to give it up."

"Idaho?"

"I don't know if it's actually Idaho—"

Margot sat for a moment looking up into the spreading canopy of the copper beech above. She could see the dark scars where
branches had been sawed off and tarred.

"Give me one," she asked. Maddy handed her a cigarette and
they smoked together for a moment.

"I can ask someone I know," said Margot, thinking out loud.
"He's kind. The kind who would be kind about this, I think. He's at
Harvard Med School."

Bidden, Dick Merryweather drove down from Cambridge.
Found the path on the other side of the fence in the woods and
met them at the pinball machine the following Sunday morning.
The girls had an hour and a half after chapel before they would be
missed for lunch. He took them to a diner on the outskirts of Hartford. They ordered three cups of coffee and waited until the waitress
was out of earshot like bank robbers in a movie.

Dick said, "Call me Richie," and was grave and sweet and said
he wouldn't tell a soul, don't worry, he knew what to do theoreti-
cally, he was in his final year before residency; but he would prefer
to take Madeleine to a real doctor, someone he trusted, who could
do the operation off-hours at his clinic in Boston in hygienic conditions. Madeleine—he used her full name—should come up on the
train and could stay over at his apartment. He would arrange to be
away for a night or two. He said it would be better if Margot came
with her, to be a friend, because Madeleine would feel sore and blue
afterwards.

"Soon," he told them, charging his voice with urgency. Margot
and Maddy nodded mutely. "Thanksgiving weekend."

THE PRESIDENT WAS SHOT the following Friday.

It was such an extraordinary and unprecedented event that classes
were halted and the prefects were instructed to wheel the television
set from Miss Wall's study and set it up on the stage of the assembly
hall for the students to watch. Sirens wailing, stentorian tones of the

newscasters. Everyone felt silent when Walter Cronkite took off his thick black glasses and announced Kennedy was dead.

Bernie Pratt rushed from the room sobbing, other girls held hands, bent heads together in prayer circles. As the weekend unraveled, girls lined up to call home (allowed under the special circumstances) from the telephone in the teachers' lounge, there was a shortage of Kleenex in the dispensary, silence was not enforced at mealtimes, a sudden craze took hold for black armbands made from stockings. "I can't bear it . . ." "She's so dignified . . ." "Oh those poor fatherless children . . ." "It's always the oddball loners you have to look out for . . ." "My uncle, you know, was at Choate with him . . ."

"I don't feel anything," Maddy whispered to Margot. "Isn't that terrible? Am I a selfish brute?"

Margot watched the striated, fuzzy television pictures: Dallas, DC, hospital parking lot, airport runway, convoys of black cars, back to the studio. The whole world was waiting: everything was liminal, contingent, up-in-the-air; as if the operator had pulled out all the telephone lines and the silence was filled with the disconnected hissing static.

The chapel was cold and dank on Sunday morning. The visiting deacon's voice intoned up and down, his vowels stretched interminably between consonants so that meaning was lost in incantation: afterlife, everlasting, obedience, God's will, gone, unto—*unto*—the word hung upside down in Margot's head, sounded only like a sound.

She pressed her hands together but no prayer came. Her eyes were dry. Maybe Maddy was right, no one truly cries for another's loss, we cry for our own, and then she cried because she couldn't cry.

Because the tragedy occurred so close to a holiday weekend, routine and regulations were suspended, classes were canceled, timetables ignored, some parents even came to collect their daughters early. Margot had been nervous about their Boston plan, but the national drama veiled their schoolgirl subterfuge. Maddy told Miss

Wall she would be spending Thanksgiving weekend with Margot's family. Margot then telephoned her mother on the afternoon of the funeral.

"I'm watching it now," said her mother. "Dotty Merryweather says they had a Hollywood producer organize it. Look at Joe Kennedy standing there as if butter wouldn't melt! I never met such an indecent man. Unless it was Black Jack Bouvier. Jackie is so *theatrical*—I wouldn't have put the children on show like that—"

Margot gently interrupted to tell her that she had been invited to spend the weekend with Madeleine Clements's uncle in Back Bay in Boston. "Madeleine's mother was a Cabot," she added.

"Well, off you go to your better invitation. Goody has had one of her episodes again. Perhaps it's best this way. Do *try* to get along with everyone, Margot. And don't forget to tip the maid."

MARGOT AND MADDY TOOK the train from Hartford to Boston on Thursday morning. Margot bought a newspaper at the station. STOCK MARKET UP ON RECORD DAY. JOHNSON BACKS EXISTING POLICY: WHEAT NEGOTIATIONS GO ON.

"It seems weird that life just continues as if nothing happened," said Margot, to say something.

"Hope is dead," said Maddy, in a small voice. "The idea that everything is going to be alright."

"Things will feel better soon, you'll see," said Margot.

"Or they will feel worse—"

The train shuddered into a siding. Margot saw green circles under her friend's eyes.

"I suppose you're wondering who, and why don't I just marry him," Maddy said, looking out of the window.

"No, I'm not actually. I'm not interested in gossip. Maybe that's why I'm not popular at school. I mean I don't find it easy to say such-and-such about so-and-so."

"People think you're a loner. For a while I thought you might be depressive, like my mother," said Maddy, ever candid. "But you're not like that. You keep your own counsel. That's why I could confide in you."

"But you're popular," Margot said, perturbed by the compliment as much as the information that people thought she was an oddball. "Not because you're a gossip, I didn't mean to say that. I think that you are popular because you don't mind about being popular. You don't care what people think. I mind too much, so I am always trying to please people. Halfway through a conversation, I stop and think: What should I say next? What do they want to hear? Then I forget my train of thought and stand there gasping like a carp."

"Oh Margot! No one could ever be as hard on you as you are hard on yourself."

"Yes, but that's worse, don't you see?" Margot took off her hat and shook out her hair. "It's all my own fault! If I just changed the way I thought about myself, people would change the way they thought about me. I'm sorry, I am going on and you must be very anxious."

"Oh please keep talking!" Maddy laughed and passed her a fifth of bourbon she had wrapped in a drugstore bag. Margot shook her head no-thanks. "Your conversation is distracting me."

"Oh, well in that case—" Margot laughed and began to tell Maddy all about her family.

She told it like a fairy tale, a bedtime story to lull a sick child: "Once upon a time there was a very rich man . . ." in a way she never had before. She mimicked Goody calling for her nightly brandy-and-molasses, described all the characters of the Big House: Mathilde, who must be seventy if she was a day, but who still wore her hair in ringlets and ribbons; Mrs. Ambrose, fussing over the shape of butter pats. She did not spare her mother, "Nothing is ever good enough for her. Even when everyone always tells her how perfect everything is," or her father, "I think something happened to him in the war. He drinks his apple brandy alone in the den, and I don't think he likes my mother very much because he basically plays golf *all the time*."

Maddy laughed too, "Families! Mine is just as crazy!" And she told Margot about four generations of Clements ranchers—a biblical tale of promised land, floods, and internecine struggle.

"My father," said Maddy with a long whistling sigh. "Big bear of a man. Straight-talking, straight-shooting. Silver belt buckle as big as a prizefighter's. He married my mother because she was the first girl he laid eyes on the first time he ever went to Houston. Total disaster!" Maddy rolled her eyes. Her father was leather, her mother was a feather bed. Her father had wanted sons, her mother gave him two daughters. "Basically I take after my father, but the old boot can't imagine a girl can be any kind of rancher. I was forbidden to wear trousers—can you imagine? There was nothing to do but rebel. And my sister, of course, darling apple-of-his-eye Lila, is the spit of my mother, primps and pours her tea so nicely and is his ideal idea of what a girl should be—which is basically obedient."

"It's funny to look at your family from the outside," said Margot. "As if they were characters in a novel."

"When you're a child you love them close-up, you can't really see who they are. Then you grow up and see that they were ordinary fools and monsters all along."

The New Hampshire woods blurred greenish dun beyond the window. Maddy took a swig of bourbon and pulled her knees up to her chest. Margot watched her eyes grow black and deep as onyx.

"They tell us we are never, under any circumstances, to have *intercourse*," Maddy said, looking out of the window. "Because we are nice girls and sex is beyond the Pale and the Pale is a place where they send you *away*—did you know it actually exists? I think it's in Ruritania. They send you *away* if you are a hussy and bring shame on your family, when three Hail Marys won't cut it. I was a tomboy, always running wild, in and out of the bunkhouse. I galloped as far as I could, begged to eat with the hands in the mess hall. One of the young cowboys, a boy, not much older than me, said we could learn it together. Can you imagine, Margot, the great wondrousness of the wide Texan sky, and the stars as bright as anything, winking at you. Johnno would walk me back from the mess hall to the ranch house, we would stop by the south corral and he would lean against the fence and we would kiss and kiss and kiss for hours, as if it would never end. My mother saw us one night. She didn't tell my father; the old man would have—god knows what—but that was the end of that and I was sent three thousand miles away to the Ethel Walker School for Girls in some cold and rainy place called Connecticut. Of course, the problem is that there are boys everywhere. Johnno taught me that there is nothing to be ashamed of. Not of your body, not of pleasure."

Margot looked at Maddy askance. "You're not ashamed?" she asked.

"I am determined not to be ashamed," Maddy said firmly.

RICHIE'S APARTMENT WAS IN a Victorian house behind the divinity school. It was a small one-bedroom; he had tidied up, putting his books in one pile and his clothes in another.

"I'll take you to the clinic," he told Maddy. "Margot, you should come and pick her up at eight this evening. Here's a map. Afterwards, give her aspirin and hot tea. She'll be quiet after the sedative; she'll probably just want to sleep."

Cambridge was cold before snow. Almost without thinking about it, Margot walked over to the Radcliffe campus. Her feet seemed to know where they were going. At the gate a porter in the porter's lodge asked her what her business was. Margot hesitated at the marble threshold. The porter looked her up and down. "No tourists!" Margot retreated around the corner, looked in through the railings. Girls were going to and fro across the green quad between classes. Chattering in twos and threes, mittened hands clasping heavy books against their chests. Margot noticed one girl in particular because she was wearing a sky blue coat that stood out among the camels and tans. She was also too tall; her hat was askew and she was laughing, and the girl beside her was laughing too. Margot pressed her forehead against the railings and wondered if she could belong like that, laugh like that, find happiness a breeze instead of an effort. Wondered if happiness was her decision or one made for her. (It did not quite occur to her that she could decide this.) She admired Maddy's ferocity then, to be able to kill the thing that would hold her back. Margot wished she could have experiences instead of exams. She wanted to do things. To be—

She had to pee.

Diner across the street. She ordered a coffee she didn't want and went to the ladies'. She came back and perched uncomfortably on the red vinyl stool at the counter. A policeman sitting across, badged cap on the counter next to a plate of hash browns, looked up from his newspaper.

"Be sure they'll never get to the bottom of anything with Hoover's people mudding about. And now we've got a Texan in the White House!"

Margot realized it was the first time she had ever been to a restaurant alone. Thanksgiving midafternoon, the diner was almost empty. No other women, she noticed.

The cop looked over at her and asked, "So what do you think about it, little lady? Was it the Mob or the Russkies or the under-the-covers G-men?"

Margot had never in her life been asked for an opinion about anything by an adult.

"I don't know."

The coffee hit her stomach with a bitter twinge. She made a small grimace.

"Fight with the boyfriend?" asked the cop professionally, perhaps even kindly.

"No. Nothing like that."

"With your parents maybe?"

"Well, I'm upset, of course everyone is," said Margot, taking cover in the national mourning.

"No one knows what to think," said the cook, wiping the counter with a rag. He was an older Negro, with white hair and a white moustache. His voice was rich and creamy. "It's like what happened in '41. Nothing'll be the same again."

He looked at Margot's undrunk cup of coffee. "No good?"

"I'm sorry, I don't feel very well." Margot put two dollar bills on the counter; she didn't know how much to tip and she couldn't bring herself to ask.

Outside the air was cool on her neck. Her thoughts looped like a swift swooping through the sky, alighting now on the pillar of her mother, now on the statue of her grandfather, gateposts that barred her future—or framed it—now flitting to the branch of a tree, holding there, cockeyed, as Sarah might have once, ready to fly away forever—before the wind blew up and she felt herself falling like she had fallen from the old rotten rope ladder—*Stop thinking so much!* said a voice in her head, half her mother's, half her own.

She found the clinic easily with Richie's map. Sat in the waiting room, picked up a copy of *Newsweek* and opened it by chance to an article about the Strategic Hamlet Program in Vietnam. *There's always a war going on somewhere.* Somewhere far, as far as you can wish upon a star hanging upside down in a sky on the other side of the world. She tried to configure the variations of orbiting constellations, triangulations, sine and cosine and pi-in-the-sky (Margot smiled at her silly muddled thoughts) and other mathematical truths. She stared at a photograph of a Sandyful GI, bareheaded, dangling his helmet by the chin strap, exhausted, as if he would like to throw it away. The soldier was looking up at something about to arrive from the sky, incoming, just out of frame: enemy mortar fire, helicopter, death, deliverance—impossible to tell—his expression was blank, as if he had surrendered to whatever blessed blasted luck or unluck might befall him.

Finally Maddy emerged. She had a bitter-grim expression and

signed the release form white-faced and silent, changed, Mad. It began to snow in sympathy as they walked back to Richie's apartment. Margot put her to bed as she imagined she might one day tuck in her own child. Then she lay down on the sofa with a blanket, stared at the white snowflakes building a wall on the windowsill.

Richie came in the morning with donuts. Mad was still quiet. She tried to make a smile but the corners of her mouth didn't curl up. Richie held her wrist to check her pulse. Margot watched his long, elegant fingers and felt a quickening and just as quick let go of it; his nose was long and thin and his mouth was narrow and scarred.

Richie held up a brown paper bag and shook it so it rattled. "This is for both of you."

"Is it the Pill?" guessed Mad.

"Yes."

"I thought you had to be married."

"You do," said Richie, "but I know some of the guys at the lab who developed the dosages. Take one every day, stop on the first day of your period for a week. There is a year's supply for both of you here."

Margot was embarrassed. He clearly thought she needed the Pill too, he must think she was as loose as Mad, *by association*, added her mother's trombone treble.

But Richie said, "If you need more, you can write me and I'll send you some—just don't tell all your friends. I don't want to turn into a mail-order pharmacy."

"I don't think I need—" Margot tried to dissuade him of his assumptions.

"Take them, Margot," Richie said. "You don't need them yet, but don't you want to be able to decide when you do?"

8

O~N THE MORNING THEY WERE DUE TO HAND IN THE OUT-~
lines of their science projects, Margot went into the lab in a red-
rimmed panic because she had been up all night reading back copies
of *Scientific American*, desperately trying to come up with an idea,
and had only come down with a cold. She waited until the end of
the class after everyone had left, stood in front of the teacher's desk,
sneezed.

"The rhinovirus," said Miss Pubis. Her eyeglasses hung on a gold
chain around her neck. "Study that."

So every day for a week, Margot pricked a bead of her own
blood and pressed it between two glass slides. She had looked at
plant cells under the microscope before, but this was different. At
×40, her blood looked like rivulets trickling through sandbanks. At
×100, she could see the circular outlines of the blood cells jostling
like crowds of people on a sidewalk. Turning the lens, click-click
to the big ×400 scope, cells became rings, like Cheerios bobbing
in a bowl of milk. Miss Puzio had told her to count the number of
white blood cells. These were rounder, without a hole, and looked
like softballs.

Margot bent over the eyepiece (atchoo!), clicking the mechanical counter once for each softball. She focused, traveling her eyes
methodically left to right, memorizing the variations of flow and

shape. When she concentrated very hard, the world and its noise fell away and she disappeared into the microcosmos of the infinite. The voices in her head ceased, quieted by the silence and wonder. Unknown galaxies are as much in us as they are everlastingly expanding into space.

Margot diligently recorded her white cell count every morning and evening, and plotted the numbers on a graph. On a separate chart, she recorded her symptoms—blocked nose, aching limbs, headache, cough—grading them one to five, from mild to severe. At the end of the week her white cell graph was a zigzag. Margot was despondent and her nose was still blocked.

"You should have seen an even gradient," said Miss Puzio.

The science project was part of the College Boards. And she couldn't apply to Radcliffe with an incomplete.

Numb, Margot put on her winter coat and her earmuffs and walked into the woods. Stared dumbly at her feet shuffling through the frosty leaf litter. Felt the sharp pang of failure, of despair. Unconsoling bare winter branches barred the sky.

Mad found her sitting in the armchair by the fence.

"I heard what Pubis said. She's a witch. Don't feel bad. Margot, there's always a way. You taught me that."

Mad handed her a slim fifth of bourbon. Margot took a timid sip.

"Bleuch! Mad, this is strong."

"Don't let Pubis get you down. You just have to look at the problem in a different way." It sounded like a Sandyful idea. "I think you have just encountered your first lesson in medicine," Mad continued, lighting a cigarette and blowing dragon smoke from her nostrils. "You see the world in black and white. As if it were a neat diagram with everything labeled. But there is so much that scientists and doctors don't know. They just put on their we-know-better voices, like teachers, and tell you this-means-that and you believe them because you want to, because the alternative is not knowing anything and that's totally scary. But think about all the new discoveries they are making all the time. If you really want to be a scientist, you have to give up the idea of a perfect answer. We don't even know what we don't know."

This was a new and frightening and enthralling idea for Margot. It seemed to expand in her like hydrogen, the lightest and most abundant element. At night, she lay in her narrow bed listening to Bernadette whistle through her nose and the maple branch swish against the window, quiet, not quiet, the sounds of two hundred girls dreaming.

Margot turned onto her tummy, tucked her palms between her legs, felt the soft wet intimate secret folded there. She was trapped in a bombed-out hamlet in Hai Phong and her soldier-poet was coming to rescue her. She hugged the pillow, felt his arms around her body as he lifted her up. A germ of something tickled. She felt its outline delicately, fingertips in the dark, slippery, self and something beyond, a tantalizing void, hmmm, trip into unknown territory, skip a heartbeat and wander over the edge of the map—no one could see—oh! and there—where? Oh! a little more a little more Oh! something melted into sense sensation sensational, into liquid plasma radiating fizzily. Unbuckled, unseen, Margot lay very still.

9

When they were in the apartment at 655, in the city, Margot's father watched television alone in his den, a balloon of apple brandy in one hand, a cigar in the other. At Farnsworth, over Christmas break, he was obliged to sit down with his wife and daughter to watch the evening news on an old Bakelite set in the shagreen study.

Peggy disliked Walter Cronkite. "I don't know why that man has to take on a hectoring-lecturing tone." World events were irritations, interruptions, the result of ineptitude, idiocy, and foreigners. In any case, there were bound to be Igbo bugaboos killing each other somewhere in the world. Meanwhile there were errands to attend to. Peggy sat with her customary vodka on the rocks sweating on a coaster, her crocodile notebook opened in her lap and a sharpened pencil in her right hand, making lists: invitations to be sent out, invitations to be answered, bridge dates, dinner guests, menus, grocery lists, a repaired necklace to be collected from Tiffany. Let that grim-faced newscaster talk all he wanted in his overblown way: wheels of progress, winds of change, cultural earthquakes! The greater tectonics, the forces underfoot that Old King Vanderloep had once mined, smelted, hammered into railroad ties, and sold as future stock options, had been banked and subsumed into assumption. Peggy signed checks as blithely as she pulled on a new pair of panty hose.

There was a report on the progress of the Civil Rights Act, which Johnson, honoring Kennedy's legacy, had vowed to enact. Accompanying the political analysis was footage from protest marches over the summer.

"I don't know why they insist on broadcasting these pictures night after night," said Peggy, looking up from her lists. "It's all so much fear-mongering and hand-wringing."

Margot watched the scenes: German shepherds straining at their leashes; solemn Negroes in dark suits and narrow ties linking arms; three teenagers pinned against a wall by a fire hose jet.

"It's the television age, my dear," said her father, who, from time to time, liked to snag at the sheer of his wife's prerogative. "There cannot be change if there are no cameras to witness it."

A young black woman, about the same age as Margot and who wore her hair curled under at the nape of her neck, like Margot did, held her head up and her books tightly across her chest and walked through a tunnel of jeering faces.

"You see, Mother," said Margot, "how important college is. Look at that brave girl."

"Well, *I* didn't go to college," said Peggy.

The college conversation had stalled in this fashion for more than two years. Peggy said college was a fast track to a *reputation*, that no man ever wanted to marry a Radcliffe girl, that biology was of *no use* to anyone but doctors, and since she wasn't going to be a doctor what was the point? Four years consorting with *unattractive* people from god knows where, she was bound to pick up all sorts of *unsuitable* ideas.

Margot knew better than to remonstrate. Bit her lip. Tried to hide her ambition, that unseemly, boastful word, buried it close to her heart, lower, deeper, at the base of her sternum where pain and hope clenched together, the location, according to anatomical diagrams, of her xiphoid process, the bone at the bottom of the breastplate named after the Greek word for sword tip; conjugated, in Margot's latent imagination, with her lost champion, Sandyful.

The news report turned now to our correspondent in Vietnam; Peggy segued too:

"Well, the Dow Jones is up despite everything," she said, suddenly all singsong. "And Clarence Merryweather has got Runny a job at J.P. Morgan. Dotty made sure to mention it to me."

"They will bring in the draft," said her father, "if this goes on."

"Dotty is simply sick at the idea," said her mother. "I told her Dr. Dome can always be relied on to diagnose a disqualifying condition—oh I'm sure Runny will be alright, he's the kind to slip through any net. Dick is protected by his medical status; I never thought I would live to hear Clarence admit it was a relief to have one of his sons a doctor. Then there is Hal, and I don't believe even the US Army would stoop to take such a lowlife as that boy has turned out to be. Trip is the main worry. But I told Dotty that married men are always the last to be called up—"

Margot felt her ears redden.

"Hold your horses, Peg," said her father. "The kids are still in high school."

GOODY HAD WEAKENED INFINITESIMALLY to skeletal, virtually transparent, but her decline had been many years slow: as if her dying was a diminishing half-life, like uranium, that would never actually be extinguished. "She'll bury us all!" was a Farnsworth mantra. A masseuse was engaged, and various equipment installed: an electric hospital bed, a thalasso-therapeutical water-jet bath, and an electric chairlift, the installation of which ruined one wing of the double ducal staircase. Her medicine cabinet overflowed with brown glass vials, indigo pots of tincture, silver blister packs of pills, rolls of linen bandages. Goody's skin was mottled with brown liver spots and deep magenta bruises. At night Mathilde tied silk bags around her hands because her skin was so fragile that she often tore it with her heavy jeweled rings when she turned in her sleep.

When Margot visited her, Goody feebly waved a white parchment hand roped in thick blue veins.

"Sarah," she whispered, and smiled a sad, long-lost smile. "You've come back! Sarah!"

"It's me. Margot."

Goody's head sank back into the soft berm of swan's-down pillow. She had forsaken her wig for a bed bonnet fringed with lace, and Margot could see her tortoise scalp through white wisps of hair. Her eyes were closed, but the folds of her eyelids twitched faintly, as if she were watching a movie behind them.

"You always were a foolish girl!" A voice out of time, dialogue for an unseen scene. Goody's lips made soft shapes; the wattle of her neck wobbled. "I warned you not to bookworm. Never any good that came from reading. Words are only dream-catchers and candied fancies! Now you've learned your lesson in all that love mush!"

Goody reached for Margot's hand and stroked it. "I know it ain't pretty to hear the scuffed-up truth of it: men is all of 'em liars and carney tricksters. Oh, to remember Old King a-courting as charming as a prince, jewels and furs and private railroad cars, all mine! He promised me long and tall as the skyscrapers of New York City. Everything glittered in his glittering eyes, like mica in the dark mouths of his mines—'cept when you crossed him. When you cross him, he's straight for the hammer and the anvil; iron is all he wants and is. Sarah-child, mind to tiptoe with your father's humor, tell him sugared almonds, even if they taste like sulfur on your tongue to speak 'em."

"It's me. Margot," Margot repeated, softly, hesitant to admit herself.

Goody's eyes remained closed and her breath shallowed, but she kept Margot's hand hostage in hers.

"Goodness got its limits. There is no beauty that doesn't wrack and ruin itself. Old Mother Hubbard told us that 'fore every performance, eyeing the jackasses lined up at the bar for their after-shows. 'Take your pick between the kind man or the rich man,' she warned us. 'Make your choice as you would make your bed, but don't be mistaking the idea you would be the first women in the history of the world to marry them both.'"

Goody opened one clear blue eye, thawing ice, brimming. "Fool as I am for optin' for the gold-lace life! More fool you! Thinking kindness can take the place of a soft bed in a warm room. Kindness turns sour soon enough when the wallet is empty and the grate is cold. Learned the hard way, didn't ya, same as me." A tear spilled onto her cheek. "Tried to run, see how far you'd get, eh?"

Goody's good eye slipped its focus and she closed her lids again. Margot remained at her side, hand still in hers, sensing that to withdraw it would be to wake her. She felt her grandmother's pulse slow, diminuendo, heard her breath slow to tarry beside it. Life was trapped and beat frail wings against the ribs that held it. Margot's shoulder ached; she wanted to move but didn't dare; accustomed to endurance, endured it. The carriage clock chimed every quarter hour, the seconds tick-tocked and the pendulum invented time and then ignored it, swinging back and forth back and forth forever.

Goody jolted, full of sudden urgency:

"Well, it wasn't my fault! Saddle the bay up! I'm going after her! She'll not get further than Hangman's Bluffs in this snow!"

"Goody, it's not snowing."

"No, dear," Goody smiled up at her, now clear-eyed again and full of apparently peaceful innocence, "it's deeper."

MARGOT LISTENED TO THE nighttime noises of the Big House carefully, as if through a stethoscope: a slammed door, the discreet metallic tumbling of a key locking or unlocking, the clatter of her mother's heels on marble, the heavy tread of Mathilde on the back stairs. Moods and humors, rumblings, subtext.

Tiptoed past her parents' room, heard her mother's unmistakable shrill invective on the other side of the door: "Not the *right* husband! And she is so—" Margot held her breath. "Ungainly. Homely." Her father answered in a mumble she couldn't catch, but her mother's voice was clear as a bell. "Girls are so *susceptible* at that age—college girls! . . . Loose morals! Anything goes!" She heard her father again, low and inaudible. Interrupted by her mother, "It's too late! She needs to be settled *now*. I should have organized power of attorney before the lawyers took over."

There is a certain privacy in loneliness. The feeling was very familiar to Margot and she found false comfort in it, drawing it around herself like a blanket.

The telephone rang near midnight, but it was as if someone had been waiting for a call because it was answered after a single ring. The driveway gravel crunched. A small *pick-puck* sound of a stone hitting her bedroom window.

Midnight, cold and clear, full moon, Margot went down the back stairs in her nightie and slippers and dressing gown, as if to get a glass of milk from the kitchen, and slipped out the back door.

Stevie was huddled in the shadow of a holly bush.

"I've come to rescue you. My folks have gone into the city for the night."

"Out of the frying pan, you mean." Margot shivered, hesitating, felt the prickle of impropriety. She couldn't bring herself to be rude.

"Don't worry, it's not like I got some kind of Sabrina complex." Stevie wore a leather jacket. His hair was thick and chestnut and he had brushed it forward in a heavy mop fringe. He was just the type Mad would go mad for.

"I don't know—" said Margot.

"Just for ten minutes. I've got a record I want to play you."

Back when they were ten and eleven, before they realized that one of them was a boy and the other was a girl, that one was poor and one was rich, when they were just pals, Stevie had invented a game he called "recording." When Nice Noreen was over at the Big House and they were left alone in the estate manager's apartment.

Stevie would say, "Do you want to hear a record?" He had a record player with a needle that you had to carefully drop by hand onto the record. They would go into Stevie's bedroom and Stevie would put on a rock-and-roll record and then he would take off his clothes and Margot would take off her clothes and Stevie would go first and be allowed to touch her for thirty seconds according to his watch and then it was her turn and she could touch his peter for thirty seconds. It was like a tapered finger except softer without bones and Margot didn't really mind, but she didn't exactly like it. One day Stevie told her to stroke it up and down and she did. One day it was stiff and Margot asked, "Why is it like that?" Stevie just shrugged and said, "Sometimes it just is." One day he changed the rules and told her to lie down on her back and then he was allowed to lie on top of her for thirty seconds, front to front. Margot lay very still. Stevie didn't move either. After thirty seconds he got off her and said, "I saw it in a movie but I guess you have to wriggle around more if you want it to work." "Make what work?" Margot asked. Another time he made her lie down and open her legs. Margot kept her eyes shut as usual. She felt him prod his finger past the outside part, into the inside part, inside the inside part. She yelped.

"Shh!" Stevie told her.

Margot never told anyone. She kept it on the topmost shelf of her memory. When she was twelve, Lydia Cummings told her the facts of life, about French kissing and getting a baby up there. The summer afterwards when Margot came back to Farnsworth, Stevie asked her to come and listen to a record but she said no. He hadn't asked her since. Now he was standing there and looking at her.

"It's a new thing. It's English."

"What do you mean?"

"I mean the record. Come on, Maggot."

Margot acquiesced. Perhaps to the cold. They couldn't continue to stand there, halfway. She had partly forgotten, not the feeling of unease, but the particulars of what had caused it.

And Stevie insisted. "Come on, why not, do you think I'm going to bite you?" His face looked up at her from inside the collar of his jacket, half puppy dog, half hound.

But the moment they arrived in the yellow-and-white-checked kitchen, the smell of Lysol and linoleum came back to her in a great rush and she wanted to leave. But now Stevie was playing the gracious host, getting out a couple of jelly jar glasses from the cupboard and producing a small bottle of rum and a yellow packet.

"If you stir it with banana milkshake powder, it makes a tropical cocktail." He mixed his potions with a fork.

Margot sipped. It was thick and sweet and vile.

She deliberately sat on one of the kitchen chairs so that he could not sit directly next to her on the bench. Her fingers picked at the Formica peeling at the edge of the table.

"So what's next for you?" she smiled brightly. *Always ask about someone's plans, that's the polite way to start a conversation.*

He was starting mechanics school in the New Year, he said as if it was something big and grown-up to be proud of. *Pumping gas,* countered her mother's voice.

"It counts the same as college, I can get a draft deferment."

He turned up the radio, "Hey Maggot, you gotta listen to this."

Margot listened to the *waah waah,* as her mother called it.

I wanna hold your haa—aand.

"They sound like the Everlies."

"They're British. They're new."

"You are more modern than I am. For me the music sounds—" To Margot, the electricity in the guitar sounded like an Apollo rocket firing.

Stevie turned up the volume. Margot put her hands over her ears.

"Turn it down! James will hear in his cottage."

"James doesn't care."

Stevie stood up and shimmy-bopped, wagging his head from side to side, elbows flapping. Margot thought he looked ridiculous. He knocked over a bowl of salad dressing on the counter. Margot instinctively looked for a cloth to wipe it up, but Stevie laughed as he floundered.

"Oh, this is a genius discovery!" he said, sliding back and forth in his socks. "Maggot"—he reached both hands out—"you gotta check this out! It's like skating—" He pretended to misjudge a glide and half crashed into her chair, tugged at her hands to pull her up.

Stevie twirled her around and Margot let him. He put his hand on her behind and she maneuvered away and tried to make it look like part of her dance.

He put both his hands on her shoulders. "I've got some uppers if you're—"

Margot instinctively ducked, then turned, making it look like a swing-bop step.

"Kick back! Let loose! What are you afraid of?"

Margot didn't realize her teeth were gritted. Stevie took her glass of rum and banana powder, which she had left almost untouched on the table, and tried to tip the yellow goop directly into her mouth.

"Down the hatch!"

"Stop it!"

"It's good for you. It's medicine. You're wound up too tight, you gotta let it all hang out."

His hands were on her shoulders again, squeezing. "Relax, old Maggot girl."

Margot downed her drink in a mighty three-swallow effort and put the empty glass on the table.

"Thank you so much for the nightcap," she said. "I'm bushed. I think I'll call it a night."

"Naw, Miss Hoity-Toit. It's early yet."

She moved towards the door. He stood in front of it. "OK, have it your way."

He was bitter about it. Now she felt bad. He leaned forward and kissed her closed mouth. She stood there, inert, like when they were children, waiting for it to end.

"Go back to your castle."

Margot was mad. She thought of Mad. Devil-may.

"I'm not a princess."

"So what are you then?"

"I don't know yet."

"Don't kid yourself. You're the same as the rest of them. You'll marry some rich guy."

"No I won't," said Margot, and pushed past him and opened the door.

10

MARGOT LOVED THE MULTICOLORED LIGHTS STRUNG along the driveway at Christmastime. But this year something felt different; off, discordant. Margot was preoccupied, sleepless, tossed between the fear of being rejected by Radcliffe and the fear of getting in; a terrifying pitch into the wild blue yonder. She thought it was her mood that soured the atmosphere; after all, her mother told her so. If only she could be more enthusiastic about the plans for her coming-out season. "Radcliffe or not, you'll have to come back to the city for the governor's ball, the Whitneys' ball, the entrance party of course; we can do your own gala over the summer—"

Her mother was so perennially unsatisfied that Margot did not see anything unusual in her fault-finding. The holly on the wreaths was too prickly, the tea was too hot, why were the summer slipcovers still on the couches in the atrium? Why hadn't the terrace plants been moved into the solarium? Where was the blue cashmere blanket? No! Not that one!

In the days running up to the Christmas party, Peggy marched back and forth between rooms, adjusting tablecloths, repositioning end tables, running her index finger over plaster moldings for evidence of "dust that has not been dusted." Jean Craft, with a cloth well soaked in furniture polish, followed her about, shuffling over her bad hip with the surly obduracy of a draft horse. Mathilde sighed Gallicly, wreathed in blue cigarette smoke. In the kitchen Mrs. Ambrose listened to the radio turned up loud. A great Douglas fir was set up in the well of the double ducal staircase and decorated with red glass balls and gold ribbon and glittering fairy lights that James cursed disentangling.

Margot was careful to step over the vacuum cord; Jean Craft repeated "promises were made promises were made" in time with the roaring whoosh back and forth back and forth. Margot redirected deliverymen around to the back door, she ferried, she drove her mother's car into Oyster Bay to pick up the mail from the post office, a great stack of catalogs and Christmas cards. Nothing from Radcliffe, nothing for her. The sky was gray, she felt a dismal gulf of waiting as she walked on the beach. Gray waves sucked at the stones, in the Sound, seahorses luffed. A lone sailboat headed towards Connecticut as a fine rain began to fall. *Where will I be next Christmas?* Margot asked the elements. They whispered their answer, but it was lost in the merging susurration of sea and shore.

Her new green taffeta dress hung on her bedroom door, freshly pressed. Margot pinched the puffed bow between her fingers, it made a loud rustle. At the back of her closet was a black cocktail dress Mad had given her at the end of the semester. "I bought it at Bendel's on Daddy's charge card to cheer me up. It's too-too and there's no way I can wear it back at the ranch—take it!" Margot shuggled the dress over her head. She was taller than Mad and it skimmed mid-thigh. Her mother would say her *tush* was hanging out. She turned and checked herself in the full-length mirror: no, it wasn't. The dress was heavy black silk moiré and hung from her shoulders in a sharp triangle. If she stood under a flight of steps, she might be mistaken for the shadowed recess.

The Reids arrived first, *hello hello hello merry merry merry.*

"Margot!" her mother hissed an aside. "Where have you been?"

"I'm right here."

"Your father is missing in action and Louisa Reid is *always* early.

That woman will be early to her own funeral. Margot, what are you *wearing*?" Black, according to her mother's dictum, was for funerals and Paris; never for unmarried girls.

"Wow, Margot-go!" said Chip, swanning in behind his parents, his sister Muffy and her new fiancé bringing up the rear.

"Well, you have to be tall to get away with a getup like that," said his mother.

Mr. Reid gave a whistle, "Margot, you're a knockout."

Margot watched her mother's eyes widen imperceptibly. The men had appreciably *noticed* her.

"Did Trip tell you?" Chip asked Margot.

"Tell her what?" asked her mother, stepping between them, but just then a green Cadillac crunched into the driveway and the group dispersed to help Mr. Gerald out because he had cracked his ankle with a 5-iron and was on crutches.

Guests arrived in gusts and crowded into the hall, taking off their coats and handing them to Nice Noreen, who was wearing a black skirt and a white blouse for the occasion. She hung them up in the old mudroom. Everyone duly gasped in mock awe at the twenty-foot tree: Marvelous! Simply marvelous! How marvelous! Oh Peggy, you've outdone yourself! Oh how marvelous! The brassy clamor of celebration rose in volume; cheery trombone carols, tinkly piano conversation.

Mr. Gerald gave Margot a large wink, squeezed her shoulder with his sausage fingers. "My dear, how you've grown!" Margot smiled and shook hands and curtsied. Her cousins Fay and Phyllis arrived, both wearing velvet. Phyllis's dress was navy, Fay's dress was red and ruched at her hips in the latest style, and she had outlined her eyelids in black liquid liner with a cat's-eye flourish. She blinked long eyelashes spiked with mascara. Butter wouldn't melt, as her mother liked to say. Fay had graduated from high school the year before. Now, she announced proudly, she had a job in the perfume department at Saks and was sharing an apartment in the city with three other girls. Her mother pursed her lips at this news and said, "Certainly a modern arrangement," before disengaging herself to greet a group of new arrivals.

"Merry Christmas, Margot, is that the latest style these days?" David Stern wore a bottle green sports jacket over gray flannel trousers and a black turtleneck. His German accent made it hard to tell if he was being kind or cutting.

"We are also waiting for the letter from Radcliffe. Phyllis has made an application for a scholarship."

Behind him Margot could see her mother welcoming the Merryweather clan, which included, at this time of year, a posse of cousins, all in boisterous high spirits and wearing the family Christmas livery: blazers and gray flannel trousers and matching ties printed with candy canes.

"Have you been up to Cambridge yet for the interview?" Phyllis asked her. "When I went in November, Dr. Bunting was very encouraging."

Margot bit her lip, she had not yet received any invitation for an interview.

MARGOT HAD REWRITTEN HER project thesis citing examples of scientific theories which had subsequently been debunked— spontaneous generation, the immutability of elements—and then cross-referenced these with several recent articles in the field of virology (*D. Hershey and M. Chase, Independent Functions of Viral Protein and Nucleic Acid in Growth of Bacteriophage, 1952*), which posited various ideas, both counterintuitive and counterindicative: a virus was a parasite, a disease, an antibacterial agent, an individual life-form because it carried its own DNA. "Therefore," Margot had written in conclusion, "my own investigations into the rhinovirus, although inconclusive, nevertheless illustrate the complexity and embryonic nature of this new and exciting field of study."

She felt sick when she remembered it. Her final paragraph had come to a hollow point: I don't know what my results mean. She reached for a glass of champagne. She could feel herself radiating resentment towards Phyllis, then hated herself for being so uncharitable.

"Merry Christmas, Margot lovely!" Trip came up. "What a dress! Your legs go on for miles! How on earth did dearest Mommy allow such a fine display?"

"She was going to send me to get changed," said Margot, "but then Chip complimented me and she forgot to be disapproving."

"Is that why you are red-faced? Or have you been kissing the stableboy under the mistletoe again?"

The champagne soured in Margot's mouth. Had someone seen?

Trip put his hand on her shoulder, his fingers slippered to the nape of her neck, pulled teasingly at the zipper.

"Trip!"

"Aw Mar-go-go," said Trip, never one to let a new nickname go unpunished. He gazed into her eyes faux-deeply, in imitation of Prince Charming examining a prospective frog, and immediately saw her guilt. "Oh you have! You have been kissing someone! 'Tis the season to be jolly! But who? Do tell!"

Before she had a chance to reply, Trip turned towards her cousins and asked, "Ah, the black sheep cousins! How you have grown! You are much more beautiful than your aunt Peggy says you are."

"Margot!" Peggy's shrill treble cut through the giggling.

Margot turned like a startled Bambi; her kid-soled evening shoes slid on the polished marble and one leg skidded out from under. She banged her knee and landed lumpily on her ass. Trip grinned and held out two hands to help her up in a public display of gallantry.

"Nothing broken?"

"Margot!" Stilettos clicked across the marble. Her mother towered, glowered. "What are you doing on the floor?"

"I fell over."

"Oh for god's sake. You're as clumsy as your father."

Margot stumbled upright, ungainly, humiliated, aware that a tear trembled on the edge of her eyelash, but if she wiped it away her mascara would smear. She was used to her mother being curt in private, but in public she usually kept her tone bright and breezy. Trip called it her brittle-glass voice. Now something had smashed.

"Your father—" Her mother's words sounded strangled by the effort of gaiety. Her carmine nails clawed at Margot's wrist.

"Your father," she said again. "Margot, did you invite Lydia Cummings and her *vulgar* mother?"

"Peggy, don't be mad, I invited them," said Trip. Margot had never heard one of her friends call her mother "Peggy."

"Mrs. Cummings and Lydia have been staying in our carriage house *since*—" Trip didn't have to say what everyone knew: *since* Mr. Cummings had run off with another woman and sold the house out from under them. "I just thought," continued Trip, smiling his very best humble pie, "that they could use some cheering up."

Peggy swallowed this explanation with a physical gulp but said nothing. Her red mouth maintained a straight horizontal line. Her silence and stillness were so statuesque that slowly she became the focus of the room. Conversations halted, an unease crept into the hall along with the fingers of cold air that dared to cross the threshold from the winter outside. People turned to look at the odd spectacle of an immobile hostess.

"Peggy lovely," said Trip, taking her hand, "come and let's find something to eat." His tone was low and sweet, as if coaxing a tiger. He extended his arm with an exaggerated swoop as if he were draping his cloak over a puddle for the Queen of England.

He asked, "Would you do me the great honor of showing me to the buffet?"

Margot saw a quiver of reanimation in the corner of her mother's mouth. The red line curved upwards, very slightly. Peggy followed her knight into the dining room. Behind them the crowd was drawn towards the whiff of scandal and smells of roasted goose and cinnamon.

Margot followed behind, handmaiden to the couple. The usually rigid line of her mother's spine swayed from side to side, almost a sashay. Margot exhaled, unaware that she had been holding her breath. Her banged knee stung. She stood against the wall, in the protective lee of one of the bronze Nubians, rubbed it better, wincing at the sharpness of the bruise, in the soft spot between patella and patellar. The pain was so acute that it masked, for a moment, her anguish as she watched Trip take hold of Peggy's arm, as a king might take his queen, and steer her to the punch bowl. Stevie, wearing a waiter's white jacket for the evening, ladled milk punch into silver goblets. Trip raised his goblet in toast and her mother leaned towards him and, lingering for a moment, too closely, kissed him. On his lips. Stevie caught Margot's eye with a naked look.

Margot turned on her kitten heel. Bumped straight into Richie. She had never been so glad to see his long, ugly face.

"My brother has been causing problems again, I hear," he said.

"Which brother?" Margot's head was swimming, cold, far out from shore.

"Touché!" Richie smiled, fish lips agape. "I don't know who is the worse behaved. Hal," he added sadly, "is not coming home for Christmas."

"Oh, I'm sorry," Margot recovered some measure of politesse.

"He's drying out again in Arizona. Maybe it's better that way; Christmas at Sage Hill is always soaked in booze."

"I always envied your big family Christmases," said Margot. "Here we are only four. The servants have the day off."

"You're not missing much. At Sage Hill the conversation follows a very reliable roster of old favorites, as worn out as Bing Crosby." Richie counted them off on his fingers. "William F. Buckley Jr.—a particular favorite of my dear twin brother's, the state of the fairways at Piping Rock, God deliver us from Democrats and their taxes. Let's nuke China!"

Margot laughed.

"Am I too cynical?" asked Richie.

"No, not at all."

"How is your friend?" he asked.

"Recovered; well, physically—"

"But she's different somehow?"

"Yes."

"Sad?"

"Yes."

"It takes time," he said.

"Margot—" Her uncle David Stern reappeared. Richie retreated. "Happy Christmas, dear. I do hope Phyllis gets her bursary, I do hope you can become friends at Radcliffe together."

"If I am accepted—"

"Oh you are very clever, everyone knows," said her uncle. "Your mother does not stop telling everyone about her straight-A daughter!"

"I don't believe you!"

She saw that her uncle was wincing slightly, listing to one side. "Would you like to sit down?" she asked.

"Yes, that would be better."

Margot took him into the library, which was empty.

"I am probably sitting in the same chair from whence the Old King issued his orders," said David Stern, settling himself. "I swore I would never take a cent from this family. That is what your mother cannot understand. It's not my pride. It's my promise." He shook his head. "But time passes, things change, girls grow out of dolls and dime-store treats. Perhaps this old dad should let his pride out a little, like the waistband of his trousers. But your mother is so very"— he searched for a word in the air with his index finger—"steely." He shook his head. "I just wish Peggy could—"

At the mention of her name, as if summoned, her mother appeared in the library doorway, clicked her nails against the jamb, agitated.

"David." She pronounced his name as an accusation.

"Peggy."

Margot stood up. In her party heels she towered over her mother and instinctively bent her neck to compensate.

"Can Uncle David and the girls come to lunch tomorrow?" Margot said in a sudden rush of emotion, a desire to make amends, to turn everything right again, to be a family, a big boisterous happy family, and not be marooned like every other year with her mother, who spent the day white-lipped and snippy, complaining she had to do *all* the work; her father, silently sloshed, stabbing at the turkey carcass with a blunt carving knife; Goody, garbling stories about the Duchess of Windsor, Princess Sex-Coburg-Gothic and Lucky Luciano—

David Stern looked towards Peggy, but her face was fixed. "There's really no need," he began politely demurring.

"Well, it might have been a nice *idea*—" said Peggy. She put one arm out like a traffic policemen, directing them out of the library, back into the current of the party.

Margot stood for a moment under the plaster cherubs holding up the gilded dome of the doorway. She wondered at the authority of her mother, perceived an inkling of the vanity of it, the veneer of it. What personality could grow in the shadow of Grand Old King, but one of command and control? What was in the cocktail mix of the King's tyranny and Goody's flighty narcissism that had cast her mother in a rigid mold of perfectionism? And what was her share of the inheritance? Was she Sarah? Dreamy stubborn, destined to be unhappy and lovelorn? What was inborn and what was taught? What was modeled after example and what was created by an opposite reaction to it? Grandmother mother daughter. *What are we going to do about Margot?*

The party flowed from the orchestra playing carols in the atrium to the milling cocktail chatter in the yellow living room beyond. Bernadette Pratt was talking to Lydia Cummings, who was looking past her shoulder for someone more interesting. Mr. Reid bent over the buffet table scraping an oyster to death with a small silver trident. Larry Gerald bellowed at something Trip said, his big bowling-ball head falling back with his mouth open to the ceiling. Long-limbed Lydia Cummings was entertaining a circle of admirers, admonishing one, now teasing another. Margot noted with dismay that Richie was among the group.

"Margot, Happy Christmas, my dear!" said Mr. Gerald, wriggling his moustache.

"Have you seen Chip?" asked Runny Merryweather. "A bunch of us were planning to take the traditional Christmas Eve midnight plunge in the Sound."

"No, I haven't—"

"Spotted your future husband yet?" Stevie breathed in her ear as he went by with a tray of champagne glasses.

"*Margot!*" Her mother, again, imperative.

A wave of nausea, of anger too, if she had known how to name it, rose in Margot. All this politeness and polish, the mores and bores and chattery nonsense—she would like to be a witch to vanish it! Banish it! Whoosh! Into the black hole of the night sky, far beyond relativity, to the stars, to a place even the ancient Greeks had not foretold.

"*Margot!*" her mother repeated, coming up to her. She stood so close Margot could see the clench of her jaw and a faint smudge of lipstick against the powder of her cheek. "Goody is insisting on walking down the stairs and cannot be allowed or she'll break her *neck*. Mathilde is having no luck in dissuading her. Margot, go up and tell her she *must* use the electric chair. The will of that woman will be the death of us all—right now it's more than I can stand along with everything else—"

Margot went through the swinging door into the servants' wing, the back stairs were a faster route to Goody's rooms. Waiters jostled, she caught sight of Stevie draining a champagne glass, and he saw her and licked his lips with his fat pink tongue. She pretended not to see, stopped in the corridor on the other side of the outer pantry to light a cigarette and take the taste out of her mouth. As she ascended the stairs, the commotion receded behind her. She drew the smoke into her lungs, soothing, one step after another . . . Stevie Runny Richie Trip . . . counting-climbing . . . David Stern and

Sarah and Fay and Phyllis. A crowd of faces with open mouths, Lydia's elegant swan's neck, Trip's sly and treacherous kiss, she sucked on the tarry filter, filled her lungs with smoke, and realized she had walked up a flight too far, as if she were going to her own room. She stopped at the mezzanine, turned to go back down, and heard a wooden banging coming from the old servants' room tucked off the half landing.

One of the wild Merryweather clan had probably gotten lost, with a sophomore no doubt. She knocked, no answer. She heard huffing-puffing and a small shriek. Worried, she pushed open the door. At first she did not understand: naked pink flesh, pumping savage rhythm. She stood dumbly appalled. The monster stopped rocking and began to thrash about in a mocking mirror image of her own alarm and horror. Her father's backside reared up as he tried to disentangle himself. Margot saw his furry potbelly, and below, for a terrible split second, his red welted penis, before he snatched at the bedspread to cover it. Mrs. Cummings put her hands over her pendulum breasts. In her shock, Margot dropped her cigarette on the carpet. Before this awful awful beast could speak, she slammed the door behind her and clattered back down the stairs.

Rushed into the library, where her flight was checked by Grand Old King's big leather-backed throne. Margot stopped, held it fast by her shoulders to steady herself, let out a breath like a long train whistle.

A white-gloved hand held out a glass of champagne. "There you are! I was looking for you!"

The bearer wore a dress uniform, sky blue trousers, navy blue tunic with red piping and gold buttons. A sword hung from his waist and there were two shiny medals on his chest. He looked thinner and older than when she had last seen him, and for a moment Margot tripped over her memory.

"Sandyful!"

"I wish I could say 'Just the same'"—there were new lines across his forehead, crinkles in the corners of his eyes—"but as you see, I am not." His smile drooped. Margot saw his left tunic sleeve was folded up and neatly pinned to his shoulder.

"Oh!"

"You look like you've had a fright."

"Oh! Yes. No. Not—"

"I'm sorry to be so dis-arming." He tried to make a joke of it. Margot fell silent. She couldn't think of any words.

"Sorry," said Sandy, "I guess I'm tired of making light of it. If one more person thanks me for my service, I am going to punch their lights out." He sounded almost serious.

"Don't do that," said Margot with alarm. "I don't think I could handle another drama tonight."

Sandy took a step back. "You look mighty fine. Let me wish you Happy Christmas properly." He leaned forward and kissed her cheek softly.

Margot felt tears in her eyes, but she held them at bay with the back of her hand and a swallow of fizzy champagne; she didn't want to cry in front of him. Sandy took her hand in his only hand and stepped closer, very close, put his arm around her.

The woolen collar of his tunic scratched her neck. He smelled clean, of iodine and limes. Behind his ear was a pink raised scar, the shape of a rain spatter on a window. She touched it, he shuddered as if electric, she withdrew her hand, but he picked it up and kissed her fingertips and put it back against his skin again. His whole body pressed tightly against her whole body so that there was no light between their two shapes. His medals clanked cold against her breastbone. He stepped one leg into the space between her legs, closer, tighter. Holding, holding, held. Her head fit exactly into the space between his chin and his shoulder. She did not let go. He did not let go.

A loud crash. All the party noise of orchestra strings, chatter, clinking crystal, abruptly stopped. They heard a woman scream. Sandy went to the doorway to see, Margot stood behind, still holding his hand. In the hall, Mathilde, her hair in disarray, her blouse torn, a livid scratch on her neck, was bent over, shaking. Peggy stood over her with an expression of sheer fury.

"That old woman attacked me!" Mathilde cried, pointing wildly up the staircase. "She is *dérangée*, completely mad!"

The audience stirred and heads began to look up. As if part of the theater, puffs of black smoke began to issue from the gods.

Peggy called out, "Someone call the fire department!" No one moved.

"Margot! Call the fire station in Oyster Bay. The number is on the typed sheet beside the telephone table in the study."

Ever a cool head, precise, directive. Margot rushed to carry out the command. Richie pushed through the throng towards Mathilde and helped her towards one of the spindly gilt Louis Quatorze chairs flanking the doorway.

"Not *that* chair!" Peggy called out, and Mathilde was conveyed instead to the library.

General chatter resumed.

"Did you see?"

"What happened? The band was playing 'Hark! the Herald' and then something went bang!"

"Oh poor Peggy, the maid is bound to sue."

"That's a lot of smoke for a wastepaper trash can fire—"

Slowly it dawned on the assembled that the smoke in the hall was increasing. Mrs. Reid wrapped her cashmere stole around her nose and mouth. The waiters had all suddenly disappeared.

"Where's my coat?"

"I gave the girl my coat."

"She disappeared into the closet with it."

"The closet is full of coats. What was yours?"

"The mink."

"They're all mink in here—"

"We've got to get out—"

"Oh don't be a drama queen."

"You know what they say: there's no smoke without—"

People began to move faster, jerkily, with urgency.

The front door was open and cold air seeped into the hall. Inside blackening, outside softly falling white snowflakes. Margot came back from calling the fire department.

"The Oyster Bay engine is out on a four-alarm call in Hicksville. Nearest I could raise was Lloyd Neck Harbor—"

Sandy was looking up into the dense black cloud that now obscured the top of the double ducal staircase.

"I'm going up," he said.

"You need a blanket or something—"

Margot looked about. Her mother was waving her arms at the servants shouting for buckets, water, "All hands on deck," but the waiters had skedaddled and Mrs. Ambrose stood her ground, palms up, "I've said a hundred times we need a fire extinguisher in the kitchen."

A clutching maul of people crowded by the mudroom, Larry Gerald was passing coats over people's heads—"No, mine has a black velvet collar . . ." "Can you see a sable?" Flurries of snow blew inside with the wind and mixed with the black motes of char. Margot couldn't see any kind of cover or cloth she could use. She coughed. Sandy echoed her cough. They looked up together. At the pinnacle of the staircase was an ebony finial carved in the face of a Grecian muse. Orange flames danced on its head.

"Goody!" Margot cried.

A glimmer of white shone through the black thunderhead of smoke, two pale hands gripped the banister, a head followed: a skull set with one milky eye and one as clear as a laser beam. The mouth opened into an empty red hole. Appeal, prophecy, curse—no one ever knew, because no words could be heard above the giant shattering explosion as the great chandelier crashed down.

PART

TWO

———

INTERMEDIATE

11

FARNSWORTH BURNED FOR TWO DAYS DOWN TO THE WALL studs. Very little was able to be salvaged from the sodden, charred wreck of carbonized mirrors, furniture reduced to tinder spindles, cracked marble busts with blacked noses. For days black snowflakes of scorched paper, remnants of the great library, floated around the site, settling in drifts in the corners of the empty swimming pool. Grand Old King's lead-lined safe was so warped by the heat it took two firemen with sledgehammers to break the locks. Inside: a stack of share certificates for defunct companies, bundles of pre-Weimar German marks, the deeds to a million acres of Utah which had since been domained as a national park. For several months afterwards local boys scavenged the site at night, kicking over burnt lintels, raking their fingers through soft heaps of ash, filching twists of melted silver forks.

Goody's will had been drawn up to rectify the injustice of Sarah's disinheritance. Old King Vanderloep's exclusionary codicils were at last defunct. Promises and principles were relegated to the past; David Stern did not contest the windfall. Farnsworth and its grounds were given wholly to Peggy. Two-thirds of the balance of the family shares in United Union Steel were apportioned equally to Sarah's two daughters, Fay and Phyllis. The estate in totality was valued at $13 million. Mr. Penny from Bankers Trust helpfully provided a balance sheet of liabilities. Inheritance tax would be calculated at 15 percent. Unfortunately, since Goody had died three hours before the Big House had been declared legally destroyed, the value of the house for tax purposes was calculated at the time of her death, as if it had been intact. Furthermore, Mr. Penny cautioned, drawing his mouth into an upside-down smile of gloating opprobrium, there was an outstanding mortgage of $1.2 million, issued seven years earlier by Bankers Trust at a rate of 8 percent per annum, on which not a single payment had been made and which had therefore compounded to a sum owed, to date—Mr. Penny looked up from his balance sheet and enunciated each number separately, as if hoping to ameliorate the enormous sum by breaking the news into single digits. In addition, Mr. Penny continued, no payments had been made pertaining as to insurance since 1948.

Probate took three years. In the end, when everything was set out in columns of black and red, totals neatly typed into boxes, Fay and Phyllis Stern each received $2.3 million and Peggy was left with a deficit of $350,000 and a final-notice lawyers' bill for $44,358.15.

Margot and Phyllis were both accepted to Radcliffe, but in the end it was Margot who needed the scholarship and her cousin Phyllis who was able to pay her own tuition. Fate had swapped their fortunes. It was so neatly plotted that Margot found it unbearable to read novels anymore.

12

IN HER FRESHMAN YEAR AT RADCLIFFE, MARGOT WAS wracked by dizzying bouts of vertigo. It was her fault because she had willed the destruction. It was her fault because she had dropped her cigarette on the back stairs. It was her fault because she was selfish, just as her mother had always said. There was something in the inverted symmetry of the impoverished rich girl and her poor cousin's sudden windfall that felt like a karmic realignment. Sarah was not willful and weak but wronged; her children would inherit their rightful place. She, on the other hand, was the child of pride and privilege, and according to all the fables, must be brought low.

Margot's guilt was unspeakable. She did not know it was guilt. She did not speak. She took refuge in withdrawal, nervous and hesitant, wrong-footed by the interrogative aggression of male professors, confused by corridors and staircases that led only to more corridors and staircases. In atonement, in compensation, she took too many classes and wore herself out studying until two in the morning.

At first, Sandy sent her letters from Fort Hood, and then from Saigon, where he had been assigned to Army Intelligence. "A desk job," he wrote. "You can't imagine the number of forms to fill out, the memos and checklists, the sheer bureaucracy of war! I am confined to a cubicle, a lazy fan swishes the flies around to the sound of one hand typing, clunk clunk—there are so many reports, my fingertips are lacerated with paper cuts." Margot was ashamed to admit how overwhelmed she felt by everything and wrote back banalities, this class, that snowstorm, a football game. Her sentences were short, her sentiments and sensibility terse.

In her sophomore year, Margot decided to broaden her mind and read everything Mad told her to: *The Autobiography of Malcolm X*, *Anti-Intellectualism in American Life* by Richard Hofstadter, *On the Road*, and Camus's *L'Étranger*. She hoped to find some insight in the company of other outsiders, but their wanderings lost her and their anger disturbed her. She went back to the orderliness of her textbooks. Her heroes were the scientists who labored in obscurity: Mendel the monk tending his peas; Barbara McClintock recording all the variant colors on ears of Indian corn, her discoveries of genetic transposition ignored for decades. Margot hankered for the same concentrated solitude; a focused life, that would do. She was her most calm and happy—although that was not a word she would have used—at least, she might have said, she felt her most herself, alone in a lab staring into a microscope.

In the lab she was an astronaut looking down on a new planet. There was a boundlessness to the infinity of size, look closer, zero in on multiples of zeros, to the nth and nano, smaller and smaller . . . "Process is progress," Dr. Bunting told them in Bio-Chem 101. "It is in the proteins, in the molecules, subcellular, even subatomic, that's where to look. Life is basic chemistry."

Sophomore year, Margot ended up sharing a room with Shirley Gulliver as a result of a mix-up in the preferential lottery. Shirley had a mop of curly hair and an embroidered Afghan sheepskin jacket she had bought hitchhiking over the Khyber Pass with Tony, her English boyfriend. At any time one of these shaggy items was lousy, in the original sense of being full of lice, Shirley would disinfect her head and the mites would flee to the jacket, then she would wipe the jacket all over with a solution of vodka and DDT and they would jump back into her hair. Despite the itching, Shirley could not be persuaded to get rid of her long matted hair or her long matted jacket, although she was happy enough to burn her other possessions—bras, male chauvinist textbooks, patriarchal sanitary products. Shirley would never have been Margot's friend in a million years, but for their assigned proximity.

"At first you look like one of those conventional good-grades girls," Shirley told Margot spring semester, "but you're less aggravating than most of the dudes in this place, you, like, slow-grow on people."

Two or three times Margot received a postcard from Saigon with a poem written in ballpoint on the back. No greeting, no signature. Jottings posted to oblivion.

> *The jungle is full of life,*
> *Full of greens, each individual,*
> *That blur and blink and coalesce.*
> *The jungle is full of death too—*
> *not in the shadow,*
> *like some dumb metaphor*
> *but revealed in a flash of blinding light.*

In her junior year, Margot finally got around to reading *Sex and the Single Girl*, ditched wearing skirts and cut her hair short like Mia Farrow in *Rosemary's Baby*. She shared again with Shirley that year, in a room overlooking the Quad. Chlorophyll filtered sunlight through the chestnut canopy of waving palmatisected petioles—she was taking a botany class; plants seemed slow and plodding compared to the fizz of chemistry, but she loved them for their glowing greenness nonetheless.

Sandy had been transferred to Washington, DC, assigned to the Pentagon. His letters became infrequent and prosaic. "Hope all's well in the land of learning, and winter isn't hanging on too long in Boston. Here it's snowing cherry blossoms." Soon they stopped altogether.

During the long summer vacations, Margot taught summer school and did lab work for postgrad researchers. She didn't like to remember Farnsworth, long easy days, buzzy-bees, flagstones warmed by the sun, diving into the deep end. Summer's lease, all too short. These childish things, she put away. She went back to the apartment at 655 Park as little as she could. The atmosphere was eggshells, brittle and smashed. Anything Margot said about Radcliffe seemed to crunch against a hollow silence. Her father was increasingly absent. Her mother, increasingly bitter.

Life was separated into before and after. For Peggy it was a monstrous injustice. For Margot it was a natural division, between childhood and adulthood, between home and parents, between school and college. She had gotten, as her mother reminded her, "what you wanted all along." As if she had planned it. Her mother's opprobrium echoed her own self-reproach. No amount of penitence was enough. She knelt at her mother's feet and swept up the broken glass, but in the morning there was always a glint of shard she had missed, winking, ready to draw blood.

On cloudless nights when she couldn't sleep and the moon shone as bright as a torch through her window, Margot would recall that lost moment in Grand Old King's library, but she remembered it falsely, as a nostalgia, a longing for what might have been. She remembered a kiss that had not quite happened, imagined the full depth of it; a kiss that went on forever in a library that was still full of books and possibility, of love, of redemption, rewards and awards—and she dreamed she was walking again along the driveway dappled with sunlight, all recriminations rescinded. The Big House was still standing, and there, in her future perfect, in the middle of the library, by sheer coincidence, was Sandyful, ready to take her in two arms and cradle her against all the bad thoughts even as she woke smiling to frown to find herself only herself.

At the start of her senior year, was Margot, at twenty-two, a different girl than she had been when Sandy had last seen her at eighteen? She was still a virgin. Still heard her mother's voice in her

head. Still carried shame around like a lipstick, ready to be reap-
plied at any moment. She still hovered at the back at mixers and
parties. Applied for a single room in her senior year. Maybe Shirley
the psych major was right when she diagnosed "classic avoidance
syndrome."

Quiet, kept-to-herself, wouldn't-say-boo, intellectually stubborn, a bit spacey—from what others saw, Margot did not stand
out much in the Radcliffe Class of '68. As Larry Gerald, who was
in Cabot House at Harvard, complained in line for the Coffee Can
in the Yard one morning, "I can't figure out you gals from across
the street, you are a mix of shy weirdos, women's libbers, hockey
heifers, Jewish princesses, gum-chewing Californians, bra-burners,
Bunsen-burners, fast girls, slow girls, and sometimes two or three
of these in the same girl—"

"You mean we're goddamned individuals," Shirley had retorted.

13

At the beginning of her senior year, Margot signed up for Introductory Genetics, the first undergraduate class of the recently inaugurated Department of Biochemistry and Molecular Biology. It was given by a new professor, rumored to be the youngest member ever of the science faculty.

"Call me Dr. Fred," said Professor Merlin, chalking his name on the blackboard.

"What are we doing here?" he asked.

A few heads looked up, nonplussed; existentialism was the philosophy department.

He put his hands on his hips. "Anyone?"

Margot thought of several answers, but she knew none of them were right. Dr. Fred let the silence hang. No one put their hand in the air. No one wanted to fall into a trap on the first day.

Finally Dr. Fred answered his own question: "We are *here*, biologically speaking, to procreate."

The students looked at each other—this guy was a nut, right?

"We are *here*, scientifically speaking, to understand, and possibly improve, our inheritance. DNA, genetics, the code of life! How is it written? Can it be rewritten? What are the biomechanics of DNA, the biochemical reactions or interactions that affect it, change it, mutate it? Does the environment play a part? These are the questions that all of *you*"—he beamed his blue eyes at them expectantly—"are here to answer. We are at the dawn of a new age."

Then Dr. Fred pulled up a folding chair and, leaning back in it, lounging, asked them to answer back, to question everything he had just said. Still no arms went up.

"So what do you guys think? Is the genetic code a technical problem or a moral problem? What are we going to do when we can read our own instruction manuals? Because you know that day is going to come. You think biology is nature and physics is war—OK, Flower Power generation: What happens when we realize that our power to manipulate the human genome is more dangerous than the atom bomb?"

Dr. Fred had gone off the map, deep into uncharted territory. Margot's pencil stopped at the edge of the page, hovered. Should she make notes on the putative? Speculation was risky, wasn't it?

Finally one guy put up his hand and asked. "OK, but like, can you explain how this class is going to work?"

"Excellent question! I am a big fan of questions, no matter if you think they are dumb. I worked in the Cavendish Lab in Cambridge—the other Cambridge—where they discovered the helical structure of DNA, and I can tell you it's a poky place, half underground, wrought-iron spiral staircases, like something out of Bram Stoker. What did I learn there? That it's not about the surroundings, it's not about the equipment, it's about the *people*. Jim Watson was a failed zoologist with a hunch. He needed a Crick to listen to his ideas instead of dismiss them. Together they needed Rosalind Franklin's crystallography expertise."

Margot sat up. Everyone knew that Watson, Crick, and Maurice Wilkins had won the Nobel prize; she had never heard of Rosalind Franklin.

"Rosalind Franklin," continued Dr. Fred, zagging along his digression, "was a perfect example of a diligent and methodical scientist, but she was also diffident and prickly—it will come as no surprise that she died alone, an old maid—she rebuffed collaboration, didn't realize that she needed Watson's leap of imagination just as much as he needed her X-rays. This is the point I want to impress upon you: yes, observation and experimentation are important, but talking, sharing, questioning, discussing—these provoke the great breakthroughs. Good science is good scientists. Emphasis on the plural. One idea meets another. There's no point in being Mendel, laboring in the garden of obscurity."

Margot squirmed uncomfortably in her seat, pencil halted mid-air. Was he looking straight at her? Dr. Fred got to his feet, restless. He didn't lecture from behind the podium as other professors did, but paced the dais, gesticulating in big circles, riffing, informal. He had a messianic glow about him. Long hair, blue jeans (!), lanky, gangly, arms thrown about everywhere. A shaft of late August sunlight caught him in its beam. His audience was rapt. He did look a bit like Jesus.

MARGOT EMERGED FROM THE class dazzled, amazed, zingy. She felt an odd lightness, like the freedom at the end of the semester after the numbing tunnel of exams, and yet it was "just the beginning." *Just* seemed a small kind of qualifier for this expanding helium of possible. Margot had spent three years in self-imposed sequestration; head-down, diligent, methodical study. Three years of holding herself apart from (and perhaps imagining herself superior to) Shirley's shaggy crowd, Mad's eccentric friends, playing the role—as Mad had accused her once—of the "meek dumb-ass Jane Eyre."

Margot sat down on a bench in the courtyard, near the coffee cart. Students stood about, book bags slung over shoulders, juggling hot paper cups of coffee. Margot knew three or four of the girls and she thought to go up to them, right here, right now, and *just* begin anew, *just* say hello—

Then she saw Phyllis at the center of the group.

Margot hadn't seen Fay or David Stern since the night of the fire. Her mother had made it very clear that the travesty of Goody's will precluded any contact. Even the mention of their names provoked a mute, clenched jaw.

"It's not their fault," Margot had countered.

"Oh it's nobody's *fault!*" said her mother, slamming a chafing dish down so hard that a wave of peas rolled out and plopped, almost slowly, one by one, over the edge of the table and hid in the green rug.

Margot and Phyllis had both matriculated the fall semester of '64. Rich and pretty, Phyllis was always surrounded by people, and among a student body of more than twelve hundred, it was easy enough for them not to run into each other. By their senior year they had fallen into a pattern of mutually repelling magnets.

"Like, Phyllis Stern is your *cousin?*" Shirley had been taken aback. "Jeez, Margot, you are a dark horse. Have you been in her ginormous private apartment? Cordelia Chatsworth is living with her this year, Tony was at school with her brother, who's like a lord-earl or something. Plenty of silver spoons up plenty of asses. Have you heard about their throwback dinner parties? Everyone has to dress up in twenties costumes and they drink champagne cocktails and after dinner the ladies retire to the *drawing room.* My friend at Lowell went once and was totally weirded out by the whole scene."

"I've never been invited. We're not close."

"Geez Louise, is there like some family feud or something?"

There were plenty of wealthy girls at Radcliffe, but Phyllis's largesse garnered more publicity than others. She once rented a bus to take her whole dorm to hear Dick Nixon talk in New York. In her sophomore year she lent her patronage to "The Salon," a women's forum for progressive libertarian ideas ("The counterculture is counterclockwise"; "Coed housing is just another way for the male Harvard to subsume the separate but equal identity we maintain here at the Annex"). Junior year, Phyllis had been appointed to the Coordinated Student Council the dean of Harvard had set up to mollify campus activist groups. Shirley, who was big into the whole antiwar thing, called it "the Shut-Up Committee."

Phyllis wore Pucci and chiffon scarves that flowed behind her in the wind. Through one winter she sported a white mink hat. One of the against-animal-cruelty Maoists from Cabot House accosted her in front of Widener Library and asked her if she wasn't ashamed when there were children starving in Vietnam. Phyllis had replied, "Let them eat my hat!" a remark which was widely repeated—by some with moral outrage at her callous imperialism, by others with admiration for her neat skewering of Ivy League moral outrage. Margot thought it curious how traits could skip generations and hop laterally. She had always felt herself closer to quiet Sarah; Phyllis seemed to take after bold Peggy.

Outside the Science Bloc, Margot watched Phyllis throw her head back and laugh. Her bronzed arms merrily tinkled with bangles; in one hand she held a single white rose, a gift. Two guys were leaning forward, supplicant knights, ready to perform any task she might command. The vignette caught Margot sharply. She stepped back. She had so wanted to fulfill Dr. Fred's assignment, but now she saw that his new approach meant approaching people, talking to them, making friends. "Getting over yourself," as Shirley might have said.

Margot laughed to herself at the irony, could it be that her mother was right all along and life really was just one big cocktail party?

14

A COUPLE OF TIMES A SEMESTER, MARGOT MET RICHIE for dinner at De Sousa's Portuguese bistro. They were friends now, not quite equals; Richie had assumed the position of an elder brother. He advised Margot on which courses to take, warned her which professors were brilliant theoreticians but useless teachers, told her not to worry about math. "Unless you're going to be a mathematician or marry a mathematician, you don't need that theoretical advanced stuff. And don't for god's sake marry a mathematician!" It was kind of Richie to talk down math, she had very nearly flunked sophomore calculus.

Richie was in the middle of his PhD and had just started interning at the Cyclotron Lab, working on a proton beam that would zap brain tumors. Margot hadn't seen him over summer vacation. He'd gone to visit his girlfriend at Stanford; she had stayed in Cambridge, incubating starfish eggs, lab tech-ing for a research project on meiosis.

Richie had grown a beard and it hid his misaligned lip. He was wearing a new corduroy jacket.

"You're looking very professorial!"

Richie raked his fingers through his moustache, an unfamiliar gesture, but one, pensive, deliberate, that seemed to suit him.

Richie laughed and showed her his elbows. "They say a patched varsity sweater is the best way to fast-tracked tenure."

They both ordered the chorizo clam chowder and shared a carafe of red wine. Richie caught her up on family news. Lydia Cummings and Trip had spent the summer in the south of France.

"My mother is expecting him to ask her for one of my grand-mother's rings any day now, but she doesn't know that my father has forbidden any engagement until he graduates. Lord knows Trip can't concentrate on more than one thing at a time. Meanwhile Runny got himself fired from Drexel Burnham, and Dad had to pull some heavy strings to get him a new position at Lehman."

Margot didn't ask about Hal. He had vanished hitchhiking in India almost two years ago.

Conversation turned to the infighting in the science department. Jim Watson stalked the halls like a giant stilt-legged crane pecking at E. O. Wilson's bees. Richie observed the debate from the medical sidelines, Margot was thrilled molecular biology had been given its own department.

"The zoolies can go and catch all the animals and study the shapes of their ears and pick up poop from the monkey cages," she told him, "but it's only taxonomy. Sooner or later they've got to understand that getting into the nuts and bolts of the chemistry of amino acids and proteins will unlock the answers to everything. Everything that's anything is at the molecular level—even the answer to your beloved cancer."

"And life and the universe and all that jazz."

"I know you are not convinced, double-doctor Merryweather."

Richie smiled at her. "Have you ever seen a cancer cell under a microscope?"

After dinner they walked back up to Kirkland, Richie showed his pass to the night porter and unlocked the door to his lab at the Cyclops Laser Center. Margot always thought there was something romantic about laboratories at night, illuminated by the blinking lights on the panels of all the electric machines, drying, freezing, incubating. They reminded her of the multicolored bulbs strung up in the trees at Farnsworth at Christmastime. There was a quietness too, a submurmur of gestation and expectancy. Unobserved, bacteria subdivided, molds spread across agar fields, blood samples denatured their proteins and leached into clear and clot. The business of transformation continued while people slept, dreaming hows: How does a cell know what it wants to become? How does DNA tell it what to do? How do amino acids join up with other amino acids? By mechanics or organics? By switchers or levers or floods of enzyme juice—

Lubricated with wine, at ease with Richie, looser than she normally allowed, Margot found these thoughts had escaped her head and she had said them out loud.

"Enzyme juice? One question at a time!" Richie pulled out a box of slides from a drawer and flipped on the microscope light. It was a fluorescent Zeiss, very snazzy. "It's a medulloblastoma, midline," he told her.

Margot bent over the eyepiece, let her eye scrunch and her pupil dilate, her right hand groped for the focus dial, on the Zeiss it was a little further back than she was used to. The cells looked dead and static. Margot allowed her eyes to adjust.

"Do you see the whitish lumpy areas?" said Richie. "They look like an aerial view of mountains." Margot nodded. "Now look at the darker valleys, and the houses in a web of villages strung through them."

"It's like you are describing a different country," said Margot.

"In a way I am."

"But is it helpful? Metaphoring everything. I mean, it's not Switzerland, it's a tumor."

"Maybe the only way we can understand anything is by analogy."

"Then we are limited by what we already know." Margot heard herself echo Dr. Fred. Her eyes continued to roam the pointillist landscape.

"Well, think about it: of course we are. What do we even

call something newly discovered?" said Richie. "We give it a Greek name."

A neuron in Margot's brain tugged a memory synapse, *Sometimes I think everything has already been thought up before by some ancient Greek guy staring at the stars.* Richie leaned over her shoulder, close enough that his beard brushed her neck. It felt softer than she thought it would.

"It's beautiful," said Margot.

"It's from the brain of a four-year-old girl called Melissa."

"Melissa, I think, is Greek for honey."

15

THE THIN AND TENSILE OUTLINE OF THE CELL MEMBRANE
wobbled, undulating. The chromosomes began to ball up, con-
tracting like prodded slugs. The cell membrane cinched its waist,
tightening tightening, until the moment of separation when all the
cytoplasm spilled out in spots and dots that blotted together like
raindrops on concrete. And then there were two. The division of a
cell is a beautiful and mysterious process. Over the course of two
hours Margot watched one of her own white blood cells jimmy, jig-
gle, and separate. She watched herself propagate herself. She didn't
even want to blink.

The Introductory Genetics class was split into lab groups of five
students each. In Margot's group, Lab Room 1123, she was the only
girl. Over the semester they were to learn how to count and identify
chromosomes and design a methodology for categorizing observa-
tions and discrepancies. The very first afternoon, Margot distinguished herself by finding a double Y.

"You got Superman," joked Marvin, one of the other students,
tall, broad-shouldered, sexy lopsided smile, unshaven. "It's a shame
the samples are anonymous, or we could track him down for you."

"You don't want a Superman," said Flashman, laconic, chin
tucked in, hair falling into his eyes. "They're aggressive and covered
in acne."

"Where do the samples come from?" Margot asked.

"Where all samples come from," said Flashman. "Med students."

"Explains why so few females," said Margot under her breath.

The second week of September, Marvin asked her out. "Not exactly a date," he qualified, "no hassle, friend of mine is giving the Friday lecture on sea slug chromosomes at Woods Hole."

"Sounds sexy."

"Sea slugs are hermaphrodites," said Marvin without any inflection in his tone to indicate irony or not.

For Margot, an invitation to the Marine Biological Laboratory at Woods Hole was better than backstage with the Beatles. It was legendary, a place where all the top scientists gathered over the summer and on weekends throughout the year. Less formal than academic conferences, Woods Hole was sea and beach and barbecues, a chance to schmooze and discuss, sound out theories over lobster rolls and ask crazy questions: How does an anemone see the world? How do starfish regrow whole arms? Do octopuses have emotions? Why do lobsters turn from blue to red when you cook them? From the shallow shore of the famous (in biological circles) Stony Beach, ideas, like life, crawled out of the sea and into scientific papers. Woods Hole was the rock pools Margot missed from the North Shore, and it was Dr. Fred's round table too. Margot nodded enthusiastically, yes please.

"Cool, I'll pick you up at the Quad Friday lunchtime."

Marvin arrived in a lime green Pontiac with rusted wheel hubs. He looked embarrassed. "My old high school car, still runs pretty well."

"It's enormous!" said Margot, running a finger down a long tail fin and dumping her bag in the trunk.

"Your bag is enormous," said Marvin.

"Well, you didn't tell me. Are we staying overnight?" It was still Indian summer warm but she had packed (ever her mother's daughter) for every eventuality: a dress and high-heeled sandals in case there was a dressy dinner, a warm sweater for the evening, shorts, a bathing suit, a bathing cap, beach shoes, and two extra blouses.

"Can't you just wear the clothes you're wearing for two days?"

"Spoken like a true man."

"XY all the way."

Marvin was scruffy, kinda cute. He wore faded blue jeans, Ray-Bans, and a leather bracelet around his wrist. He was never in a million years anyone she could take back to dinner at 655 Park.

"Let's get the introductory-chapter crap out of the way," he said as they navigated the south side towards the highway. "First thing: I'm Jewish. I guess you guessed."

Margot had not. It had not even occurred to her.

"Lapsed." Marvin shrugged. "But I grew up Orthodox. Two years at Yeshiva University in New York before I was tempted by a bacon cheeseburger. Once you're 'pork inducted,' you can't go back. I mean, obviously, it wasn't just the bacon, New York was so crazy full of people, it was just so much life, you know? Like your first petri dish in grade school when crazy-ass life-forms just start blooming before your eyes. New York was like that for me. I just couldn't imagine spending my whole life quietly contemplating the Torah in the company of a limited gene pool."

"You were really Jewish?" Even as she said it, Margot knew it was a dumb question.

"I'm still Jewish," said Marvin, affronted. "But yeah, I had the kippah, the tefillin, the tallit katan, the whole nine yards."

Margot had no idea what any of these things were.

"And lobster. I mean, what kind of religion bans lobster?"

"Jews can't eat lobster?"

"Or shrimp or any kind of shellfish—or meat with milk. Kosher, man, my mother had two blenders in her kitchen. What a drag."

"My uncle is Jewish, but my cousins aren't. Is Jewish inherited?" asked Margot, knowing that it was rude to ask, but curious and emboldened by Marvin's breezy openness.

"That's a very contentious question for a shiksa."

Margot fell silent, she didn't know what a shiksa was either.

Marvin took a long lungful of smoke and winked at her, "Now wouldn't that be fun: to find a Jewish gene! The question is: Would I be hailed as Hitler or Jonas Salk?"

Margot didn't answer. Her thoughts unspooled like the open road before them. That morning she had opened a letter from her mother: the weather was fine, her father sent his regards, she had run into Fay Stern on the street in midtown wearing a miniskirt so short it was obscene, they were digging up Park Avenue and the dust was horrendous, she had fired the old trust lawyers and let Mrs. Hanna go, and she had received, finally, the official fire department report. "It is now conclusive," her mother had written, "it was Goody's fault after all. They found a burn pattern on her bedroom wall 'consistent' with the bed curtains catching fire from a naked electric bulb."

"What are you thinking?" Marvin asked her.

Margot had not yet managed to articulate her exoneration, even to herself. "Actually I'm trying very hard not to think," she said. "My old roommate says thinking is a mental construct, and that in order to experience real consciousness we have to stop doing it."

"Sounds brainless."

"For me," said Margot, regretfully, "not thinking is usually impossible. But today it's different."

"Why?"

Margot didn't want to wreck the feeling by trying to explain it. She only knew that she felt buoyant, like floating on the surface of the Farnsworth swimming pool, ears underwater, the world muffled and the blue sky suspended above. She felt, for the first time in a long time, untangled.

"Dunno," she told Marvin.

After a while he asked:

"So what's your story?"

"The opposite of yours," Margot replied. Marvin lowered his

sunglasses a tad, side glance. "My mother never used a blender; that was the cook's department."

He waited for her to elaborate but Margot had stopped at the end of the sentence.

"Ah, wryly deflective, private. OK."

"No, it's not that, it's just—"

"You see you stopped again. It's OK, you don't have to say. Families are weird. I get it."

Excused an apology, Margot sat back, propped her feet on the dash, and let the ribbon of road rush towards her, her toes bare against the windshield, flush to the future.

THE LECTURE WAS TITLED "Nervous Systems of Nudibranches: How Memory and Neuron Response Can Be Mapped in Aplasia." A brown-speckled sea slug, with a frilly foot and two long extendable eye antennae, smiled on the poster. The hall filled up with an odd assortment: grungy boys, distinguished white-haired professors, women in sundresses, every kind of geek in between. Marvin's friend, Cosimo Case, gave a talk in which the phrase "gill and siphon withdrawal reflex" recurred often.

"What did you think?" Marvin asked her as they came out of the auditorium.

"Super interesting."

"I know, right?"

"Cosimo, meet Margot. She's smart. She knows her RNA from her DNA. She's good at counting chromosomes. She found a Superman this week."

"Stay away from those guys," said Cosmo, "they're loco."

"Hello," said Margot, putting out her hand, *She's smart!* still smarting. "I enjoyed your lecture."

Cosimo bowed low. "I'm glad it's done! Now I need a drink."

There was a clam shack behind the Stony Beach parking lot

where everyone always ended up after the Friday night lecture. It
was still warm enough to sit outside. Picnic tables, a couple of lopsided red Coca-Cola umbrellas. Styrofoam plates of littlenecks on
the half shell, bottles of Tabasco on the tables, a big Igloo cooler full
of Budweiser. People pulled up stools and a small crowd gathered at
their table. The conversation quickly got down to the nitty-gritty:
ribosomes histones peptides amino acids RNA. How to turn a sea
slug inside out and dissect its nervous system and then reverse engi-
neer nerve cells back into stem cells.

"What makes them nerve cells? What turns them on?"

"Have you tried Swedish girls in a hot tub?"

"Imagine what we could do with a big fat test tube of pluripotency."

"Everything gets shuffled during meiosis; but how? Like, what's
the chemistry of that?"

"You mean, what can cut all those covalent bonds?"

"Could you use voltage?"

"Yeah, like Frankenstein."

"Where else are you going to get the energy?"

"Mitochondria?"

Margot opened her mouth to offer an idea, but a guy with a
blond moustache said what she was about to: "What about viruses?
Viruses alter DNA," and was immediately shot down.

"Viruses don't just alter it, man, they blow up cells with a billion
replicants. It's like Hiroshima for the host DNA."

"Maybe man is just a complex virus."

"It's been said by many."

"Ah, the age-old battle between viruses and bacteria."

"It's what I've been saying all this time! War is written into our
genome."

"It's encoded in all of us."

"Perfect theory: you see, it incorporates memory and reproduction and violence."

"Well, it's one way of explaining Vietnam—"

"Are you going to the antiwar rally?"

"Nah, I can't. I've got an autoclave full of protein broth."

"I have a friend who fought in Vietnam and lost an arm," said Margot, to say something, and then wished she hadn't.

The sun went down. The sea striped blue to indigo. Beer bottles piled up, someone pulled out a guitar, strumming Dylan. Maybe the answer was blowing in the wind. The corners of her mouth ached from smiling; everything was clear and fluid. The conversation turned to the headlines: antiballistic missiles and Oakland burning, would RFK run? Marvin squeezed her knee.

"What do you think, Margot?" Cosimo asked her directly. "Is the world going to hell in a handbasket, or is all this riot and color and noise necessary to clear out the old for a new age of peace and love and chilling out."

Margot opened her mouth to reply, but Marvin interrupted:

"Depends if you believe history is a progressive ladder or a Hegelian struggle."

"Depends, in other words, if you are an optimist or a pessimist," said Cosimo.

"I'm an optimist," said Margot, surprising herself. "Scientists have to be optimists because science is about discovering knowledge and the idea that knowledge is going to make something better."

"Like nuclear fission—"

"Yeah, and look what that led to—"

"Or penicillin—"

"Or the double helix—" said Margot.

"Or how to edit DNA—" said Marvin, "because if you could understand how recombination works, you could write our own genetic recipe. You would be God in the image of man."

"And one helluva megalomaniac," said Cosimo.

Everyone laughed and Margot laughed too and Marvin leaned over right in front of everyone and kissed her.

Fear of the unknown was drowned in beer, awkwardness comforted by the blanket of night; Margot couldn't see in the darkness, it didn't matter what her hair looked like or if her skirt hitched up as she stumbled over the stones on Stony Beach. At the far curve a group of people were leaping naked into the sea. Marvin's hand was around her waist. Insecurity banished by "She's smart." His tongue felt like a sea slug in her mouth, squashy and warm. Her own sea slug foot swirled against his and she leaned into him, closer. The sea lapped their bare feet. Time sucked away on ebbing waves. For a moment the moment hung around waiting. Its successor tarried, savoring its nano-blip time slot, stared right into the black and perfectly round pupils of the young woman and the young man, as those mirrored portholes simultaneously held an answer and posed a question. Nano-blip hesitated to move on (to where? where do tiny increments of time go when they are done? are they extinguished— or do they just continue "to be" somewhere else?), and all the nano-blips strung out at regular intervals behind it piled up like cars at an intersection. Black holes appeared in the space-time continuum and were swallowed whole. Margot closed her eyes. The wedge of his thigh fitted between hers, pressed close. Have you ever seen snails making love? Squishing their whole slimy bodies together?

A deep knowing, further back from whence the waves, beyond history, out of time, yet remembered from primordial, even before the oceans, when we were stars blinking at each other through space. Marvin entwined his fingers with hers, pushed her back against the weathered clapboard. Margot felt the pressure of his intent, put her arms around his neck and ran her hands under his shirt, up his back, smooth underneath the fur. The slime spread from her mouth to his fingertips, touched her breasts that tipped towards his hand to catch his palms. Encouraged, he reached lower, and when he slid his index finger past the delicate elastic edge of her panties, she realized the slime was everywhere, slipping away any friction to make a vacuum in her that was aching now aching to be filled.

It amazed her that she wasn't embarrassed, and this new feeling unfolded into all the other amazings. She had returned to a state of liquid being, swimming, sweetly salty aqueous; his mouth against her vulva, an anemone against an oceanic volcano vent; and the memory of this, waking in a motel room two miles out of town, her legs scissoring in a moil of bedsheets, which might have mortified her in another life, yesterday, now only made her smile and want him to do it again.

Marvin woke, "Hey gorgeous," and laid himself against her snoozing back, spooning, snuggling his chin into her neck. It was late morning, it didn't matter at all, they had nowhere to be but here. He pushed her into the bathtub and climbed in behind her, his balls slapped gently against her bare ass, naked seemed only natural. Her mother's voice in her head fell silent, powerless against the flooding dopamine. They went for pancakes at a diner. Marvin ate his with butter, syrup, and ketchup, and Margot watched him glob the Heinz out of the bottle and thought, That is completely gross, but naturally she didn't say anything. "You're such a sweetie pie," Marvin told her. Margot felt herself growing into the sunlight of his compliments: smart, gorgeous, sweetie pie. "Snow White—Walt Disney drew the lines of your body, the curve of your neck—" The curve of my neck! Margot grinned with her mouth full, instinctively held up a napkin so that nothing might spill unseemly. Princess Margot again.

16

KARYOTYPING, COUNTING CHROMATIDS VISUALLY, WAS like diagramming a photograph of a tray of eels.

"I have given up trying to be scientific about it," Margot admitted to Richie at De Sousa's. "I have my favorite chromosomes, the tall ones, 1, 2, and 3, waving their long arms."

"Because they look like you."

"Yes, I admit, I identify with them!" Margot poured herself another glass of wine, boldly, without waiting for Richie to do it for her. "But 10, 11, and 12 are boring middlings. Could be anyone, average, you couldn't pick them out of a police lineup—and then there's X and of course stumpy little Y, almost an afterthought, an appendage."

"Careful about impugning the Y chromosome! All the old dinosaurs still trying to fix gender traits in the genome will drown you in testosterone."

"Genetics is the new feminism, haven't you heard? We are all female, until Y comes along."

"Have they found the gene for distracted-while-driving yet?"

"For god's sake!"

"I'm only being observational," said Richie, unwilling to concede. "Statistics show that if you take males aged between sixteen and twenty-four out of the equation, the majority of accidents are caused by women."

"Facts," said Margot, "Dr. Fred says, are like atoms. You can arrange them to configure anything you like: from a submarine to a blue whale to a sun. In and of themselves, they are useless."

"Now you're just borrowing someone else's metaphor."

"I know. But he's very good at them."

"If I didn't know better, I would say you had a crush on Dr. Fred."

Margot looked down at her plate, yellow rice grains spilled over pink shrimp. Why did he have to deploy a cheap shot just because he was on the wrong foot in the argument?

"What's eating you this evening?"

Richie didn't look up from his plate. Margot felt bad; maybe she had overreacted. Was it that time of the month? She watched Richie shovel two big forkfuls of paella into his mouth and elaborately swallow.

"I hear you've been seeing a lot of Marvin Cohen."

"Oh." Margot was not sure why this sounded like a reproach.

"I mean," said Richie haltingly, "it's your life."

"You mean because he's Jewish?"

"No—I don't care about that—it's just—"

Margot looked at him not looking at her. She saw how pale his skin was at his temple where the faint blue of vein was visible, tender and exposed. She waited patiently for the second half of his sentence, for his reason.

"I just thought you might have told me—"

"Oh." This hadn't occurred to Margot. She wasn't the type for confidences.

Richie drained his wine and asked for the check. Margot tried to fill the gap by saying something about McNamara coming to talk at Harvard, stirring up the antiwar groups. Richie listened distractedly. He held the door for her as they were leaving.

"Don't mind me. I'm in a funk." He ran a hand over his beard, smoothing. "Sage Hill stuff."

"News of Hal?"

Richie shook his head. "Mother wants to go to India to look for him, Father refuses to let her. And it turns out Runny has run through another twenty grand at Saratoga, and Dad's old pal at Lehman told him he's on probation—some kind of discrepancy in his sale slips."

"That's a shame," said Margot, aware of the lameness of this response.

Richie made a sour smile. "And that girl in California? Well, it didn't work out. So I guess I'm sore about that too."

"I'm sorry," said Margot. "What happened?"

But Richie wasn't the type for confidences either. He made a dismissive waving motion with one hand. In the moonlight his narrow face hung morose and plaintive. For a moment he looked as if he wanted to ask her something, but then he seemed to think better of it and continued walking up Mass Ave, with his long, even stride.

17

AFTER A FEW WEEKS OF PEERING AT CHROMOSOMES DOWN the microscope, Margot was able to discern individual characteristics. She learned to divine shadow from shape, to separate the jumbled mass, like picking out sticks from a pick-up sticks pile. Like counting-climbing.

A concentrated calm, Shirley would have called it "Zen." The world receded. Questions wandered into her head like the fleeting auguries of dreams. How did they decide? How do these funny-looking bendy-wiggly chromosomes merge or meld or mix to make a whole new living loving walking talking individual person, my mother or me or my daughter or anyone?

It was a Thursday afternoon, October New England weather, azure skies and yellow ginkgo leaves. Margot laughed, "Did I say that out loud?" She pulled the ring tab on her can of Fresca, let the fizz burr pleasantly against her top lip.

"You are asking about the origins of life!" said Flashman.

Margot had discovered happy. Lab 1123 was a sanctuary of oddballs in which Marvin was king and Margot, by extension, was—well, not queen exactly, but perhaps consort. Flashman was mild and kind; concave-skinny, looked like a puff of wind would blow him over. But once, when Marvin had mocked Adam's entomological obsession, gangly-dancing and singing "I'm a grasshopper, come and kiss me," Flashman had fixed him with a stare and said, "Just don't, OK. Not funny." Adam was the baby of the group, a sixteen-year-old whiz kid who had finished high school when he was twelve, didn't need to use a razor, and kept an aquarium of stick insects in his dorm room.

"Don't be bashful, Margot," said Flashman, pulling up a stool. "Geneticists have spent whole careers breeding generations of flatworms, fruit flies, jellyfish, bacteria, all those strains of influenza—tracking traits, measuring inheritance—and all of them had the same basic question: What evolutionary mechanism is running the show? How does the genome shuffle itself? And to what end? It's the basic eternal question—"

"Not the meaning of life!" Marvin interrupted him. "Let's leave that old saw to novelists and philosophers and priests. They can make up whatever bedtime story they want. Looking for the meaning of life is nothing but an analgesic."

"It's a journey," said Margot, to agree with him.

Marvin did not agree. *What's the meaning of life?* It's a stupid question! It's the *how* of life that matters!"

"That's what I meant," said Margot, but quietly.

"*How* life is made: what is the order of the base pairs, what makes up a gene, identify, decode. Because if we can understand the sequencing, we can edit it, get rid of all those mutations—"

Flashman kept his tone even, amiable. "Aren't mutations how nature improves itself?"

Margot hugged her shoulders, hunched inward. What about her *genetic mutation?* Would she have chosen to be shorter if she could have? If she could, would she choose for her own daughter to be shorter? Hadn't her mother once tried?

The scar on her forehead had faded, but the imprint of the fall from the treehouse remained. Margot startled at the sound of any sharp sound, shied from heights. Almost more than the terrible stretched-out second of falling, Margot remembered the crunch of landing, CRACK and blackout, the searing pain and the terror of finding herself blind and alone. In consequence, she preferred to be close to the ground instead of high up, was not accustomed to asking for help, tended to hunker down. Shirley called her "ostrich" and rolled her eyes. Sometimes Margot worried, in a Psych 101 kind of way, that in that second of falling, which must have been only a split second, she herself had split. From a before-self—the fearless girl who had reached upwards counting-climbing towards her egg prize—to an after-self: hesitant, scaredy-cat, oversensitive.

Margot went back to drawing ideograms with a pencil on a pad, carefully separating stripe from striation. The sameness was hypnotic, double step, quick quick slide together, like dancing—until there was a stumble, a mutation. What syndromes or brittle bones or bubble boys resulted? No one knew who they were because the samples were anonymous, labeled only M or F, for male or female, with a number. M-343. F-565. Marvin gave them nicknames like Pluto and Mickey, Daffodil and Erasmus. He said he couldn't bear to give people numbers instead of names, because that's what the Nazis had done at Auschwitz. Margot thought this was a kind of joke, and she reached out and tickled him under his chin and teased, "Oh my great humanitarian." But Marvin detached her hand from his face and got up and walked out of the room. She didn't understand what she had done wrong.

There were other odd things: Marvin could spend a whole hour in bed in the morning, singing summer tunes along with the radio, running his fingertips up her legs, apparently rapt, but then Margot would knock on his door late at night and find him cold and irritated, "I was trying to get some work done." One time he couldn't get the radio to tune properly and he punched it so hard one of the knobs gashed his knuckle. A couple of times he yelled at some tiny thing: an unwashed coffee cup, he couldn't find his sock. When his anger passed, he would make a kind of wounded animal whimper as a signal that he would let himself be petted again.

But then again, there were counterfactuals: Wasn't she sleeping in his room almost every night, almost as if they were married? Hadn't he given her a ring made of a cowrie shell glued to a metal band? Weren't all these indications of love? Margot had been bowled over with the speed and intensity of sexual intimacy, by the ramming fuckingness of it. Walking around in the nude, she was finally inhabiting the mind-set that Mad had once insisted upon, defiantly insisted upon, as *unashamed*.

18

HER MOTHER HAD MADE IT CLEAR THAT MARGOT WAS expected at 655 Park for Thanksgiving. She took the bus down to New York but went to see Mad before going home.

Mad's father had bought her a town house on Washington Square Park, and she lived there in grand bohemian style. There were no doors, an ancient claw-foot bathtub stood in the middle of her bedroom. Mattresses and cushions and carpets were heaped around low tables strewn with hubbly-bubbly pipes, ashtrays, strings of beads, and glasses crusted with dried-out red wine.

But a cleaning lady came three times a week to clear away the party detritus and swab the decks, and there was a newly installed boiler and gleaming radiators in every room.

"I'm from Texas," said Mad, "I can't be cold."

"It's perfect for you," Margot had laughed. "Pretending to slum it."

With her wild red hair and a body that curved around corners before she did, Mad was a voluptuary, a word Margot had yet to come across. She loved warmth and glow, candlelight and sunlight. She loved to be admired, to be caressed by her admirers, loved to make love, to say "love" and "lovely," to lie back and pass a bong around, and hum old show tunes. She teased Margot to take off her cardigan, for god's sake, and stop being so uptight!

Mad's crowd freaked her out. Black fingernails, nose rings, hennaed hands. "Oh they're harmless," Mad insisted. There was always a guy strumming a guitar, someone who was "a majorly talented artist, he just needs a place to crash," a handful of surfer dudes from Connecticut, a beautiful woman with an Afro tied up in a batik head scarf, and a Black Power boyfriend in a revolutionary beret, strung-out skinny girls, boys with long hair and bandannas, some random lost British banker, a Mexican guru with a fake Indian accent.

"Don't worry about me, Margot-so-sensible," Mad laughed everything off with a full-throated ease. "I'm as happy as a dolphin swimming in the deep blue sea."

Margot knew that Mad would be alone; Thanksgiving was a holiday she did not celebrate. She came to the door barefoot, wearing a kimono, and wrapped Margot in a great enveloping embrace. Her body was warm and soft and smelled of chocolate and jasmine. "Come, come—" she ushered Margot into the living room and sat her on a pink velvet beanbag in front of the fire. Margot took off her shoes and socks and nubbed her toes in the sheepskin rug. Mad poured wine into jelly glasses and drowned the Flintstones.

"Don't you think it's odd that Richie has never made a move on you?" Mad asked, filching a cigarette paper from a roll and laying it flat on the steamer trunk coffee table.

Margot shrugged. It had never occurred to her.

"Maybe he plays for the other team," said Mad. "I mean, that would explain *a lot*."

Mad had a tan from Cancún; in the firelight, the planes of her face were striped terracotta and black like a goddess on a Greek urn.

"He was dating a med student all last year," said Margot.

"I think Richie would be good for you, you're like the mirror image of each other—Margot! Don't look at me like that; not *physically*—you know what I mean."

"You mean my mother would approve."

"Hasn't she still got her sights set on Trip for you?"

"He's still going steady with Lydia."

"Yeah, but she's such a ball-breaker."

"And anyway, I have . . . I am . . . finally—" Margot dropped her chin, embarrassed, grinned.

Mad's eyes grew wide, "You got laid!"

So Margot told Mad all about her new boyfriend, how he was tall and strong and handsome, that he was a fellow biomolecular geek, but not geeky, that he was kinda cool actually, totally laid back, Hendrix fan, voted Democrat but generally thought all politicians could go take a flying leap. She didn't tell Mad about Marvin's temper or the way he always had to have the last word, or his habit, in bed, of patting her butt as soon as he had come, as a signal to disengage.

"I could never take him home to Mother dearest. I don't think she would let him into the apartment without a coat and tie."

Mad slipped the kimono off her shoulders and shook her breasts free. The resinous smoke wreathed her bronze body. She wasn't wearing panties. Margot looked, looked away.

"Don't be such a prude!" said Mad, handing Margot the joint. "Marvin sounds like the perfect first boyfriend, but he's not a keeper."

"How do you know?"

"I can tell by your face."

Margot's face fell.

"All I am saying, is that Richie is not as hot as Trip, but he's by far the better Merryweather."

"I am beginning to think that happily-ever-after is a confidence trick made up by novelists."

"Because you've never been in love, my darling."

"And you have?"

"I fell in love on June sixth. I can tell you precisely the moment: we'd had a long night in the village, *trop de l'herbe*, we couldn't sleep. Solomon Grundy hails a cab and tells the driver: Idlewild! Solomon Grundy says: Let's fly away! And right then, I knew. It was six in the morning, dawn coming up and it doesn't matter where we are going, just that we are together. We go inside the Pan Am terminal

and he says: Look up at the departures board and pick the first destination that speaks to you. He's got this spiritual side, you feel it?"

Margot had met the famous Solomon Grundy one Sunday afternoon at the Mad House. He was eating scrambled eggs sitting at
the big refectory table, half asleep, bare chested, a tie-dyed sarong
draped around his waist and a dragon tattoo curled on his bicep.
His half-moon eyes were focused on a distant horizon somewhere
between sage, somnolent, and stoned. If they looked at her directly,
Margot knew she would turn into primordial jelly. He was the most
heart-stoppingly beautiful man she had ever seen. She had sat down
on the furthest chair and unfolded the science section of the *New
York Times*. Without a word Solomon Grundy had come up and
taken her wrist in his big warm paw, pressed his fingers against her
pulse and felt her heartbeat racing. "You've got a congested chakra,"
he diagnosed. "I prescribe: marijuana, an orgasm twice a day, and
complete nudity for a week."

Mad continued: "So I looked up at the destination board, at
all the letters revolving on their electric spindles making nonsense
words. And slowly they began falling into place with the names of
destinations. Marrakech glowed back at me, somehow cosmically
brighter than all the others. So I went to the ticket desk and put
down my Diners card and we went to Marrakech with only the
clothes on our backs."

"You just got on an airplane?"

"That's what I'm saying: we can go *anywhere*—we are not like
our mothers. Our choice is not between marrying Billy or Bobby
and spawning a tribe of ankle-biters. Our choice is between following our parents' example of same old same old, or cutting loose,
making a break."

Mad stopped for a moment to relight her joint. "Well, anyway,"
said Mad, "think about your future. I'm just asking: What's next?"

"Grad school," said Margot easily. "MA."

"And then?" Mad twirled her joint, smoke rings spiraled upwards,
drawn to the escaping draft of an open window.

"PhD," said Margot defiantly, knowing this was absurd.

Mad rolled her eyes. "I'm just saying you could do a lot worse than Richie Merryweather."

"I can't believe you of all people are advising me to get married. What happened to your free love commune."

"Oh, we're still going to have one," said Mad, "Solomon Grundy says it will realign my inner consciousness."

"Realign it to what?"

"I don't care," said Mad, with a sudden pang of despair.

Margot caught the edge, wondered at its sudden intrusion, but then remembered the date.

Mad lay back on the shag rug, stared up at the ceiling.

"It just hurts all the time, like it just hurts to be alive."

"Try to describe it to me."

"It's an ache, but acute."

"Where?"

"In my sternum. Deep in."

"Did you tell the shrink about Boston?"

Mad lit a new cigarette from the ember of the one she was smoking.

"Of course not. Daddy thinks it's all about my insomnia. I couldn't bear it if he knew."

"Why don't you get your own shrink?"

"Because then I'd have to tell them the truth."

They fell silent for a while, each gently tapping at the hollow spaces in the self. The fire played merrily with light and carbon. Thoughts shimmered like oases. When they hugged goodbye, Margot felt an emptiness in Mad; she didn't want to leave her alone.

19

HALF AN HOUR LATER SHE WAS UPTOWN, SITTING UPRIGHT at the kitchen table.

"I need to talk to you," said her mother. Margot sipped her tea and waited. When Mrs. Hanna had been in residence, there was always shortbread in the cookie jar. Now there was nothing in the refrigerator but a bottle of seltzer and half a tub of cottage cheese. Peggy was rail thin, her forehead ironed with neat new pleats, each perfectly parallel and equidistant. Her hair was still styled swept up from her face, but it was now secured not with hairdressing lacquer, but with a plastic tortoiseshell hairband. Margot noticed she was worrying her wedding ring around her knuckle; the sapphire engagement ring had evidently been sold too.

OVER THREE YEARS OF financial ruin and social humiliation, Peggy had maintained her fixed smile, her erect bearing, chin thrust forward, ready to berate or to insist. She filed and polished her fingernails into red triangles, the better to threaten, declaim, and to point, point out to the world that they were wrong and she was right. They, them, all of them: the shyster lawyers, the idiots at the bank, the incompetents at the trust, the parvenus at the corporation. For three years Peggy had not flagged in her campaign of certitude, rectitude, outrage, and injustice. She had stood inviolable against them all. I. Will. Not.

It was only her husband and her daughter who saw her true wrath. Knew the power and the fury of it. The smashed plates, the scrubbed-out bloodstains on the carpet, the cracked bathroom tile where Peggy had hurled the porcelain toilet cover when the flush had broken on a Sunday when no plumber would come.

When she had shouted herself hoarse, Peggy would weep and howl and curse all their uselessness. Margot and her father tried to soothe her, offered blandishments, brought her her favorite almond cookies, never mind the expense, suggested she call a friend, get some fresh air, walk in the park, give herself a break—Peggy would not be mollified.

Invitations dried up. Peggy had never made intimate friendships, and now, club memberships canceled, Social Register dues unpaid, society had rescinded its associations. Only Dotty Merryweather, whom Peggy continued to disparage, mistaking kindness for condescension, still called. Memorial Day weekend, when they still had the car, they had driven out to a cocktail party at Sage Hill, but on the way back Peggy declared it was the last time. "All of them, smug as pugs with their so-sorrys, and not one of them offered any *help*. Lawrence Gerald suggested that I could call one of his partners to ask about a secretarial position!"

Over time, the distractions and hope of the probate process diminished and were replaced by the exacting details of loan application forms and IRS liens. As the pile of envelopes mounted, Peggy grew ever more taciturn, grinding her cigarette butts into the ashtray with a violence that sought to crush the whole world of petty bureaucrats ranged against her.

At some point in her junior year, Margot understood that her father had lost his job. Without voting shares, sold to pay the IRS bill, United Union Steel had no use for an executive to run a philanthropy department, signing checks to his wife's favorite charities. That Christmas her mother had opened the small present from her father and, finding only a single cotton handkerchief inside, threw the box in his face.

"You're a waste. You're a drain. I'm counting pennies, selling my jewelry. And you do nothing! Sit there with your newspaper! While I work myself to the bone cleaning up after you like an Irish maid! And as for your *daughter*! Up at college, no *help*, no *use*. And you *encourage* her! The selfishness of it all! I haven't been to the hair-dresser in months. I haven't had new stockings in a year! And you sit here and drink your apple brandy and watch the television as if nothing has changed!"

They had eaten their turkey in silence, dry-mouthed, without gravy.

MARGOT TOOK HER ELBOWS off the table. Peggy said, "I need to ask you about your future plans because—"

Margot waited for the rest of the sentence, head bowed, examin-ing the cloud of tannin collect on the surface of her cooling tea. Her bag was still in the hall, she hadn't had a chance to splash water on her face and gather herself; she was still a little wobbly-wavy from Mad's weed. Her mother looked uncomfortable sitting at the small wooden table in the drab kitchen which she had never decorated because, before, she had never had reason to spend any time in it. The pause lengthened.

"Maybe you could paint this room," suggested Margot, to say something. "Yellow, something cheerful."

"Decorating costs money, Margot."

"I could do it."

"And make a complete hash. No. I am asking if you have given any thought to your future."

"I don't know, I guess."

"You don't know, you guess." Peggy tapped her spoon on the side of the teacup, an insistent piano note. "Well. I think it's high time you got married."

Margot tried to fix her eyes beyond her mother's moving mouth. Behind her was a window, but the kitchens in prewar buildings were all built at the back, because that's where the servants' quarters were, and it looked out onto a brick wall.

"I have a boyfriend," said Margot flatly.

Peggy did not hear her. "Trip Merryweather is in his final year at Yale, an attractive boy, the best of the litter, and you have been such pals since childhood."

"Trip has a girlfriend," said Margot. "They're practically engaged."

"Lydia Cummings! With that harlot mother and a father who upped and moved to California and *lives-in-sin* with some groupie and *her* brood of children? I don't believe for a moment Clarence Merryweather would allow such a match!"

"Trip doesn't want to marry me," said Margot.

"He will. He must!" But there was something cracked in the steel of her mother's conviction.

"Why does it have to be Trip?"

Margot thought of Marvin being the answer to her mother's prayers, and almost giggled.

"No." On this point Peggy was firm. "The other Merryweather brothers are a bunch of doozies. Dick has gone his own way—oh I know you're pals, but a doctor's wife is no life, and Clarence has already decided that Trip is the heir apparent. The bulk of the fortune and the Sage Hill estate—which cannot be divided according to the rules of the Whitney Trust—this Dotty, mealymouthed one evening, sopped to the gills on Martini, let loose—will be signed over before Clarence dies, for tax reasons, to Trip, *when he marries.*"

Margot stared at the brick wall as her mother continued to talk of plans and parties and people and presents. She was more animated than Margot had seen her in a long time. Peggy took out her old crocodile notebook and resumed her to-do list, as smoothly as if she were simply picking up where she'd left off that breakfast morning at Farnsworth when she had begun to plan Margot's debutante year.

Margot swallowed her tea. A butterfly appeared in the bottom of the cup.

When Peggy had completed her list, she said, "Well, that's all settled then," and cleared the cups and saucers and stacked them in the sink. Margot washed them up and put them back in the china closet and waited for her father to come home for dinner. By seven o'clock he had not appeared and there was nothing in the icebox to eat. Her mother sat in the den watching TV, cracking ice cubes with her molars.

"Where's Dad?" Margot asked eventually. Her mother feigned silence, as if she could not hear. "I'm hungry," said Margot. No reply.

It was Thanksgiving. Everything was closed. Margot walked all the way to Rockefeller Center before she found a hot dog cart. The frank was salty and sweet with green relish and yellow mustard. Margot ate it walking back up an empty Fifth Avenue. She walked very slowly, the blocks accumulating, each number a little higher, a little heavier, a little closer to home.

MARGOT COULDN'T SLEEP THAT night. Addled, strung out, she half suspected Mad had laced her doobie because everything looked surreal and lit up like a stage. Orange streetlights cast strange veering shadows on her bedroom walls. Four in the morning, the witching hour, Margot kicked off the sheets, lit a cigarette, felt the hot coal burning against her ring finger. She began adding, subtracting, recounting. In order to do an MA she would need money for tuition and living expenses. During the semester, she could earn a small stipend as a teaching assistant. Over the vacations she could do lab scut work at two bucks an hour. She thought of Sarah, as Jean Craft had once described her, with red hands from scrubbing laundry.

Freshman year, Margot had written an essay on marriage as a plot device for a Nineteenth-Century Literature class. Balzac and Dickens; *Buddenbrooks, Middlemarch*. Fortunes lost and then regained with a wedding. But Margot did not imagine herself any great literary heroine; she half suspected her mother had framed the whole story as a way to push the Trip thing—

The Trip thing.

It tickled sometimes. Margot wondered what it would be like to run into him and Lydia with Marvin; Harvard-Yale game, or a deb ball—but Marvin wasn't clubbable like that—he would end up showing off and Trip would just laugh because everything in life was laughable if you could pull off the trick of not taking anything seriously. "Poor old Pine Tree," she could hear his voice, mocking. "Look what the cat dragged in!"

Last summer, at Chip Reid's wedding, Margot had seen Lydia flip out at Trip for flirting with one of the bridesmaids. Trip, deep in his cups, wasn't the least embarrassed.

"Oh Pine Tree, you would never give me such a hard time, would you?" They had danced sloppily, Margot fizzing with champagne and nostalgia for the sound of a big band, swing and croon and dance-floor swoon. Princess for a moment, relapse. She had smiled encouragingly as Trip had said things he shouldn't have said. Till Lydia came back for him.

Till the image of Trip kissing her mother beside the buffet table at Farnsworth rose up from the slurried depths of memory and was overlaid with Stevie's sneer. Then followed the ghosts of all the other hurts. *Not good enough.* The familiar litany lined up to take their turn to scratch the ditch deeper: a C in calculus, "She's not our type" overheard in the Quad, a yucky, sweaty kiss freshman year, a stabbing finger in her solar plexus out of nowhere on the bus, the forgotten batch of slides left to degrade in her lab locker, the rank stench when Marvin had pushed her head into his crotch, her mother's voice: *What are we going to do about Margot?*

Margot got out of bed and opened the window. The moon had risen high and shone like a spotlight.

She wasn't a child anymore to be done with. She was her own doing.

"I am not a child I am an adult!" she said out loud.

The moonlight was very clear and bright. A siren wailed. Margot heard her father's key turn in the lock and his lumbering tread in the corridor as he made his way to the empty maid's room at the back.

20

It happened at the beginning of December that Margot found an intriguing repetition of stripes on chromosome 4 of M-747, which Marvin had nicknamed Gustav.

"I think it could be a mutation," Margot told Flashman.

"Let me have a look," said Marvin.

"You see, it's not a happy haploid. Look at the slight wriggle of the centromere, the way the bottom telomere seems to droop."

"Happy?" Marvin chided her. "Let's not anthropomorphize our chromosomes."

"What's more anthropological than a human chromosome?" asked Flashman.

"I just want to know if you can see it too," said Margot. "Maybe I'm crazy, but—"

Flashman peered down her microscope. "Yeah . . . kinda."

Then Marvin looked. "Nope. There's nothing. You've been staring at those things so long you're seeing things that aren't there."

"Maybe it's an indicator of a disease or a syndrome," Margot persisted.

"You're overreaching," said Marvin in a low, personal tone; he wasn't talking about a chromosome.

After the lab session, they all went for a beer at the Crimson

Cup. Margot automatically sat next to Marvin in the booth, but he bent away from her, didn't touch her or meet her eye. She felt the proximal warmth of his body as a cold reproach. Flashman and Adam kept up a stream of patter running over the rocks of Marvin's mood. Margot endured the crispiness, potato chips crunching very loudly in her head.

Margot thought she knew Marvin because she knew his penis. But sitting beside him, regarding his mouth, so recently kissed, now pursed in condescension, almost daring her to react to his studied indifference, she thought back to the moment she had first seen it: penis-by-daylight, purple-headed, a bead of viscous sperm at its eye and a stiffening insistence that pushed against her palm. Her first reaction had been disgust: How raw and bald! How can Mad want to put that in her mouth?

They settled the tab. Amid the leaving bustle of putting on jackets and goodbyes, Flashman said to Margot, sotto voce, "Don't let him get to you, he's just exerting his alpha."

Margot didn't want to be disloyal. "Don't say that."

"Look, he's a big stud, I get the attraction. But trust me, he's not the nicest guy in the world."

Flashman touched her elbow. Margot didn't see the puddle of spilled beer he was trying to guide her away from.

"And you are?" she asked pointedly, slipping on the mess on the floor.

Flashman shrugged, "Whatever"— and pushed through the swinging door without holding it open for her.

Marvin was in combat mode. Still, Margot followed him. At the intersection he caught her forearm. Why was it men were always tugging at her?

"Margot! Car!"

"I saw it!"

"Don't argue."

Were they arguing? Margot instinctively took a step back onto the curb. Despite her retreat, she wanted him to know she wasn't defeated.

"I'm just saying the shadows on the chromosome could be an illustration of something."

"Just drop it, will you?"

"Why are you so mad at me? What did I do?"

"Look, you're a nice enough girl, but."

"But I'm not Jewish." Margot supplied the reason herself, even though it didn't make much sense to her. "I thought you weren't Jewish anymore," she said.

"I can't stop being Jewish. That's what I'm talking about. You've got no idea."

She watched his eyes turn from caramel to coal.

"I can never marry a shiksa," he said, stepping onto the street away from her.

Margot followed him. When they got back to his room, Marvin pushed her onto the bed and flipped her over so that she was on her stomach. He pushed her skirt up over her waist, pulled off her panties, pushed himself inside her, suddenly fully erect and urgent. She felt the punishment of it, that he was doing it *to* her, but as the rhythm repeated harder harder, it made her shudder with the buried depth of it.

The glow from the lava lamp swam across the headboard. Margot let her mind heave thoughts as slow as molten wax in oil, through the dreamy sloppiness of aftermath, Marvin snoring gently and the bruising burn of him still inside her. She lay very still while he slept with his hands cupping his balls like a baby chimp, long eyelashes fluttering under REM. She whispered, "I love you."

The next day it was over.

"I think we've taken this thing as far as it can go," Marvin told her at the door to the lab. Margot felt slapped and stupid, because what idiot would have mistaken a lab affair for anything more serious. How totally retrograde, in this day and age, to get hung up on love and happily-ever-after.

Margot walked back to the Quad through the oddly consoling hummocks of the Old Burying Ground, catching her fingertips on brambles. There was a sweetness in the pain that still carried hope. She coddled her disconsolate self; lonely and independent were two sides of her newly minted ego—or was it her id? Which one had Mad told her she was supposed to develop?

21

Richie took one look at her face. "As bad as that?"

Margot nodded.

"Don't take it too hard. Marvin Cohen is no great shakes. Honestly, I can give you the names of half a dozen girls he's screwed over."

Margot bit her lip to hear that she was only one of many. Her xiphoid process stabbed.

Richie tried to cheer her up. He ordered fizzy wine and shrimp with garlic and changed the subject.

"How's Madeleine?"

"Up and down. She has convinced herself that her moods have a physical cause—unbalanced hormones, an overactive thyroid, an allergy to milk. She goes to doctor after doctor. Each one has a different explanation and gives her a different pill."

"As far as I can tell, all they're doing is prescribing her tranquilizers."

"And she's smoking a lot of pot. Probably other stuff."

"I'm worried about her. I saw too many nice girls OD when I was doing my rotation in the ER, washed out, washed up by some guy."

Margot dug her fingernails into her palm. He could have been talking about her.

"They're like empty bottles after a party, after all the sex and drugs and guitar-twanging and letting-it-all-hang-loose." Richie jangled his bony forearms to illustrate letting-it-all-hang-loose.

He looked so silly trying to bop like a teenager in his tweed jacket, Margot actually smiled. Richie made a self-deprecating grin.

"I know I am an old fart," he said. "I feel like I'm already too old to swing."

"Me too," said Margot. "I can't dance all by myself, it feels weird."

"We'll have to find some old-fashioned dance hall where we can waltz to the golden oldies like we were taught by Miss Waverly."

Richie leaned forward across the table. Margot leaned back. Too soon, too something. His beard hid his scarred lip, but his big teeth still shone through. His eyes were kind, but they were bulbous. She looked down at his hand walking on fingertips across the tablecloth towards her own. It looked disembodied, like Thing's hand in *The Addams Family*. She sat back, demure, as she had been taught.

"I don't remember how to waltz," said Margot. "It's been an age."

"Trip always said you were his best dance partner," said Richie.

"Did he?"

"He said Lydia Cummings couldn't carry a beat, but you were a real glider."

"A glider! Me?"

Now it was Richie's turn to sit back, disconsolate.

"Ah. I see."

"What?"

22

How does the nematode on the flea on the dog look up and understand the moon? Margot zoomed between microscope and telescope, extending, retracting—never quite sure which would give the better view. DNA was smaller than the wavelength of light, too small to see, even with an electron microscope, but it was also of unfathomable unraveling dimension. Wound in its spirals was the history of a man and mankind, the memory of meteor showers and ice ages, bacterial infections and prehistoric wolf attacks. Each human genome contained three billion base pairs. Too many to count in a lifetime. Longer than a lifetime; a record of every lifetime.

What are we doing here? What was she looking for when she stared at chromosomes, scanning for markers that marked only another unknown; Margot wondered if she would know it even if she saw it. Wondered if the process was all there was. What if counting-climbing never led anywhere (no nest, no blue eggs), and there wasn't any destination but the helical ladder that you kept hauling yourself up on, clinging to the slippy mossy rope, tripping on gnarls, buffeted by the wind, losing your grip, falling backwards, falling, CRACK, hurting, but not dead apparently, not yet; pick yourself up and keep climbing.

There was a secret space inside Margot, in all women, she

knew—knew it from Mad's hollowed-out pain, from her mother's anger and ambition, from Sarah's sacrifice, from Goody's dying words that hoped to recall her daughters to her. Harbinger, womb. Margot wanted . . . wanted very much to fill this secret space with babblings, tidings of joy, with love—yes, yes, exactly that! Shh . . .

Chromosomes were a clue to the mystery of life, but what is life if not love, a word not found in any textbook, but more elemental than carbon or oxygen or deoxyribonucleic acid. Part of Margot wanted to solve the mystery and read the code, part of her didn't want to know the trick behind the magic. She loved the scientific process, the counting-climbing. But she also wanted to hold and be held and all the fairy-tale princess crap. She was furious (as much as Margot could admit to fury; it was more likely expressed in self-excoriating angst) that love was apparently dependent on Marvins who only used it for sex. Begone, the whole sex delusion! After all, intercourse was just an evolutionary device for introducing sperm to egg; there were plenty of other nudibranch-ish ways of doing it. Asexual, hermaphrodite sea horses, pathogenesis—*Gerrantry and Müller, Reproductive Homogeneity in Whiptail Lizards: Cloning in Female-Only Populations of Squamate Reptiles, 1963.*

It occurred to Margot that in Lab 1123 they were just a bunch of undergrads counting chromosomes, but two floors above, Meselson and his team were figuring out how to snip DNA into pieces with enzymes and jimmy its sequencing, possibly even, whisper it low, *alter it.* Maybe one day random pheromonal couplings of reproduction would be moot; sex would be for sex and when you wanted a baby you went to a baby designer who shuffled one gene from here on chromosome 12q13 and another there on Xp. Margot turned the dial on her microscope, lost in the thought of all the traits she would stir into the cocktail: from her side, Sarah's lovingness and Peggy's strength; and from the other, a multiple paternity of Trip's confidence, Richie's kindness, Marvin's roguish glint, and Steve McQueen's blue eyes—

Because if you could figure out which bits of DNA the embryo got from which parent—*how* the mysterious universe placed this gene next to that gene—you could potentially influence the process.

"Fuck that, you would be the greatest scientist on the planet!" declared Marvin, grabbing Margot's can of Fresca and taking a swig. He didn't ask. Just took, as if daring her to confront him, which he knew she wouldn't.

"Darwin would turn in his grave! No more natural selection! Man could finally determine his own destiny!" Marvin held up both arms in the air, already victorious, as if the audacity of the idea was triumph enough.

"Don't look at me like that, Margot!" he said. "Don't tell me you wouldn't cut off your left hand to be *Time* magazine's Man of the Year."

Woman of the Year, thought Margot, and bit her lip.

It was the last lab session of the semester. Margot made some lame excuse not to go with the gang to the Crimson Cup. Flashman said, "Come anyway. Don't let Marvin chase you away."

She nearly did, but—"I'm sorry, I've got a ton of tabulating and all the graphs to plot up by tomorrow. It's going to be an all-nighter."

Walked away alone, ordered a grilled cheese to-go from the diner on the corner of Mass Ave where she had once been too nervous of her own company to finish a coffee, ate it sitting cross-legged on her bed and felt like crap.

She remembered something Adam had mentioned a while back—maybe it was a long shot—but in any case, the next morning Margot went to see Dr. Fred in his office. She found him shuffling through papers on his desk. She stood, waiting for his attention.

"Sorry, end of the semester, drowning in paperwork." He looked up, hazel eyes slanting through his lashes.

"I'm sorry," said Margot, automatically apologetic.

"Why? What happened?" He waved at her to sit.

"Nothing, I just. I just wanted to ask about the DNA graduate class I heard you were putting together next semester—even if you don't have a place for an undergrad, I wanted to say that I could be a lab assistant, researcher, errand boy—we've been working on chromosomes. And. I mean. I found a double Y. There are a lot of gradations in the striping sequences, I think they could be significant."

Margot held out her project report, hand-drawn ideograms and graphs attached by paper clip in several sheets of appendices. "Here are my final conclusions. And. There are one or two, well, speculative, findings—"

Dr. Fred flipped to the last couple of pages and was silent for a few minutes reading.

"What's your undergrad thesis?"

Margot answered decisively: "Anomalies on the X chromosome."

"What are you looking for?"

"Well, that's just it. I don't know what I am looking for. I thought—perhaps, maybe"—her habit of caveat made her hesitate— "it would be better to keep the subject exploratory. If I prefigure a result, I could end up with nothing to report."

"Hedging your bets," said Dr. Fred with half a smile.

In Boston in December he was wearing a Hawaiian shirt, open-necked to show off a fading tan and a necklace of amber beads. His hair was long, down to his shoulders.

"This way my research can be purely observational."

Margot had thought it over and decided to keep her thesis conclusion open ended; that way Dr. Fred would have less to object to.

"Well. You see. I would like to be considered as an MA candidate in the new microbiology department."

A silver dollar fell from Dr. Fred's hand onto the desk and Margot followed his gaze. It landed heads.

"OK. Margot is it?" Margot nodded. "Let me level with you. Meselson is working on a restrictive enzyme. My genetics grad class isn't exactly a class. It's more of a research group without funding, because—well, it's easier to fill in the forms this way, less scrutiny. Meselson needs a secondary group to verify his promising leads and knock out some of the less promising dead ends. I said I would help out."

"You're going after recombination," said Margot, her heart sinking, clutching at her ego for good company on the way down. This was far more ambitious than she had thought.

"I understand," she said, thinking this was his way of letting her down easy.

"But I have another agenda for this class—and that's where I have some extra spaces. It's a pet project of mine. I want to mix up undergrads with DPhils and postdocs, students at different levels doing different projects—it's part of my collaboration-is-king idea, trying to break down academic boundaries"—he looked her up and down.

Margot waited hopefully.

"But it's got to be on the down-low," said Dr. Fred, leaning forward. "No chatting in the common room. Your ears only. Double-oh-seven and hope-to-die."

Margot nodded dumbly.

Dr. Fred looked her straight in the eye and said: "OK. If you want in, you're in."

23

MARGOT PASSED THE PEAS. HER MOTHER HAD MADE A stab at Christmas dinner, despite the fact that there was just the two of them. Sliced turkey, kept warm in the oven, curled on a serving plate. "I didn't think it was worth it," said Peggy, sour and irritated, "to buy a whole turkey. Deli slices were more practical."

A lot was more practical these days, Margot noticed: paper napkins; Crisco, not butter; plain bars of Dove soap. A small Christmas tree quietly shed its needles in the corner of the dining room; there was no silver on the sideboard. Her mother's hands looked old without her rings, her earlobes were bare and there were purplish shadows under her eyes.

Margot gave her mother a small Crown Derby porcelain penguin for her collection. Her mother gave her a leatherette case of nail scissors and cuticle clippers secured with elastic loops.

"I thought you would find it useful." Useful, like practical, was a new addition to her mother's lexicon. Her father, it seemed, was not.

"Your father and I." Peggy did not finish the sentence, instead she swallowed another draw of vodka. Ice clanked.

"Are getting a divorce," Margot supplied.

Peggy pushed her food around the plate. At length she said, "He's at the carriage house at Sage Hill."

Margot remembered that Mrs. Cummings had once stayed at

the carriage house in similar circumstances. She remembered, too, the image she wished she had never seen.

"Clarence"—Peggy spat out his name like a piece of gristle—"has been oh-so-generous."

Margot had seen the check on her mother's desk, signed C. G. H. Merryweather, paper-clipped to a handwritten note on a monogrammed card, for services tendered and rendered. She half guessed, didn't want to know. A memory tugged—years ago—one summer pool party, Trip had made some crazy comment in front of everyone: how his father and Peggy Vanderloep had very nearly made the real estate marriage of the century—think what a golf course you could have built across the two combined waterfront properties! And Lydia Cummings, in her yellow polka-dot bikini that had been the talk of Piping Rock all that summer, had said, "Oh don't joke, Trippy! If that had happened, that god-awful Mrs. Thornsen would have been your mother!"

"Mr. Merryweather?" Margot prompted her mother, curious despite herself.

"An old admirer of mine." Peggy twirled her highball glass. "But my father forbade it. On account of Old Granite Merryweather. They were rivals for years. And then the war came along and your father signed up for the infantry and they shipped him off to Europe. I sometimes think," said Peggy, tipping the vodka iceberg against her lips, "he never really came back."

She shook her empty glass. "Margot, freshen my drink, will you?"

Margot went to the bar in the living room and poured out a heavy glug from the bottle of Smirnoff. Her father's Calvados sat beside it, undrunk, dust on the cap. She added ice and the lemon slice her mother always insisted on. She poured herself one too with ginger ale. 'Tis the season, Christmas spirit, down the hatch.

The dirty plates were still on the table, in another time they would have been cleared and dessert served, coffee brought on a tray to the living room with mint chocolates. But there was no dessert and no servant to fetch and carry. Peggy was oddly voluble, and

Margot realized, another glass refilled with a wobbling wrist, her mother was drunk.

"Never marry a man thinking you can change him, Margot. I married in wartime and there was no silk for a dress because it was all taken to make parachutes. Your father was over in Europe more than a year, came back wounded. The moment he got off the train I saw he was changed. He couldn't look me in the eye. I am sure he had some French floozy like they all did. Summer of '44 and Paris had fallen; everyone said the war would be over by Christmas. We had only eight days and then he was shipped back again."

Margot knew her mother had not seen her father again until the end of 1945, when she was already six months old. At this part of the story, Peggy's tone turned bitter. She had been left to have her baby alone, "a ghastly, shocking business. And when your father finally came back, he sat in the den and drank his rotgut apple brandy and would barely look at you!"

"He never helped when I was a baby?" Margot ventured. Perhaps this was the nub of it, if she was not good enough for her father, she was not good enough for her mother, because what is a woman but a wife to give children to a husband?

"Of course not!" Peggy slammed her palm on the table so that the peas jumped. "When it was the nanny's day off, I had to do it all!"

Margot took the plates into the kitchen. The dishwasher was broken. She opened the cupboard beneath the sink to look for the dish soap and saw a cockroach lurking there. Her mother was still talking through the swinging door; a slurry of complaint. Margot turned on the tap and began to wash up. There was consolation in a clean plate, in tidiness and order.

In the afternoon they watched an old Cary Grant movie on TV and Peggy reminisced about the time Cary Grant had come to Dotty Whitney's coming-out ball because he was stepping out with

Babs Hutton at the time and he told them all to "just call me plain old Archie" and all the girls swooned even though everyone knew he was light in the loafers.

When the nightly news came on, Peggy said, "Change the channel, Margot, I can't bear to watch that man."

Margot got up and turned the big clicking dial until she found Bob Hope entertaining the troops with a Christmas special in Saigon. A woman in a sequined leotard and a top hat high-kicked across the distant stage.

"God, it's so *vulgar.* I don't know why they have to *broadcast* this kind of *trash.* There's no *decency*, no *respect* in this country anymore. Everyone does as they please. *You* do exactly as you please, hightailing it back to your *college*, insisting on this new *independence*—let me tell you: you'll find no independence in penury. My father always said: There is no pursuit of happiness without the pursuit of wealth! Sarah ran off with that *Jew.* Love will find a way! *Nonsense!* Mark my words, young lady"—Peggy pushed a sharp nail against the bridge of Margot's nose, cutting into the flesh—"you better get a move on and marry Trip Merryweather. Money is the most important thing in life."

Her mother's green-eyed glare was categorical.

As a child Margot had run from this glare, clattered upstairs, down the garden path, running as far as the pebble beach; staring up at the sky wishing it could lift her higher than the clouds, into the expansive blue wonderment of a world that might, on closer examination, return concrete and satisfactory answers to the questions "Why?" and "Why me?"

Now Margot stared straight back at her mother.

Her mother's eyes were famed as green, after Old King Vanderloep's, the coloring of dragons and witches, likely a mutation on chromosome 15 (*Fuller, Wright, and Omato, University of Chicago, 1964*), but holding her gaze Margot saw the murky jade of a heavy ocean in winter; stormy, confused.

Peggy retracted her pointed finger, looked away, rattled the ice cubes in her glass.

"Turn to Channel 2. That dreadful Cankerman and his news should be over by now."

Little Women had just begun. Marmee was setting the table for Christmas breakfast.

"I can't bear this movie," said Peggy.

24

MARGOT TOOK THE BUS BACK TO BOSTON, QUIET. THE white winter sky had nothing to say either.

She walked back to the Radcliffe Quad from the station, the suitcase handle chafing her hand. Among the holiday mail in her cubbyhole was a plain envelope, inside a page torn out of a reporter's notebook, quickly written in blue ballpoint:

—Monday 31st: If you're around this evening, and by some miracle don't have plans, come for New Year's at the Sea-Side at 7 p.m., Sandy Full

Is it chemistry or electricity that quickens a heartbeat? Margot found that she was running, it was already past six. She tripped over the little wooden sign that told people to keep off the grass and skinned her knee, but didn't realize she was bleeding until she got to her room. Which meant she had to decide: go casual in blue jeans or wear the red dress that swayed mid-thigh. *I am my mother's daughter*, she thought ruefully, worrying about the dress code, applying lipstick (badly, she had never mastered the precision sweep), and pinching her cheeks to make the roses bloom. Genetically speaking we are all our mother's daughter, until a Y chromosome comes along and sticks a penis on an embryo.

The Sea-Side was a lobster place on the other side of Beacon Street. It was a Harvard student favorite; long trestle tables, Chinese lanterns strung up along the walls, a jukebox that still took nickels. Margot walked in quickly, breathlessly, toes squashed into her kitten heels, Band-Aid stuck on her knee.

"Margot!"

With dismay Margot saw her cousin Phyllis, hair shining in a glossy wave, wearing a flowing turquoise dress and gold sandals. Her boyfriend George was next to her, next to George was Larry Gerald, next to Larry was Lydia Cummings, next to Lydia was Trip with his arm around her waist. Larry Gerald introduced her to Magnus, who had flown in from London that very morning with his sister Cordelia, Phyllis's roommate. Margot knew Cordelia only by reputation: titled and entitled; her father was an earl, whatever that was, and lived in a castle.

"Jet lag is such a drag," said Cordelia, leaning her head on her brother's shoulder.

Margot had a terrible feeling that she had accidentally stumbled in on a party she had not been invited to. She turned to go—and then a figure she hardly recognized, shaggy-haired, wearing a battered fatigue jacket with one arm of his shirt pinned up, stood up and there was Sandy.

"Hey Margot, glad you got the note. I was at my uncle's place after Christmas and heading up here for the antiwar march tomorrow. Larry asked if I would give him and Trip and Lydia a lift."

"What's cooking, Pine Tree?" said Trip. "We missed you last summer in France, it would have blown your mind. Richie says you have devoted your life to science—"

Magnus ripped the foil off a bottle of champagne, unwrapped the wire, and carefully twist-popped the cork.

"You're very practiced at that," Margot told him.

Magnus had rosy cheeks and was wearing black tie. "Well, I am the one dressed as a waiter," he said.

"Poor Magnus," said Cordelia, "I've been trying to Americanize him. This afternoon he did try to loosen his tie."

"It felt most unnatural!" said Magnus, laughing, pouring champagne into everyone's glass.

Larry Gerald passed her a glass. "So, Margot, all geared up for the final semester?"

"From what I hear, she never leaves the lab," said Trip. "Richie has been singing your academic praises. Your father," he added, "was very impressed."

"He was?"

Sandy hugged her hello. He smelled of woodsmoke. When he kissed her cheek his beard felt soft.

"I'm sorry I've been out of touch. I've been out of everything, really. I don't know if you heard, but I left the army."

"He's totally left!" said Larry. "He's so far left, my father denounced him as a Red and practically threw him out of the house."

"I lost myself in the wilds of Arizona for a few months. Now I'm involved with Veterans Against the War."

"My father says he's a Commie peacenik."

"Well, it was a bit of a radical crowd in the desert," admitted Sandy.

"Ah, the alternative lifestyle," said Cordelia, "do tell! Is it all free love and nudity and guitar-twanging and mind-bending substances, or is the reality a little more dig-your-own-latrine."

Sandy half smiled, half blushed. "Well, there's a bit of all of that," he said, "but it was mainly a lot of discussion around the campfire, how to change things, how to shake up the system. We can't go on letting the military-industrial complex determine our foreign policy."

"Well, I, for one, believe America is doing a fine thing in Indochina," said Magnus, who sounded like David Niven, mildly interested in everything and nothing in particular, "keeping the world safe for the rest of us."

"I bet you were just trying to get out of doing another tour!" Trip grinned with the even white teeth and confidence of a Kennedy.

"I don't see *you* signing up anytime soon," Lydia pointed out, ruffling his hair with her long fingernails. "You've piled up so many deferments you're practically a draft dodger."

"I'd love to go," said Trip. "I hear those girls in Saigon are like ripe peaches."

"When I see it on the news," said Phyllis, "I always think the orange explosions look like blooming orange roses against the green of the jungle."

The paper lanterns cast glowing shadows against the walls, votive candles scattered on the table twinkled like stars. Sandy reached his hand towards Margot's, laced his fingers with hers and squeezed. Margot withdrew her hand, a delicate extraction, unhooking knuckles, the pads of Sandy's fingertips brushed hers, soft as cashmere. The pain of Marvin still stung, Trip mingled with the hope of it too—

A platter of steaming red lobsters was set in the middle of the table. Phyllis clapped her hands delightedly. The waitress brought baked potatoes and bowls of melted butter, and Magnus made a great show of taking off his jacket and rolling up his sleeves and saying, "When in Boston!"

"More champagne!" Trip called out. Everyone began to eat noisily and messily, cracking and dunking pink knuckly lobster into drawn butter, reaching over each other for wedges of lemon and extra napkins.

Sandy turned away from Margot and was caught up by Phyllis asking him why he had quit the army.

"I believe," she said, with emphasis on the first-person pronoun, "it is an American duty to fight the Reds."

"The Viet Cong are not Stalin," said Sandy. "Khrushchev isn't even Stalin. Politicians are always fighting the last war."

"Well, I don't know," Trip parried with the received wisdom of his class and upbringing. "Being antiwar is just the same as saying you're on the left, and in this day and age, you might as well say you support the other side."

"Look at it another way: the Vietnamese want their independence the same as we did," said Sandy.

"Freedom!" said Cordelia with nasal contempt. "That's what they said in India, and just look at all the dreadful violence that followed the British withdrawal."

"But you can't be against freedom!" said Phyllis, taking Republican umbrage at the colonial oppressor.

"There's money to be made in war," said her boyfriend George, pragmatic.

"That's the American way," agreed Trip. "Buy up stock in Lockheed!"

"Blood money!" said Lydia, who liked to be provocative.

"Where'd you get that? Reading a slogan at a march?"

"Oh, all these marches. I can't bear them!" said Phyllis.

"Aren't they marching for freedom?" said Cordelia, batting Phyllis's "freedom" right back at her.

"Not if it's anti-American. Not if it's violent. I mean, we're not living in the Soviet Union, are we? I don't see why people feel the need to protest in a democracy. They're just protesting the will of the majority.'

"There are those," said Sandy directly to Phyllis, "who would say that democracy is about the protection of the rights of the minority."

"Well, it sounds very clever when you say it," Phyllis told Sandy, unwilling to let go of his attention.

George said, "Phyllis, quit running for office; we're not at one of your GOP fund-raisers."

"That's OK," said Sandy, "it's my job to try to explain."

Thwarted, George turned to Margot on his other side.

"You're Margot Thornsen, aren't you? Phyllis's cousin. I don't think we've met." They had, briefly, at least twice that Margot recalled. "I don't know if you know that my father has bought the Farnsworth estate." Of course she knew. "How funny to think that you grew up there. Phyllis is very taken with the swimming pool. She insists it must stay! She's got quite a lot of ideas about the place—my father says it's going to be worth a fair chunk of change when the zoning laws get redrawn and we can subdivide it into plots. Have you seen the redevelopment of the Phipps estate?"

Margot shook her head. Undeterred, George continued to talk, glancing from time to time at Phyllis, who was engrossed in Sandy.

Sandy looked different, older. His high forehead was finely lined with experience, pain was etched there too; crinkles at the corners of his eyes, his cheekbones were sharper. Something of his smooth and rounded youth, plumped by enthusiasm, was gone, scraped away, leaner. Now Margot wished she had squeezed his hand back.

"We can build three houses on the East Meadow, I am sure," George continued. "Families are moving out of the city, looking for homes in the suburbs with room for a swimming pool in back—"

"It sounds fascinating," said Margot.

"Well, you of course know better than anyone how much acreage there is if you cleared the woods. It's all about location, Farnsworth is only a ten-minute drive to the railway station at Syosset, a commuter's dream."

"So you plan to follow in your father's footsteps into the real estate business?"

Next to her, Sandy was nodding at something Phyllis was saying. Margot could feel the heat of his body. Across the table Lydia was ruffling the hair at the back of Trip's neck, where it grew in pale gold whorls. Larry Gerald and Trip were hawing about the wine in Provence and nothing but rosé José!

"That's the plan. He's got fifty acres north of Hicksville, another twenty-five adjacent to the Piping Rock Club, the old Honeycutt place—"

"It must be very comforting to have your life already mapped out," said Margot.

"My father is a genius. He came from humble beginnings, made everything himself. Sure, it's a tough act to live up to."

"You'll do swell. You're a Harvard man."

George bowed his head. Margot saw that his hair was thinning at the crown.

"It all adds to the expectations," he said with a dropped smile. "How can you fail when you're a Harvard man, as my father likes to remind me, when you've had every advantage?"

"Remember what they say: failure is just a part of success. Don't worry too much."

"Who says that?"

"In the lab, ninety-nine percent of experiments are failures, so we pretty much get used to it."

"I'm not sure they apply the same philosophy at Harvard Business School."

"Maybe they should. Read the biographies of the old titans—see how long it took Rockefeller to find his way, how difficult it was consolidating the Cleveland refineries and how many setbacks he suffered."

"You're sweet, Margot. Not like Phyllis says at all."

Margot started to say something in reply, but George put one of his big hairy hands on her bare knee right on top of the Band-Aid. Margot stifled a wince. She looked down at it, pale with wiry black hairs. His waistline bulged a little over his belt. George acted as if nothing was happening. He looked over to Phyllis again, she was holding her hands up, this big! to illustrate something to Sandy, laughing and showing her pretty white teeth.

"'Oysters down in Oyster Bay do it!'" Phyllis was saying. "'Even lazy jellyfish, electric eels.' Those are real lyrics, they are clever, you see, internal rhyme and whimsy. Now it's all just screaming and I can't understand the words."

"It's the rage of a generation," said Trip, who had never known a moment's anger in his life. "I read it in *Time* magazine."

"Well then, it must be true," said Lydia.

"Everyone is burning things, protesting things," said Trip, "but what they don't understand is that they've never had it so good."

"Trip, you sound like a dinosaur," said Lydia. "You sound like my grandmother."

"I happen to think your grandmother is a very fine lady," said Trip. "No need to rock the boat. I am a simple creature; a few comforts and I am as happy as a clam: a decent martini when the sun is over the yardarm, pretty girls in short dresses, sailing when the weather is fine. The sum of my ambition is to secure a partnership in a good firm and slope off to the links every Friday afternoon."

"And a wife, and children," prompted Lydia, a perfect semicircle of eyebrow raised, as it would be for the rest of her life, simultaneously a half-mast protest and an acquiescence.

"Oh well, of course, wife, children, all the usual accessories."

Everyone laughed. Ah, good old Trip. Nothing could dent such armored charm. He leaned over and kissed Lydia, and Margot felt as lonely as a hermaphrodite aplasia. Marvin was mean. Trip was taken. Sandy appeared and disappeared like a conjuror's trick. And now he was engrossed with Phyllis, who had rested one of her pale, elegant hands on his forearm and was looking up at him. Cape Cod clams, 'gainst their wish, did it. If even oysters and jellyfish and electric eels could fall in love, why the hell couldn't she?

Trip turned up the volume on the jukebox. Burr of electric guitar, a double chord they all knew, even Phyllis—"Oh Sandy! This is the only Stones number I can deal with—let's boogie-woogie!" And everyone got up and began to dance, no rhyme no reason, grinding their feet in old twist patterns, banging elbows, abandoned to the great paradoxical paroxysm that was the greatest feeling in the world and the shared admission that they couldn't get no satisfaction. *No! No! No!*

Margot slipped her pocketbook over her shoulder to slip away. Maybe she was a bit drunk, maybe not drunk enough, preoccupied with an imaginary broken heart, a confused heart, she surrendered to the familiar sensation of being the only sad person at the party.

She got as far as the corner of Brattle Street. Trip came running after her.

"Hey Pine Tree, don't do your disappearing sulky act."

"I'm not sulking."

"Yes you are. I'm sorry you got stuck with George, he's a bore but he's harmless. He sent me after you, 'Go get your pretty neighbor back!'"

"He didn't say that."

"He did, I swear. Come on, Margot, come and dance, don't be Piney-Whiny, Lydia has got some tequila. And you don't want to disappoint Sandy. You're the only reason he agreed to come out with us kids anyway."

"Looks like he's pretty into Phyllis."

"Naw—she's just putting on a show for George so he'll pony up a ring."

Margot smiled. Trip smiled too.

"It's not the same at Sage Hill without you next door. Richie spends the whole time singing your praises; we're all ne'er-do-wells and Mother is always saying, Take a leaf out of Margot's book, there's a gal who knows how to keep her nose to the grindstone."

"OK, hold your horses." Trip's compliments were always over-blown, always irresistible. "I'm coming."

Everyone was drinking tequila shots. Cordelia showed Margot how to tip her head and close her eyes "and think of England!" Larry Gerald (who knew?) had some moves, knew all the words to "Paint It Black." Lydia shimmied like a pro, everyone formed a circle around her and clapped as she limberly limboed. George was a ter-rible dancer, red-faced, sweating, thrashing his arms, but he didn't care. He dragged Phyllis away from Sandy, and Phyllis, perhaps weary-wary of what she had wished for, gamely bopped opposite him. Trip shuffled his Miss Waverly two-step to every song, even to "Wild Thing." Sandy stood off to one side, swayed to a different tune, murmuring low-down to the Supremes. *YouJustKeepMeHangin'On. Baby-Baby.* Margot swayed opposite him for a few beats, but he didn't reach out for her, his eyes were closed, as if he were some-where else.

Lydia shook out her long blond hair from its tie-back. Her dress slipped off one shoulder, exposing the fine angles of her clavicle and the lace edge of her bra strap. She pulled Margot into the dance, come into the circle, spin here awhile. There was something deliberate in her attention to Margot, as if to accentuate her disattention of Trip, who stood by, drinking glugs from the tequila bottle, bleary, grinning because his face knew no other expression. Margot perceived the triangulation only dimly, through the mazy thump of the music, but she wanted to do something nice for Trip, to make it up to him, to salve Lydia's sarcasm. She reached out to him to make a group of three, but as she did so, Lydia broke away, tossing her hair with exaggerated abandon. Trip put his right hand on Margot's left shoulder and his left hand around her waist and counted one-two-three-four to the bang-bang in "My Baby Shot Me Down." She rested her head on his shoulder for a moment and saw Sandy turn away just as Trip turned her in a twirl—

"It's like old times."

"A little more booze than we managed in the Armory."

"Thank God. Imagine if we had to go through adult life sober."

"Are we adults yet?"

"I never want to grow up," said Trip.

He pulled her closer, cheek to cheek. He smelled of wood chips, like the woods at Farnsworth in winter. Over his shoulder she could see Lydia making a pistol out of her pointed finger and mime-shooting George as Phyllis sloped off and sat down.

"Did you have a fight with Lydia?" Margot asked him.

"Oh, there's always a fight with Lydia. She has terribly high standards and I'm always failing to meet them. I think I am going to end up marrying my father."

"You don't have to marry her," Margot whispered into his shoulder. She sounded different in her own inner ear, husky, conspiratorial, confident as her mother hovered and pushed through waves of champagne that she would very much like to keep drinking forever.

Trip pulled her closer, brushed his lips against her earlobe.

"Who should I marry instead?" he asked. Breath caught in her throat, breathless. She left the question unanswered, answered in her heart, leaning closer in, didn't realize that the song had changed. The beat slowed to what they called at the house socials "necking tempo," and Trip pulled her even closer, so that his whole body was pressed against hers. There, unmistakably, in the middle of it all, she felt his erection.

She tried to pull back, delicately, subtly, but he tightened his grip. If he let go of her now, everyone would see; closer, it only got harder, pushing. She clenched, straightened herself up, tried to stand distinct from his embrace. He sang into her ear, *Pine Tree, ma belle*, so loud it made her eardrum ring and itch. She let herself be swayed. Embarrassed, confused, how to extricate?

Lydia came up behind Trip, put her hands around his waist and made a sandwich. Still Trip did not release her. Lydia put her hands in his pockets, felt what was to be found and hissed, "You fucking asshole!"

Lydia stalked off. Phyllis closed George's mouth with her hand and led him out into the street, hailing passing cars in hope of a taxi. Magnus and Cordelia made their excuses. The party was breaking up. Still Trip did not let go, only drooled gently into her ear, dribbling nonsense. Margot looked for Sandy but he had gone. Larry Gerald was counting out a roll of twenties to cover the tab.

Margot called out, "Larry!"

Larry looked at her with sleepy eyes, "I'm going to leave you two lovebirds to it," and got into a taxi with Phyllis and George and went off too.

"Just us," said Trip, opening his eyes as if he had been sleeping, dreaming, and was just waking up. He put his hands on her breasts and murmured "mmmmm."

"What are you doing?"

"I'm making love to you."

"I've got a boyfriend."

"No you haven't."

No she hadn't, he was right. Trip swayed to kiss her and she let him. His tongue looped in her mouth just as it had a hundred years ago in the rain in front of 655 Park. It was like being kissed by a windmill. He tasted of spoiled wine, sour grapes. She heard her mother say very clearly in her head, *You must suffer to be happy.*

Margot took another step back and pushed his hands away from her chest and said, "No."

"Yes."

"Trip, c'mon. I'm tired. I want to go home."

"Where am I going to sleep? Can I sleep with you?"

"No."

"You're going to leave me on the street?"

Margot began to walk away. Arguing with herself with her mother. Almost changed her mind, turned back to look. Trip was following her, stumbling, jogging to keep up. She felt an odd sort of gratification even as she lengthened her stride. The divinity school was a series of dark courtyards, eerily empty.

Halfway across the cloister, Trip called out, "Wait up, Pine Tree!"

She stopped to let him catch up. Stopped, but did not turn.

"I'm all out of breath. You're too fast on those giraffe legs. Don't run away from me."

"Lydia must be wondering where you are," Margot said, but didn't turn, didn't look at him.

"She will have gone to her cousin's in Beacon Hill and locked me out again. She thinks she can keep me keen, keep me on my toes. I'm tired."

Margot turned to face him.

"Beacon Hill? You've got the address? Let's get you into a cab."

"Oh Pine Tree. I'm so tired." He slumped towards a bench and splayed himself across the wooden slats.

"Come sit by me," he said, and patted the bench.

Margot sat down. He resumed kissing her, his hands on her

breasts, under her blouse, finger snapping her bra strap, his tongue twirling round and round.

He clutched her tightly, uncomfortably. Margot didn't kiss him back, but she couldn't bring herself to push him away, it would have been too abrupt, too rude—the skirt of her dress was hitched up, Trip was crushing her breasts with his palm, moaning, pushing her against the back of the bench, hard, pinching her nipple, ouch, ow, don't, fingers wriggled into the space between her waistband and her panties, inside her thigh, prodding the soft mound, tricking tickling against the lace edge of her panties, underneath, into—

"Don't you like that? Oh I bet you like that, Lydia always said you liked me, I know you do."

And then he shifted, pulled himself away. Margot thought he had stopped and a wave of relief went through her, like a wash of clear, stinging alcohol. She watched, blinking, unmoving, silent, as he unbuckled his belt and yanked it through the belt loops of his trousers with a crack like a leather whip. He unbuttoned his fly, pulled down his trousers, leaned forward, hitched her panties to one side and pushed his penis inside her. Again and again again again again again. Even the stars were embarrassed and hid behind a curtain of cloud. The inside of her eyelids was dark red. "Move a little, Pine Tree, help me out here." She tilted her pelvis so he could fuck her more easily. Again again again again again. "That's right, I'm coming I'm coming, I'm coming home." He came. Margot said nothing. When he withdrew, she got up and ran ran ran all the way home home home without looking back.

SHUT THE DOOR BEHIND her. There was a sink in her room and she ran the faucet in a cold torrent against her wrists, splashed off the rime of sweat on her face, at the back of her neck. The water felt good washing away. She stripped off her dress, balled it up and threw it in the wastepaper can, but it sat there red and accusing, so she stuffed it in a paper grocery bag to hide it. She brushed her teeth as hard as she could, rubbed her tongue with a soapy wash-cloth but couldn't reach the back of her throat, not far enough, not even with the toothbrush angled to scrub every last molecule away in a stream of vomit, pinkish, fishy, lobster redux. She opened the medicine cabinet above the sink, Band-Aids, purple merthiolate antiseptic, Bufferin, blister packets of the Pill, no Listerine. She wondered if nail polish remover was toxic in small quantities. Lit a cigarette, smoked it down to the filter, lit another. Soap nicotine acetone vomit. Anything that would take the taste away. She hung her head upside down and let the water flow into her mouth, not thinking, not thinking about her private interior, not even daring to touch herself. For a long time, she stayed like that, leaning upside down with the water running into her mouth.

Didn't sleep, slept in a curled-up ball like a cat, woke up to the early dawn chorus, the new day washed pale blue, and remembered, stopped herself short of rewinding the full memory, but just the tip of it was enough to flood shame through her whole body. She wrapped her bathrobe around her, slippers on her feet, packed the toiletry bag with soap, shampoo, washcloth, nailbrush, Q-tips, and went down the hall to the last bathroom at the far end that had a bath and a lockable door. Locked the door, wedged the chair under the handle.

On the shelf under the mirror someone had left a glass jar of dried-out black eyeliner. To wash something, Margot washed it out, scratching the residue off with her fingernails, rinsed it thoroughly with soap and hot water, dried it, screwed the lid back on—and then noticed the Q-tips half falling out of their box on the chair. She looked from one to the other, puzzled by the coincidence of these two items: swab and jar. It seemed at first a darkly cosmic joke, but she began to recognize their utility. What was inside her was a secret that no one would ever know. She looked in the mirror and saw herself: pale, raw, ugly. Said the word out loud: "slut."

Then tried to refuse it, to deny it, as Mad had, and corrected herself: "No shame!" She stood quite still staring at her face, swimming in and out of familiar and strange, not knowing on which side the seesaw would fall. Even if she wanted to, who could she tell? The dean of students? A policeman? C. G. H. Merryweather himself? For services tendered and rendered. Her mother's voice answered, *Don't be ridiculous!* Margot looked squarely into her own eyes and answered: "I am not ridiculous." Then came a quieter moment of calm. Followed by the practical consideration: even if she were to tell, she would not be believed. The secret was inside of her and would have to stay locked up because there was no proof. She-said-he-said, that's what they would say.

She took a cotton swab and reached down and scooped inside herself gently. She smeared the opaque mucus into the jar. A sample. That felt a little better, she was a scientist again.

MARGOT RAN THE BATHWATER very hot, lowered herself slowly in; scalding, red. Scrubbed every inch with a soaped-up washcloth. Ran the water out, cleaned the bathtub with bleach, ran it full again. Rinsed herself, flushed herself out with the showerhead several times. The third bath was cold. She scrubbed her scratched feet with the nail brush. Particles of dirt swirled in a vortex down the drain. Finally, pink and tingling, she went back to her room and lay down and slept with the small glass jar against her belly, perversely, to keep her evidence warm.

When Margot rewoke, it was lunchtime already. Automatically she dressed and walked to the lab. She didn't understand why the corridors were empty, until it dawned on her that it was New Year's Day.

The plans for the new Science Center building had been drawn up, Lawrence Hall was due to be knocked down in two weeks' time and all the furniture had been moved out or piled into the corridors.

Everything was disordered, her thoughts were an icy sludge, slow and numb.

Unthinking, muscle memory, Margot walked up the stairs to the first floor towards Lab 1123. She found Flashman in the process of loading slides into a cold chest, the kind you keep beers in at a tailgate party.

"Hey girl, what's cooking? Happy New Year!"

Margot ran her fingers over the wooden workbench, let her fingers trace the old scars and chemical burns. "I can't believe they're going to tear this all down."

"You look pale."

Margot didn't answer.

"If I didn't know you better, I would say you had been partying last night."

Margot moved her mouth in imitation of a smile.

"By the way, I wanted to say congrats. Dr. Fred told me you're in his hush-hush research class too. That's really major. You, me, and Adam, if you can believe it."

"Adam?"

"Yes, the baby genius himself. Don't ask me why—you OK?"

Flashman put a hand on her shoulder. Margot made a small yelp. Flashman put his hands in the air and backed up.

"Sorry, man. Look, don't sweat it. Marvin is an asshole. Let's forget that guy! It's gonna be a whole new semester. We're gonna be working our asses off."

Margot remained frozen, time's conveyor belt was stuck and all the baggage was piling up.

"Anyway," said Flashman cheerfully, "I'm trying to save my slides for my thesis. I'm taking them over to the cryrofreezer."

Margot stood for a moment suspended between voluntary and involuntary.

"Can I put something in there too?" she asked, as casually as she could muster. "It's just a personal project."

Flashman shrugged, "Go for it," and she hastily made up a vial and filled out a label with her name and the date.

"As long as there's no massive clear-out, you can probably keep it stashed here for a year or two."

Preserved, deferred.

25

Beginning of the semester, Lawrence Hall was a building site, everything was in flux. The statistics department had moved in with the economists, botany had moved to the basement where the old Galápagos Library had been, half of natural chemistry had been shoehorned into the architecture department. There were maps and arrows tacked up on the walls redirecting students.

Molecular Bio-Chem had been temporarily relocated to the Museum of Comparative Zoology. Margot got lost and was ten minutes late for Dr. Fred's introduction, turn left, left again, up and down the stairs—

"Ah, welcome!"

Margot stammered an apology. She found Flashman easily because he was standing next to Adam, who was wearing an orange T-shirt. Margot was surprised to see Vicky Jefferson, a friend of Shirley's, there too; she was always a bit in awe of Vicky, she was a psych major, she was black, and she was known for her withering put-downs.

"As I was saying," Dr. Fred continued, "this group doesn't represent natural selection so much as self-selection."

Margot looked around, a dozen of them crammed into the fossil rooms of the zoology museum. Light filtered from an ancient skylight, opaque and yellowish as old Scotch tape. Oak vitrines of trilobites and ammonites, extinct bivalves and brachiopods lined the walls, the spirals and coruscations of a hundred million years.

"I kept the class description deliberately vague, to discourage the majority," said Dr. Fred. "I wanted a mix of undergrads, MAs, and DPhils because I was really looking for a collection of different minds. I want to try a new approach. For the past decade we have been asking: What is a gene? Now we know: it is a combination of base pairs that encode an instruction to build a certain protein out of amino acids. Meselson thinks he's pretty close to proving that a bacterial enzyme can cut up DNA. Coming down the pipe, ready or not, we are going to be able to slice and dice the human genome. We are going to be able to reconfigure—rearrange—rebuild nature."

Dr. Fred paused for a moment. His audience formed a semicircle around him. Margot felt a small shiver. There was something about the way Dr. Fred had said "*we*" that was simultaneously inclusive— all of us, the whole human race—and exclusive: you chosen few, gathered here in the Precambrian gloom of this basement, sur- rounded by life's early efforts.

"All of you are here because you stood in my office and stared at the rug, second-guessing yourselves, wondering out loud about some question that's been bugging you. Like Darwin out on a limb, all alone, asking, 'What? What if?'"

Dr. Fred opened his long arms wide to welcome their pink and glowing faces into his grand design. "Maybe this dark and dingy repository is the right kind of vibe—it's like rewind, back to the very beginning, before we crawled out of the sea. Because what you are going to be encouraged to do is to follow your question- ing impulses. There's no class project; some of you are working on Meselson's leads, but pretty much everyone has their own individual thesis to research, experiment, workshop. In this class, I'm going to protect you from the skeptical world of academia that wants you to cite a hundred sources. Here were are going to provoke, promote, and procreate."

Margot followed his gaze as he looked at them, at each one of them. They were a motley mix of phenotypes: tall, short, myopic, hirsute; one guy was wearing a three-piece suit as if he were going to work in the Eisenhower administration, another had a flower painted on his forehead. Next to her, Adam gulped his giant Adam's apple, Flashman gave her a look, like, What the heck?

"Oh and don't tell anyone, but for the undergrads and MA candidates, you've already got A grades"—Margot held her breath—"just by being here."

Flashman and a couple of others high-fived. The guy in the three-piece suit put his hand up in the air to ask a question.

"We're not adhering to pedagogical tropes here," said Dr. Fred, waving him down, "we're all in the same boat. Frankly, I'm not teaching you anything. I'm using your status as students to further my own grandiose ambitions. I want to see what crazy-ass ideas you come up with that I can exploit or take forward. Any resulting papers, you'll be cited as coauthors. It's like profit sharing, incentivization. But hey," he made a joke, "the Nobel Prize is mine."

THAT FIRST DAY THEY pushed the fossil cases against the walls, covered the library carrels with sheets of plywood to make workbenches, strung up cables and adapters to plug in centrifuges, autoclaves, oscilloscopes, a microwave oven, and three Zeiss microscopes. The space was cramped and Margot shared a bench desk with her fellow undergrads, the suit, an MA student called Thomas Cleverly, and three aquaria of Adam's stick insects. After a while it seemed perfectly normal for her to come to class with a few leaves in her pockets to feed them.

Margot was looking at X chromosomes and trying to convince Dr. Fred to convince the lab at the med school to give her access to corresponding medical histories so she could try to match anomalies to pathologies. Thomas Cleverly was doing something totally far-out with polymerases as some kind of amino acid glue. Adam was trying to extract DNA from his stick insects, which was messy and spread insect viscera glop all over the desk. Flashman was tracking mitochondrial DNA from different generations of women, looking for similarities. Vicky said she was doing something "more, like, theoretical," and sat in an armchair in the corner writing in a notebook.

No one wore white coats; Dr. Fred didn't care much about protocols.

There were no fixed class times, no syllabus or reading list, no midterms to worry about. Students came when they wanted, stayed all day, half an afternoon, late until midnight. Flashman said it made him want to come to class more often, not less. Adam was discovered very early in the morning wandering about barefoot as if he had been there all night. Thomas Cleverly brought in a hatstand to hang his jacket up and a teapot to brew tea in. Vicky said, "People's different responses to a new environment are very interesting."

Margot found the lack of rules disorienting, the absence of boundaries alarming. Without walls there was no corner to hide in. Agoraphobia clawed at her throat, sometimes she felt her heartbeat quicken and her brain spangled faint and she had to put her head between her knees to come back to earth again. Flashman could embrace the grand enormity of the world and all its possibilities, but this wide angle frightened Margot and she was ashamed of her fear. She felt apart, as if she was floating above looking down at everyone getting on with life. She tried to get into the swim of things, but her limbs and her mind were gooey and slow and her conversation was mistimed, off-kilter.

Dr. Fred nailed up a corkboard and encouraged them all to pin their thoughts to it. "This is your free space," he told them. "Whatever idea you think is too stupid to say out loud, stick it up. A quote you like, a pretty picture. A headline that makes you mad. Let's see if we can dismantle the academic hierarchy a little, break through the walls. Don't be shy."

At first people posted slogans, *Peace Not War*, *Down with LBJ*, declarations, *I love Jane Fonda*, *Jim Watson is an alpha ape SOB*, and the usual toilet-stall graffiti overwritten with chemical formulae. After a while the jokes receded and the additions became more personal. The guy with the painted flower on his forehead, Dello, tacked up lyrics he had written and told them he was a folksinger on the weekends. Adam wrote that his parents were Christian Scientists, *They won't speak to me anymore.* Margot came in one afternoon and read Thomas Cleverly's note: *My brother has Huntington's disease. I'm trying to save his life and probably my own too.* When Dr. Fred saw it, he went straight over and gave Thomas a hug and said he was very proud to work with him. Everyone shook his hand, sorry, man, that's rough, and Adam, who found it hard to look people directly in the eye, gave him a cookie, which Thomas very gracefully received with a small bow of thanks.

Margot was humbled by the idea that someone else's *problem of me* could be physical, could even be fatal. But this only made her feel more inadequate: her own *problem of me* was all in her head, an indulgence compared with the real challenges Thomas Cleverly and his brother faced.

Margot kept her own *me* carefully glued down. Didn't put anything up on Dr. Fred's board. Didn't do coffee with Shirley or the girls on her floor. Avoided Richie. Once or twice Dr. Fred asked her, "So what's on your mind, Miss Thornsen?" but she just said, "Nothing, sorry, nothing." Flashman said, "Let her be, she's thinking up the theory that's gonna blow us all out of the water," but Margot only resented having that kind of expectation on her shoulder. She felt herself struggling, for the first time in her life, with studying.

Spring semester senior year. Finals. Thesis. Do-or-die. Margot had put her name on the list as a molecular biology MA candidate. Everything was important: credits earned, GPA, professor reports, dean's list. In addition to Dr. Fred's class, she was taking Advanced Chem, Evolutionary Science, Cell Biology, and the Historiography of Scientific Discovery. Her room was stacked with papers, manila folders, lever arch files, books and charts and diagrams and cross-references, précis, conclusions, addenda, et al., ad infinitum.

She studied studied studied. But her concentration was shot, sentences fractured before her eyes, she forgot things she knew, missed classes, which she had never ever done before. She was hungry, then nauseous, limp as spaghetti, then agitated, filled with lassitude and then furious. She saw her red stupid face in the mirror and screamed at it. So loud that Shirley came barreling down the hall and banged on her door, "Marge, what the heck is going on in there?"

"Nothing, sorry, nothing."

She found herself sleeping eight, nine, ten hours at a time, too long and too late as if she was—no: she checked, double-checked; no missed period but she was down to her last month of the Pill—she would have to ask Richie for more.

WHEN MARGOT RESTED HER eye socket against the rubber eyepiece of the microscope, the rattle and hum of the Zoo receded and a liquid calm flooded her brain. The tangle of chromosomes unknotted themselves as she stared at them. She made tiny chinagraph pencil marks with a needle point on the slide, separating the long arms from the short arms, picking out the X's. Then she blew the slide up in the copy-expander and razored the film into slivers to make a separate ideogram. Karyotyping, counting-climbing, one telomere two telomere three . . . the indigo staining striped the chromosomes like candy canes . . . unraveling into a code looped around the grand banisters of a double ducal staircase . . . a twisted rope ladder . . .

The frozen gray New England winter provided no solace. Chromosomes danced in her dreams, held hands in the shapes of proteins. Tet raged, and the common rooms raged antiwar, but Margot was too busy studying to pay attention to outside events. She worked till midnight, checked analyses, drew diagrams, reread back copies of *Cell* in the bath. Woke up to the radio, the Patriots were winning, Go Babe and the Grand Opera! Fourteen dead in Hue, an admiral's son shot down over Hanoi, the march on the Pentagon, Apollo rockets fired up from Cape Kennedy, tailbacks on the Longfellow Bridge, a cold front advancing from Canada, more snow this afternoon, folks. Margot bought a heavy pair of headphones to block out the music, the noise of cars going by, chirruping birds. Kept her focus narrow, examining the smaller and smaller, ignored the frightening dimensions of the larger and larger. By dint of working, she worked. She had observed anomalous shadows on several X chromosomes that looked promising.

Sometimes Margot would catch sight of Marvin in a cafeteria or a corridor and she would feel a stab of rejection. To neutralize this pain, she displaced it with another, the Trip thing. She had to be careful of doing this because if she kept the Trip thing in her mind too long, her thoughts got broken up and disrupted. She kept the Trip thing crouched in its silo like a nuke, radioactive, deterrent, MAD.

26

In her cubbyhole one afternoon was a letter, post-marked New York, NY. She opened the envelope walking up the stairs, footfalls ascending.

FEBRUARY 5, 1968
NEW YORK CITY

Letter To My Daughter

First, before everything else: I am sorry.

The staircase fell away. Margot stopped still. Her heart sounded like clumping footsteps, but it was someone coming up the stairs behind her.

"Marge! Where have you been? In hibernation?"

Shirley launched into a long jag about Tony and Vicky and Jefferson and an airplane taking off or arriving—Margot couldn't make sense of it, couldn't think of a response, panicked and ran past Shirley into her room and closed the door. But it slammed too loud, as if she was shutting out her friend, so she opened it again.

Shirley was still standing there. "Like, what the heck, dude?"

"I'm sorry, I'm maxed out. I've got a paper due—"

Shirley walked away. "Yeah, there's always a paper due."

Inside her room, door closed, locked, Margot sat on the floor in the crosshairs made by the daylight shadows through the window-panes. Impatient, shocked, she opened up the double-spaced typed page and read:

First, before everything else: I am sorry. I should have been brave. I was weak. I was too young and I didn't know what pain was. Or consequence. Or all those things that you wish a mother would tell you that I wish I could tell you.

When I am out of it, flying in a narcotic dream, I imagine a turned-back time without regret and I feel your little hand in mine, warm tiny trusting, and I tell you things I wish to tell the child of myself; as mothering goes, I could use some too:

Don't give in to guilt. Don't let regret fester. Don't think too much but think things through. Don't waste your time with people who drag you down. Say yes and no loud and clear. (Sometimes you may have to repeat yourself to yourself.)

Dance and laugh and drink plenty of wine. Go outside. Take your shoes and socks off. Lie down on the grass and look up into the branches of a mighty tree. Swim in the sea. Ride your horse as fast as you can with the wind in your hair.

When you feel bad, be quiet and calm. Listen to music and pay attention to the rhythm. When someone hurts you, it is like when you skin your knee, at first it stings like crazy but with time the hurt will stop and the wound will heal.

I believe in you. You are love. I am also love. We will walk together through this life.

Margot lay down and wept. Slowly, softy, wetly, rent. Tears ran down her face, overflow from a deep sinkwell, unfathomable even to herself.

These were not the heartfelt words of her mother. A draft of cold air seeped in through the open window. Margot recalled the same low gray light, the smell of snow in the air that murdered November afternoon as she had waited in the waiting room. The next morning, Mad had woken up pale as the snowfall and asked for a glass of water. When Margot put it to her lips, Mad had said, very softly, quieter than a whisper, quieter than sound, "I saw her. It was a girl."

THE NEXT MORNING ANOTHER letter came, the same neatly typed ivory envelope, and inside a single line, written in haste, in ballpoint:

> *I'm sorry, stupid me, stupid mix-up, forgive! Ignore ignore!*
> *Envelopes all look the same!—it was the new shrink's idea.*
> *Promise you will never speak of this.*
> *Mad xx*

On the back was written:

> *P.S. Solomon Grundy says we should get married, as a counter-countercultural rebellion. Be my maid of honor?*

27

On the ides of march, margot slipped on a puddle of water on the linoleum floor of the Zoo and banged her head on the corner of the bench.

"That's weird," said Margot, sitting up, feeling the trickle of blood, "it's in exactly the same place I cracked my head when I was a kid."

"Foreheads always take the brunt," said Thomas Cleverly, holding out a wad of paper towels to staunch the flow. "That's why the bone is thicker there."

Flashman took her to the emergency room and sat with her through the three-hour wait. He held her hand as the doctor stitched her up. The doctor was a young resident plastic surgeon—"It's a bit trickier because there's already some scar tissue here—what do you prefer? Jagged lightning bolt, or should I elongate it into an elliptical shape?"

"Oh go elliptical, for sure," said Flashman.

Margot tried to raise one eyebrow, but it stung.

Five stitches and a Valium prescription. Wobbly, tired, a little queasy, Margot let Flashman take her back to the Quad and Shirley put her to bed, tucking her in and clucking maternally.

"There, there. Poor thing. Don't think about classes tomorrow. Concussions need rest. I'll come by in the morning with some breakfast, but sleep now."

Bidden, Margot slept.

She opened her eyes early morning. It was quietly snowing blankets and she fell asleep again.

When she woke, it was late afternoon. Blue shadows on the ceiling, sapphire sky hung with a new moon. There was a sandwich and a note from Shirley on her desk. She ate the sandwich and went out to the Corner Bar, where Shirley had written she was meeting Vicky.

THE CORNER BAR WAS divey and noisy. Not Margot's scene, but she felt oddly light-headed and sat at the bar swinging her legs like a kid.

Shirley was riffing dream trips: after graduation she wanted to go to Kashmir with Tony and live on a lake boat and practice yogic breathing and experience all the mind-bending qualities of ganja smoked at altitude.

Vicky put up three fingers to order beers. "Wait till you get out into the real world."

"Oh I've traveled!" said Shirley defensively. "I'm a born wandering spirit."

Margot was afraid of the "real world." On the TV news it looked violent and chaotic and random, veering as if it could slam into her at any moment. Glimpsed from the train shuddering through Harlem into Grand Central was the real world of brick housing blocks, piles of smoldering trash, dead-end alleys. She knew Vicky had grown up in the real world, on "the swamp side of Newark," as she had once described it; a different color, a different America, and she was a little afraid of Vicky too.

"What is the 'real world' anyway?" Shirley asked, back-atcha, arching her arms in a sarcastic parabola. "Define your terms, girl-o! Because right about now, Vicks, you sound like my mother."

"The real world," said Vicky, settling her beer on the counter, "my hippie-dippy darlin', is money."

Shirley rolled her eyes, but Vicky wasn't giving an inch.

"Whether you buy into it or not, your life is defined by how much money you have. Most of the girls in this place"—she made a *pfft* noise like a balloon deflating—"stocks and shares, lump sums and interest—floating through life, as if banks automatically dispense money, like cigarettes out of a cigarette machine—"

Margot thought of Mad in her big Daddy-paid-for-it town house; Richie, tuition assured for his two doctorates; Trip, who would inherit Sage Hill. She thought of her mother too, evicted from this cushioned world, screaming blue murder all the while.

"But maybe," Vicky continued, "at some point, all their bank accounts will empty as mysteriously as they filled up—like the Weimar Republic, 1929. What goes up must come down, ladies! And then all the legacy Harvardeers are going to have to go and shine someone else's shoes and see how they like it." She looked as if this would amuse her greatly.

Shirley said, "You are right, Vicks, righteous right. We must shoot all the rich people *toot-sweet* and requisition all their cash."

Margot understood that Shirley wished to draw Vicky's rancor by agreeing with her, but saw too that she agreed with her unseriously, airily, yes-yes, as if being poor or being rich were abstract graphs in a sophomore econ class.

Vicky smashed Shirley's lob, "I'm not a Bolshevik and don't pretend *you* are!"

Shirley did not take offense. "My dad says he'll pay my rent until I'm married or I'm twenty-five, whichever comes first. After that I am on my own. So I've got three years to figure it out."

"Three years to find a husband to replace the Bank of Dad, you mean," said Vicky.

Shirley sighed, "I do love Tony, but—"

"My mother wants me to get married," said Margot. "For her, marriage is the be-all and end-all." The beer fizzed up her nose. "No matter that she's in the process of getting a divorce."

"Basic maternal hypocrisy," said Vicky. "Mirroring: they want you to be versions of themselves. Projecting: they want you to enact a fix for their mistakes."

"You are pretty slick with the sociology psychobabble," said Shirley.

"Sociology's basically premed for teachers," said Vicky. "But I don't want to be a teacher."

"What else can you do?" Margot asked. For most Radcliffe girls, teaching was the default career option. Teaching was respectable and acceptable, teaching could be done anywhere a husband might have to move for his work, and those nice long vacations were a perfect fit with the children's schedule. Richie had tried to sell her on it, but the idea of standing up in front of a class and talking made Margot nervous. He had even tried to encourage her to apply to med school, but women doctors were comical, it was commonly assumed patients (even women) would always choose a male physician over a female one. Margot had banked her future on academia; when Richie shook his head and told her she would inevitably get sidetracked and abandon her studies the minute her first baby came along, she had stuck her tongue out at him: "How am I going to have children without a husband? And who's going to marry a skyscraper like me?"

"I want to go into marketing," said Vicky.

Shirley misunderstood: "So you're going to swap the patriarchy of your father for a husband and spend his salary on dinner parties, how very *à la mode*."

"Marketing: selling stuff," said Vicky, explaining. "Not marketing: buying stuff. It's the sociology behind advertising."

"You got it all figured out," said Margot, wondering how she herself ever would.

"All except the part where someone hires me," said Vicky.

Shirley fell silent for a moment, there wasn't anything to say to that.

Vicky stared past Margot into the back of the bar. A group of rowdies were jammed up by the pinball machine, thumping it and yowling.

"I don't want to get married as a *compromise*," said Shirley, after a while.

"Everyone has to compromise sooner or later," said Vicky, shaking her head like an older sister.

"My parents want me to go back to Cincinnati and take a law degree," said Shirley. "They say this will keep my options open. I say: a law degree is one option, and another option is to move to Europe and live with Tony and explore multiple options. I don't want to be told what to do."

"That's any job and every husband," said Vicky.

"I want to stay in a lab forever," said Margot, "looking into a microscope. The rest of the world can go hang."

"You always want to be left alone," said Shirley.

"Like Rosalind Franklin," said Vicky. "But she did all the work and then Watson and Crick took all the credit."

"Men are such a drag," said Shirley.

At this, they fell into a silent concurrence.

As if on cue, one of the pinball rowdies came up and asked:

"Can I buy you girls a drink?"

"Buzz off! We're organizing a lesbian peace march," said Shirley, and he went away.

"I wish they wouldn't ask," said Margot.

"Careful what you wish for, we'll be thirty soon enough and they'll stop asking altogether," said Vicky.

"If you say no, you're rude, or worse, a prude," said Margot.

"If I want to talk to a guy," said Shirley, "why can't I just go over and talk to him?"

"Way too revolutionary, it'll never catch on," said Vicky, in a professional tone. "Women are the policemen of women. They'll never own their own power. They don't want it."

Margot, infected with Shirley's enthusiasm and two beers down, boldly refuted this: "No! They do! We do!" Suddenly it seemed imperative to realize this: "Woman Power!"

The rowdies at the back were leaving. They moved towards the entrance in a mass of bulky winter coats, wide-shouldered. Instinctively, the three Radcliffes inched their stools closer to the bar. Margot's statement, "Woman Power!" hung in the air. One of the guys, a big lug wearing a black leather jacket and a knit beanie pulled low over his forehead, jostled Margot, a deliberate barge.

"Dyke bitch."

Margot threw her beer in his face.

For a moment the lug stood there, unmanned. Then he pulled back his fist. It looked like he was going to hit her. Margot watched the foam slide down his face, watched his eyes go blank and red and narrow and full of hate.

The bartender said, "Hey Joe."

His friend said, "Hey Joe."

Joe walked to the door, opened it, went out and slammed it behind him.

"Right on!" said Shirley.

Margot steadied herself against the bar. She was shaking. Her breath hiccupped.

"Maybe I *am* a lesbian," she said, not realizing, hazy-headed with beer and adrenaline, that she had spoken out loud. "If I can't bear a man touching me!"

Then she panicked to hear her inner thoughts escape and pushed against the bar, as if to leave.

Shirley put her hand on her forearm. "Hey"—her voice was soft, cambric.

"It's OK," said Vicky. "You don't have to explain."

"Explain what?" Margot looked up, confused by their tenderness.

"We get it," said Shirley.

"Get what?"

"Let's just say you're not the only one."

"The only lesbian?"

Vicky turned to look at her directly. Margot stared at the floor. The oak floorboards were patinaed with grime that sparkled in places with embedded chips of broken glass. Vicky hugged her. Her body felt warm and her skin smelled like beeswax. Margot didn't want to let go. Maybe I really am a lesbian! She managed a half-mocking self-smile. As Mad would say, that would explain *a lot*.

"They think anything goes these days," said Vicky. "The old rules—no sex till the wedding night—don't apply since the Pill. There are no limits anymore. Women have been brought up to be polite, we've got no defense. Girls aged eighteen, nineteen, twenty are showing up in psych wards with no prior history of mental illness, mute, tearing out clumps of their hair, cutting their arms with razor blades. One of the young psychiatrists at BU told me they are exhibiting some of the same symptoms as the boys coming back from 'Nam with shell shock. Look, don't be mad at him, but Flashman was worried. He said he knew Marvin was the type to lash out, and he told me you were acting different, withdrawn—and at the Zoo I could see you were—"

"Was I?" Shell shock made Margot think of her father cowering from the whizbangs on the Fourth of July and her mother elbowing him, "Buck up, Harrison, people are looking."

Vicky held her hands and repeated, "It's OK."

What was OK? Margot's head throbbed and her tummy was liquidy, like when she was little and in trouble.

"No, it's not that, it's not Marvin, I mean, he hurt me, but—"

"Look, you don't have to talk about it," said Vicky.

"I just totally lost it with that guy," said Margot, astonished at herself.

"It was brilliant!" said Shirley.

"Really?"

The bartender mopped the bar, took her glass and refilled it. "On the house," he smiled. "Don't sweat it."

Margot touched the spiky black threads on her brow with her finger, marveling at how her own skin could regenerate, knitting mitosis, heal. The tails of several ideas swam forward, encountered a blue egg in a flash of light, and wriggled inside. Things broken came together again. She felt the curving outline of her wound as a talisman, a reminder of what was possible instead of what was lost. Maybe the new knock had knocked the old one away, redrawn her scar and somehow redrawn her; maybe she could be stronger at the broken place.

28

CHROMOSOMES DANCED LIKE MATING EELS IN THE SAR-
gasso Sea, mysterious and unseen. Margot turned the dial on the
microscope. To her left Thomas Cleverly was examining a rash on
the agar surface of a petri dish. To her right Adam was poking
around in a stick insect's stomach. Margot did not hear or see these
distractions. She let herself float amniotic, mysterious and unseen.
Divining the divide, the moment of mitosis when the nuclear mem-
branes broke apart, protophase metaphase anaphase telophase,
unzipping their DNA to create two new daughter cells.

By April 1, Margot had karyotyped forty samples. Or, to put it
another way, forty different people. They were all disappointingly
normal. She had hoped to find an XXY with Klinefelter syndrome,
because she had heard Klinefelter describe his discovery in a guest
lecture the previous spring, but there was none. No XYY either; her
September Superman was long forgotten. She had almost come to
the end of the available samples. Margot tried to resign herself to
the fact that she would, once again (Miss Pubis and the rhinovirus
fiasco still rankled), be reduced to fashioning a thesis out of guess-
timates and preponderances. It was all very well having a new-age
no-competition class, but Margot knew she would need a successful
thesis to get into the MA program.

This year, as part of the ongoing academic integration of the two institutions, it had been announced that master's degrees for women would be awarded jointly by Harvard and Radcliffe. Phyllis and her conservative women's movement were up in arms about such blended arrangements. Separate but equal, they cried. The Radcliffe Students' Union rolled their eyes and derided them as Queen Canutes, trying to hold back the tide of progress. Margot's MA panel interview was scheduled for two days after graduation.

One of the DPhils put salt in the sugar bowl as an April Fools' joke, and Flashman drank a cup of salty coffee trying to pretend it was delicious to nix the prank.

"Salt is supposed to heighten sweetness," said Thomas Cleverly. "Have you ever been to Brittany in France?" Margot and Flashman shook their heads. "They add seawater to their caramel." In the Zoo, Cleverly was known as the resident gourmet.

"How are the enzymes cooking?" Flashman asked.

"It's looking like a virus could be the answer."

"I was thinking of virology as my Plan B," said Flashman. "In case I can't get into the program at Imperial College London. I've heard they need virologists at the government lab in Delaware."

"What's your Plan B, Margot?" asked Vicky.

"My Plan B?"

"You have to have a Plan B in life," said Thomas Cleverly, pouring chilled white wine from a thermos into a coffee mug. Flashman said white wine was a ridiculous drink for a man from Detroit.

"One can't help where one is from," said Cleverly, pretending to be Peter Cook and aphoristically British about it, "but one doesn't have to stay there."

"If I don't get into Stanford, I'm going out to California to keep bees," said Adam. "I like bees and there is a shortage of apiarists."

"I've applied to all the big advertising companies on Madison Avenue," said Vicky, "but it's a long shot. Realistically I've got to choose between B and C: researching or teaching."

"What research? What do you scribble all day long in your little pad?"

"I should have applied to Stanford," said Margot. "I missed this year's deadline. I don't know what happened to me this January. It's like my brain had a whiteout."

"You could do a semester at Heidelberg," suggested Thomas Cleverly, because that's what he had done.

"I haven't got German."

"You don't need a Plan B, kiddo," said Flashman, trying to cheer her up. "You can always get married."

APRIL 2: DULL GRAY nothing Thursday afternoon staring swimming-eyed at the shapes of giemsa stain: discerning the blues, deep sea, high skies, a hundred shades of indigo—

Margot saw an XXX.

Said nothing, kept the little glowing secret to herself. She cross-checked the sample with its medical file: woman, Caucasian, born February 1, 1905, died September 9, 1965; cause of death: coronary. Then she happened to glance at the next file: woman, Caucasian, born February 1, 1905, died September 16, 1965. Cause of death: coronary.

At first Margot thought the second woman was simply a dupli-cate. According to protocol, the names had been blacked out, but when she looked again she saw that the length of the two names was different, and although the birth date was the same, at the same hospital, Boston General, the death date for the second woman was a week later—

Margot had been staring at chromosomes for three hours straight but was suddenly filled with energy. She loaded the second woman's blood onto the slide and began to diligently separate the chromo-somes. Slowly, flickering faster, like a neon tube coming into light, there she was! Again! Another Triple Superwoman!

"EUREKA!"

"Oh my god, I can't believe she actually said eureka," said Thomas Cleverly, looking up.

"What?" Flashman had half a sandwich in his mouth.

"TWO!" declared Margot.

"Two!" Vicky echoed, climbing down from her perch in the trilobite niche.

"TWINS!" said Margot, both arms in the air, V for victory.

"OK, who had money on Margot being the genius?" said Flashman, banging his fist on the bench.

Thomas Cleverly shook his head. "Not me, I'm pretty sure I'm the genius in this room."

Identical twins were the great genetic gold mine. For research purposes they were clones. But finding a triple X chromosomal anomaly in twins was an extraordinary stroke of luck. It was not yet understood at what point of meiosis, when the spermatozoon shed its shell and mingled its chromosomes with the oocyte's, that the extra chromosome appeared. Observing genetically identical twins with the same anomaly, it could be posited that such a mutation was hereditary, a theory that had not been considered before.

The celebratory commotion attracted the attention of several DPhils, and they gathered round. What's going on? Wow! Way out, far out, outta sight! They took turns peering at Margot's triple X through the microscope, clapped her on the back, well done, passed around the medical history files.

The female twins had died within days of each other in 1965, both, according to their death certificates, of a heart attack. The incidence of twins dying of similar causes at similar times was well known, if not well understood. Following protocol, the basic medical records listed only major operations, preexisting conditions, pregnancies and live births. There were no photographs to illustrate the kinds of physiognomies—wide-spaced eyes, high foreheads, elongated fingers—that characterized other chromosomal abnormalities like mongolism, Marfan's, or Turner's. Neither was there the kind of detailed biographical information that could describe a syndrome.

"Here, you have a look," said Margot, frowning, handing the file to the hovering Cleverly. "I can't see anything odd—which is odd."

Thomas Cleverly scanned the pages and then passed them to Flashman.

A general discussion ensued about the differences between Supermen and Superwomen. If Supermen were more aggressive, more hyper, did that mean that Superwomen were more "feminine"? And what was femininity? Passivity? Nurturing-ness? Bigger boobs?

"If masculinity is more of something, is more feminine less of something?"

"And how do you even calibrate that?"

"By measuring estrogen levels?" asked Dello, the guy who had come to the first class with a flower painted on his forehead.

"But hormone levels map behavior, not genetics."

"What's the difference?"

"Isn't behavior personality?"

"Not if it's hormonal."

"But personality is modeled. Personality is a social construct," said Vicky.

"If a girl is crying all over the place, it usually correlates to menstruation," said Thomas Cleverly.

"But not always. Sometimes those models of behavior are inherent psychopathies."

"What they used to call hysterias," Vicky again, derisive.

"The asylums are still full of them," said Dello, who was a med student in the middle of a psychiatric rotation.

"The asylums are full of women, and the prisons are full of men," observed Thomas Cleverly.

"And we know that a disproportionate percentage of violent criminals are triple Y."

"So it would stand to reason that a disproportionate percentage of the female psych population are triple X—"

"Stand to reason?" Vicky stood up tall and furious. Her Afro was backlit into a halo, her hands rested on her hips, akimbo, warrior pose. "Are you guys kidding me? You are extrapolating out of thin air. Your conclusion is that men are violent and women are nuts? That's your social construct right there!"

Margot stood beside her. For a long, dangerous moment the two women faced their male peers. No one spoke. Vicky was breathing hard, like she'd just run a lap. Margot felt hot color flush into her cheeks.

Flashman came to the rescue. "Look at the data! The fact that there is nothing odd about their medical histories is noteworthy. Think about it: two women walking around, even reproducing— it says here they both had two children—living normal lives with an extra X chromosome. That's a major chromosomal abnormality without any physical effect."

And then Margot saw it. The answer. Perfect as a shiny blue egg, trembling, fragile, as if it might crack with the effort of ideation.

She clapped her hand against her forehead. "It's the perfect confirmation of Lyonization! That's the significance! Not only one X chromosome has been switched off, apparently in this case two have!"

The British geneticist Mary Lyon had guest-lectured the previous year on her theory that one of the two X chromosomes was rendered a silent, inactive partner in females. This explained why men could do with only one, because one was what women did with too. Margot's twins were a happy corroboration.

Dello and the DPhils and even the erudite Thomas Cleverly fell silent, shut up by the sheer empirical.

29

Margot's discovery was a big deal on campus. People came up to her in the Quad to say congrats! Girls she only knew in glancing, waved hello in the cafeteria line. Shirley threw a room crush for her, and even Phyllis (!) put in an appearance. When she was toasted with Asti Spumante, Margot flushed beet red.

The *Crimson* sent their science reporter to interview her. "How do you feel, as a girl, to have made such progress?"

Vicky and Shirley, sitting with her in a coffee shop, rolled their eyes.

"Do girls have different feelings?" asked Vicky sarcastically.

The reporter, a buttoned-down Connecticut type, faced Vicky's stern bronze brow with stupefaction.

"Because, I mean, that's the whole difference between men and women, right?"

Shirley scowled as he fumbled defensively, "And in any case, what does genetics have to do with all that women's lib crap?"

Margot kinda apologized for her friends. Shirley was kinda annoyed about her apologizing. Luckily the guy wasn't a total asshole and the write-up was positive. There was a picture too; Margot thought she looked like a chipmunk, but Thomas Cleverly insisted on tacking it up on the Zoo bulletin board.

At the weekly Zoo seminar, Dr. Fred made her take a bow. He

cuffed her on the shoulder, quite the star of his little pedagogical experiment. He asked her to address his sophomore class. "He wants to show you off," said Flashman. The thought of giving a speech made Margot nauseous. As the gathering was breaking up, Dr. Fred told her, "Look, don't sweat the naysayers."

Big pink bubble popped. An image of Fay chewing gum at her birthday party came into her mind. Success engenders jealousy, but Margot didn't know that. There were those who said Margot Thornsen's big breakthrough was no great "discovery," just dumb luck. Margot Thornsen wasn't anything special, or especially deserving; she was just one of those country club girls who would probably end up marrying Christopher Robin the Third and spending her days picking out chintz. Margot perceived these unkind corridor whisperings and felt the familiar undertow of *not-good-enough* that clutched at her xiphoid process, pulling her down, inward.

THAT WEEK MARTIN LUTHER KING was shot in Memphis. Margot heard the news on the radio. Walking through the Old Burying Ground on her way to Widener, she found Vicky with her head bowed, sitting on a bench between the headstones.

"I heard. I'm so sorry for all of you."

Vicky looked up. Her face was a mess. Not shock, not sad; raw, rent, shattered; her lipstick was smeared, her hands were balled into fists.

"You're sorry!" Vicky roared. Margot stood there, words clamped up. "You're damned right you're sorry! Now we see how real is the real world. How it's got to be. Now you're going to watch this country burn!"

Margot did not answer. Felt her own useless ignorance, felt sick, screwed up inside. Lit a cigarette and smoked it, walking away slowly, footsteps echoing hollow. She walked across the Yard, wind whistling through bare branches. Tree, carbon, water hydrogen and oxygen, breathing in and out. What is life? A protein or a double helix or this thing we are moving through every mad micro-millisecond?

The next day was also hushed, in respect, but in fear too. Through open windows Margot could hear the radio repeating the news of King's death over and over. James Brown was scheduled to play Boston Garden, and Mayor White got up onstage with him and together they spoke about calm and loss and unity.

Margot walked through the quiet streets that Holy Week absorbing the sting of Vicky's anger, needled with guilt. It wasn't her fault, but it was her fault. She saw that she had been floating through life without touching the sides. Things happened around her, but she had remained apart, inert. The fires that burned Baltimore and DC and Chicago, monks in Vietnam, crosses in southern yards—even Farnsworth—seemed not to touch her.

It was ever so, wasn't it?—that bad things happened, war and poor people and suffering—injustice. She heard her mother's voice, bitter, defeated, reminding her, *Life isn't fair.* At the time she had nodded; that's the way the cookie crumbled; you could be born into a poor Vietnamese village or a penthouse, into a happy family or an unhappy one. People were subject to greater forces than their own: cyclones and dictator fathers; strokes and stock market crashes. It was just the luck of the draw if you found love, like Sarah, or lost it, like David Stern; if you were too tall and shy like she was, or beautiful and popular, like Phyllis.

Things were the way they were. What could she do about it? Margot heard her defense ring hollow. People lived in the world, didn't they? Plowed it, built it, wrote its laws. What was immutable in an age when atoms could be split and DNA spliced? The world was changing. Shouldn't she at least try to be a part of it, like Sandy, protesting and shouting? But Richie said protesting and shouting was more show than substance. And all the rowdy crowdy pushing trampling smashing-up of the campus sit-ins and occupations made Margot nervous. Some students had been suspended, some had even been arrested.

Margot had even abstained from the women's movement. She had always assumed her gender was just another part of her inadequacy. She felt it keenly, often painfully, but had formed no articulated perspective on it. Being a man or being a woman was just the way things were categorized: Harvard and Radcliffe, gentlemen's and ladies' restrooms, husband and wife. Formed (*de-formed*, Shirley would say) by these institutions, she had been sheltered by them too.

But Radcliffe was not the real world. Radcliffe was not even going to be Radcliffe for very much longer; everyone knew it would merge with Harvard and cease to exist. And then Vicky was right, they would be women out in the real world, where the fires were.

Margot tied a black armband around her jacket sleeve and took it off again. She was not sure if it signaled solidarity or hypocrisy. Everyone was upset and unsettled; but maybe she was only upset and unsettled because Vicky had been angry with her; or maybe it was the state of the world, addled, riled, inchoate. She went to the vigil in the chapel and sat at the back. Knelt in prayer, felt empty and ashamed, felt the ridge of wooden pew dig into her knees, felt alone and cold, as she always did in dank, churchy places.

"Hey Margot—"

It was Vicky with a small wave; the service was breaking up.

"Hey Vicky." Margot halted, sidestepped out of the flowing crowd into an apse.

"I'm sorry," she said, almost by default, in the same way she had apologized her whole life.

"Yeah, but for what?"

Vicky looked at her directly. Margot looked to her left, where a marble Christ lay dead in his mother's arms. She looked back at Vicky, meeting her gaze.

"For everything."

Vicky made a wry turn with the corner of her mouth.

"Not good enough."

"I mean, I'm sorry everything is screwed up. This stupid war, stupid laws, stupid people, that things are unfair and not right and not better. I'm sorry I don't know what to say or how to fix anything. I feel as stupid as the whole system."

"You really don't know, do you?"

"Know what?"

Vicky hovered, shifting her weight from one foot to another, as if she was deciding whether to tell her or not.

"Can I buy you a coffee?" Margot ventured into the silence.

"Sure," Vicky said hesitantly, as if she wasn't.

"I know I don't know anything about anything," said Margot. "Maybe that's what I'm really sorry for."

"It's a start," said Vicky. "Let's go to the coffee shop behind the Brattle Street gas station."

"I don't know that place," said Margot.

"I know you don't," said Vicky, smiling now.

30

COFFEE, CLASSES, TRIANGULATED PATHS ACROSS HAR-
vard Yard, afternoons in the Zoo. Rhythms resumed. Life went
on. Dr. Fred finally pried loose the full medical histories on the
triple X twins. Margot read them diligently. They were supposed
to be anonymous, but due to an oversight the names had not been
redacted. Meet Constance Beerbroke and Clementina Wolfer-
son, née Cooper. Both had worked as nurses at Boston University
Teaching Hospital, Constance in the emergency room, Clementina in pediatrics.

Small biographical details were revealed in the blue-black ink of
handwritten doctors' notes on the hospital admissions forms that
spanned the six decades of their lives: a broken arm in childhood,
"tripped over playing stickball," a second broken arm, Constance
again: *"Patient says she fell off her bike."* They had both contracted
polio in 1915, aged ten; Constance of the broken arms had recovered,
Clementina not so well, *"limp, dragging right leg, but not disabling.
Outpatient rehabilitation for strengthening suggested. As discussed, family means preclude."* There followed the female litany of childbirth,
miscarriages, tubal ligation. The sisters' lives mirrored each other.
But Flashman was right, there was no incidence of congenital disease, nor of anatomical abnormalities observed at autopsy. Two perfectly normal women had lived through the First World War, the

Spanish flu, through the Wall Street crash and the Great Depression. They had laughed at Charlie Chaplin on a silver screen and swooned at Rhett Butler in Technicolor and watched the Nazis march down the Champs-Élysées on the newsreels. At the beginning of their careers they had washed their hands twenty times a day with carbolic soap and still watched sepsis kill half their surgical patients; by the time wounded GIs were being shipped back from Normandy, they were routinely injecting penicillin.

Margot smiled at history's march, at civilization's rise, at the miracle of indoor plumbing. So much was better, getting better all the time. "Process-progress," Margot repeated to herself, "is counting steps, climbing upwards."

STILL SMILING WHEN SHE bumped into Richie. She was walking out of the Zoo, he was walking in—

"This is where you have been hiding!" he said.

"Not hiding—"

"I wanted to come and see what was going on in here."

"It's top secret," said Flashman, hovering, half joking.

"I keep hearing about some Frankenstein project in the basement."

Margot made introductions. Vicky said "Hi!" Thomas Cleverly said, "Dr. Richard Merryweather? Of the laser beam team?" and Richie nodded, gratified. Margot felt weird, two halves of her life meeting up, but apparently no one else did because suddenly they were all scooting around the table in a corner booth at the Crimson Cup and ordering pitchers of beer. The zoolies peppered Richie with questions: What effect does the laser have on the cellular structure? Does it atomize or disrupt it? Is it really as precise as they say?

As a second pitcher of beer arrived, Adam rushed in, late, flapping his hands excitedly.

"They've found it!" he announced.

"Who's found what?"

"Meselson's mob upstairs."

"What about them?"

"They've done it!"

"Done what?"

"They've found the genetic scissors."

"Where?"

"*E. coli!*"

"Holy shit!" said Flashman.

Margot felt light and lost, like the walls had fallen out and everything was suddenly wide open.

"You OK?" asked Richie.

She nodded dumbly. She took a sip of beer, and the swallowed coolness brought her back to the present. Everyone was talking and interrupting and excited. Her triple X twins, Margot realized, were small fry compared to this. This was the beginning of everything.

The zoolies around the table chattered like starlings. Flashman whistled. Vicky was talking nurture and nature a mile a minute. Thomas Cleverly loosened his tie and held up his palms in benediction. Of all of them, he had been working the closest on the Meselson project; he might even get his name on the paper.

Only Richie was appalled.

"Don't tell anyone," Margot begged him. "We have been sworn to secrecy."

"I'm sure you have. Because it's totally unethical."

"It's not unethical yet. At the moment it's hypothetical," said Flashman.

"That's like saying: I'm not doing anything wrong, I'm just splitting the atom, it's not my fault if people want to make bombs out of it," said Richie.

"C'mon, fission was every physicist's dream!"

"Look, of course every biologist wants to be Watson, well, OK, not Watson—who everyone knows is a lucky Jim—but Crick, everyone wants to be the clever Crick. But it's a different thing to be actually working on the Manhattan Project."

"What do you mean?" asked Vicky. "That we shouldn't make scientific progress? Aren't you working on a laser beam? Isn't that a weapon?"

"In outer space, maybe—"

"It's the unintended consequences," said Richie, stern and worried. "You know very well that the moment we can rewrite the genome the human race is doomed. People want to conform, they want to be like everyone else. But it's the very diversity of life that makes it successful. Take genetic manipulation to its logical conclusion and you will end up with a race of tall, blond, blue-eyed idiots. All edges sanded down. No spark, nothing new. The geneticists will eradicate the misery of disability and declare it a wondrous improvement, like laundry detergent. But we need the weirdos and the misfits and the oddballs. Without the outliers, the anomalies, life is just people sitting around the dinner table in an advertisement for Thanksgiving, everyone agreeing and happy. Without argument and pain, there would be no striving, no irritant spur, no grain of sand to make a pearl."

Margot was puzzled. Imperfection was useful—perhaps even vital?

IT WAS GETTING DARK. The company disbanded, headed back to the Zoo, to libraries and dorm rooms. Together, still talking, Richie and Margot, almost without deciding, walked over to De Sousa's.

Ma Sousa sat them at their usual table. It looked the same, raffia-wrapped wine bottles as candles, red-shaded lamp, a comfy fug of roasted peppers and sausage smells and cigarette smoke, but it felt different because for some reason they had changed places. Richie sat opposite the window, Margot faced the restaurant; Richie talked, Margot listened.

Richie had carried a heaviness with him from the Crimson Cup, now he held his head in his hands, almost, it seemed to Margot, as if he was going to cry. Gone was the wise older brother, replaced by a Richie she didn't know, raw and upset. Slowly, haltingly, peeling ragged strips from the label on his bottle of beer and rolling them into pellets, he told her the story.

"It's Hal," Richie said, hunching over. "He showed up on the doorstep of the American consulate in Kabul, no passport, totally out of it. Apparently he's not the first lost hippie they have ever seen; Dad wired money for the ticket and they sent him home. Mother put him to bed and they thought he would sleep it off. But he wouldn't sleep, he kept screaming and didn't seem to know where he was. They called Dr. Dome but Hal became violent when he tried to examine him, and then they called me.

"By the time I got there, he was shivering and yellow. Luckily it turned out to be jaundice, not hepatitis. But he was painfully thin. Incoherent, zoned out. He refused to let me touch him. On the second day I discovered that he had been so afraid of running out of drugs that he had swallowed four condoms of raw opium paste back in Afghanistan and then tried to drink Ex-Lax to flush them out and given himself terrible stomach cramps.

"The drugs eventually came out painfully. I got him a clean opioid from the pharmacy for his night terrors. I slept in his room for a week, kept him calm, hydrated. He was mostly out of it. My parents kept insisting he be sent to a sanatorium. When Hal saw either of them, he got agitated and started clawing at the air.

"I fed him mashed potatoes with a spoon. I read to him from Kipling's *Just So Stories*. How the leopard got his spots, how the giraffe stretched his neck. I was thinking of you and your twins as I read. Runny and I are twins too, but we are completely opposite, it's almost impossible to imagine we once shared a womb. Runny came out one weekend and we sat in the den drinking whiskey and Runny said, 'I don't know why you bother. Whatever bad gene Hal's got, it can't be fixed.' Can you imagine, Margot? He wanted to abandon him, like a junked car.

"For the first couple of days Hal was dazed and suspicious. Slowly he woke up. He began to tell me what had happened. He was angry, but it was the guilt that was chewing him up. When he talked, he turned away so that he was facing the wall. It turns out it all started that summer he was so sick."

Margot nodded, she remembered him silently screaming in the window, remembered too that she had run away.

"It began with a fever, but there was never any real diagnosis. Dr. Dome said he was infectious and had to be put in quarantine, but in retrospect that doesn't make any clinical sense. Dr. Dome came to visit Hal every day. Every day he told him to pull down his PJs so that he could give him a shot. Then he started to give him enemas—

"Hal told me Dr. Dome gave him Oreos, brought him ice cream, things that he had banned from his own prescribed 'nutrition list.' He presented himself simultaneously as torturer and rescuer. He kept Hal doped up—Hal said it was some kind of a milky liquid that was supposed to knock him out, and he thinks it did sometimes, but sometimes it didn't."

Margot reached across the table and took Richie's hand in hers to stop him from scratching at the beer label. He pressed her fingertips gratefully and then resumed his methodical shredding, one strip and then another.

"I tried to tell Hal: 'It wasn't your fault, you were a child.' But he just looked at me with black dead eyes and said I didn't understand. That summer was only the start of it. He told me he had done worse since. In Jalalabad, he said, you can buy a boy in the market. I think he did as he was done to. That's why the guilt is so bad, that's why he takes the heroin. He's an addict, yes, but he's just desperately trying to numb the pain."

"I remember one New Year's Eve," said Margot. "I was seated next to Hal at dinner and I didn't talk to him all night. I felt bad about it. Maybe if I had been nicer to him—"

"Maybe if we had all been nicer," said Richie. "But growing up Hal was always Hal-the-problem. We blamed him for his behavior instead of trying to understand why he was acting out like that. Guilt, I am beginning to see, is contagious."

"It's not your fault either," said Margot gently.

"My father wants me to go home, he says he'll buy me a local practice and I can tend to my brother. He says, What's the point in being a doctor if you won't even treat your own family? He says the word 'doctor' in the same tone of voice he uses for something you pay for, like a lawyer, an accountant, a barber. He always acted as if my profession was some kind of comedown in life."

"You should send him a bill," said Margot.

"I should send him a bill!" Richie repeated.

The thought of Clarence Merryweather sitting at the table in the breakfast room at Sage Hill, opening up a doctor's bill, neatly typed, state sales tax totaled, from his own son, was perfectly absurd. Richie almost laughed.

"I should have gone to Stanford for postgrad," he said after a pause. "I would have been out of their reach."

"Can we be who we want to be? That is the question," said Margot.

"Or do we just do what our parents expect of us?" said Richie.

"Or our genomes?

"Aren't they the same thing?"

They fell silent for a moment. The beer was flat, the crème caramel was soft.

Richie tried to explain, "We're so"—and then he stopped, searching for the right word—"*hidebound* on the East Coast. Stanford is just a different energy—no one goes to sleep, like they don't want to miss a single second. Everything is communal, shared, backyard barbecues, cooking up ideas, passing the bong around. And yet every conversation is about the work. And I'm not even talking about the politics, which is somewhere between Mao and Gandhi by way of Tom Paine. They've got a flyer for everything: Ayurvedic medicine, shamanic healing, kibbutzing in Oregon, solidarity with the Vietnamese people, exchange programs with Bolivian farmers. By the end of the day your pockets are full of the future."

Margot laughed, "I wouldn't have thought that was your scene at all."

"Because I'm such a stiff, you mean?" Richie's head dipped again.

"I didn't mean that—"

"I guess I am too old."

"You're only five years older than me."

"It might as well be a whole generation. I got taken to a party one night and everyone was out of it on psychedelics. You can feel like a real stuffed shirt standing in a corner watching everyone else tripping."

Margot made an upside-down smile in sympathy.

"I sometimes wonder if Hal didn't have it right all along—he's the only one of us who is really free."

"But lost," said Margot.

"Maybe we have to lose ourselves to find ourselves."

31

MAD MARRIED SOLOMON GRUNDY AT ST. JOHN THE DIVINE in New York on Easter Saturday. The bride wore an orange kaftan with a white mink stole. The groom wore an emerald green Nehru jacket and smiled as beatifically as a god. His groomsmen, in more traditional blue blazers and gray trousers, lined up like oarsmen ready to row his gilded barge down the Nile. Mad's father wore a ten-gallon hat and an enormous turquoise and silver belt buckle. All the Texans wore cowboy boots with their suits, but this was less shocking to the groom's relatives—the very Lorillards of Tuxedo Park; Solomon Grundy's real name turned out to be Edward—than the multicolored guests who clapped and threw rose petals as they came out of the church. Mad shimmered like a sunrise through a cloud of confetti.

The reception was at the Sherry-Netherland. The walls were hung with diaphanous purple fabric, the waitresses were dressed in baggy Moroccan trousers, and instead of round tables of ten there were low-slung couches and leather poofs scattered about. A buffet table was covered in silver dishes of shrimp and green goddess sauce, mimosa eggs, pastry parcels filled with pigeon and cinnamon, bowls of figs and tangerines and Turkish delight. The vibe was groovy and bohemian. The different tribes stood in the four corners of the room sizing each other up like delegates at a political convention; Solomon Grundy's brother was running for state senate and went round shaking everyone's hands. The Texans tried to rib him, "Are you for the Kennedy brother or more of a fence-sitting Humphrey man?" and then roared with laughter, "Lemme tell y'all that Wallace down in Alabama has some interesting ideas!" It was hard to know if they were joking or not. The imperial Catherine, née Morgan, Lorillard shadowed her son, dispensing niceties and nudging him forward, making sure he didn't get stuck too long with a maiden aunt. Mad floated about like a jeweled dragonfly, alighting here and there, kissing the air and powdered cheeks and exclaiming "Oh my!" in a southern accent Margot had never heard her use before.

"Oh my! Margot help me out! No one is mingling!"

"I'm the worst mingler in the world," said Margot. "Except perhaps Richie—who sends his regrets—" Richie had been summoned to Sage Hill again.

"That's true, I never saw a more awkward man," said Lydia, inserting herself, followed, inevitably, by Bernadette, who was now as skinny as Twiggy and wearing a pink minidress that made her look like a Popsicle.

"I had to invite some of the old Ethel Walker brigade," Mad whispered to Margot. "My new dragon-in-law insisted I needed more girls to balance the numbers."

"I just love what you've done with the place!" said Bernadette.

"It's so very *you*," said Lydia.

Mad caught hold of a passing Texan. "Eldridge, cuz! come and meet some New Yorkers, I promise they won't bite! This is Bernadette—"

"I prefer Nadia now," corrected Bernadette, batting her glued-on eyelashes.

A waitress appeared carrying a brass tray crowded with different kinds of glasses: silver tankards, highballs and flutes, each filled with a different-colored liquid, yellow, pink, and green.

Lydia regarded the array. "How confusing!"

Mad laughed, "My father won't drink anything but mint juleps, my tough-as-nails new mother-in-law insisted on champagne, and I wanted arak and grapefruit juice." She twirled with happiness. "I wanted to get married at the gardens of the Aga Palace in Marrakech, but Solemn Solomon discovered we wouldn't be legal. Oh, weddings are so silly!" she declared, decrying Lydia's greatest dream, just as Trip—dear old Trip—appeared.

Margot froze.

The noise of the room went away and was replaced with a rushing white silence like a vacuum tube.

Trip did not say hello. Didn't even look at her. Stood, arms by his side, stiff. Usually so garrulous in a crowd, he hung back.

The group formed a little circle around Mad.

"How marvelously exciting . . . You are positively glowing! . . . Oh you must be terribly happy. . . . You were never one to pay attention to what people say . . . This explains all the flurry and hurry!"

Lydia stepped back and Margot saw the object of their attention, Mad's tummy, beneath her pleated chiffon dress, described a small bulge.

"Oh my!"

Lydia clutched Trip by his elbow. Margot heard only part of what she hissed into his ear, ". . . you should, you must . . ." as she steered him towards the buffet table, a June wedding at the Piping Rock Club, an apartment on 72nd Street, two blond children, an office at one brokerage house or another, squash at the Racquet Club, lunch at the Knickerbocker, cocktail parties in the winter, dinners on the deck in summer; being good at tennis and golf and sailing and bridge and jawing about nothing while balancing a martini glass in one hand and a cigarette in the other.

Margot stood for a moment watching their progress. Lydia pointed to the dishes she wanted so that Trip might spoon the food onto her plate; at others she shook her head, "No, I don't want that!" Margot almost felt sorry for him. Maybe it was enough to know that he knew her shame was really his own.

Maybe it wasn't.

Margot walked towards the door with the thought to discreetly slip away, but was intercepted by one of the Texans. He doffed his hat to introduce himself, revealing a tan line across his forehead like a horizon.

"Howdy, I'm a real-life cowboy, name of Johnno."

Margot knew exactly who he was. His hand shaking hers felt just as Mad had once described it, like a saddle, rough in the rough parts and smooth in the smooth. They chatted about Maddy growing up tomboy of the ranch, about the relative comforts and discomforts of cities and wilderness, and then he introduced Margot to the Charleston cousins, who wanted to know what they should see in the Big Apple and was it worth going all the way up the Empire State Building? They laughed when Margot admitted she had lived in the city all her life and had never done it. After the speeches there was a string quartet. Margot danced with Solomon Grundy's father, who told her he had once met her grandfather and thought him a mean old bastard, and then she danced with an uncle and then with a Jamaican guy called Rollo with dreadlocks, and then she got talking to a tall, elegant man with brilliantined black hair who spoke with a French accent but said he was Italian and gave her his card with a Geneva address. At midnight the older generation made their excuses and a rock band set up onstage. Everyone took off their jackets and ties and began to get down.

Margot had never figured out how to dance to rock and roll; it had always seemed so anarchic. But now she saw that you could dance to your own rhythm; there was no right way or wrong step. You were free, no man to ask you (or not ask you) to dance, no arms to hold, to bind or pinch, no partner's feet to follow or tread on yours. Margot danced and danced until her feet ached, and then she kicked off her shoes and kept dancing.

Was it already two in the morning, three? Her watch had stopped. Margot regarded her bleary-blurry face in the mirror in the ladies' room with some chagrin, her mascara was smudged. Time to go home. She smiled at herself, and this smiling felt odd and she remembered that in all this time having fun she hadn't once seen Trip or thought about him.

Mad caught up with her in the hallway, as she was leaving.

"Margot, don't head off so soon!"

She spun around and her dress billowed. "You dig? I mean, I know the Lorillard tribe are stuffed shirts, but"—she caught herself and laughed—"I almost think I need your approval, Margot. Oh don't you see that he's perfect for me! I know he looks grunge-o-rama, but Solomon Grundy—I mean, Edward—is entirely grounded. Did you know? He's like a brilliant math whiz in real life, numbers just hum to him; he does all the accounts for the musicians and bands downtown."

She took one of Margot's hands and placed it on her belly.

"Can you feel the bump?"

Mad's skin was warm through the silk. "Yes! Yes I can!"

"Edward suggested I stop taking the Pill last Christmas. He kind of guessed what had happened in Boston, I think. He never said anything, but he found me the right doctor—well, I know now that everything causes a scar, visible, invisible. Don't you believe that, Margot? We can never erase our pain, but we can honor it and we can learn to redirect it—at least that's what the new shrink says. She's a woman, she's fantastic."

"Oh my!" said Margot. "She kicked! I could feel it!"

"I just *know* it's going to be a girl too—" said Maddy, Mad-ness banished. "Women have the all-healing power of life."

Margot felt the warm, taut skin under silk. She felt moved. She felt happy.

"You see, Margot, you don't have to diagnose or theorize or fantasize a baby. That's what Edward says. You just have to have it."

ERNIE TOOK HER UP in the old clanking, swaying elevator at 655 Park.

"Have a good time, Princess M?"

"Yes," said Margot, half incredulous, "I did."

Margot found her mother on the sofa in the den. An empty highball glass sat in a small puddle on the side table. Her head had fallen back, her mouth was open, and she was snoring in competition with the static hiss of the snow-screen TV. In stereo, the sound was somehow urgent, like the approach to a waterfall. Margot tiptoed towards her room, bashed her hip on the corner of a table and yelped.

Peggy woke up with a snort.

"Oh it's you. You look the worse for wear. Why didn't you tell me your friend was marrying into the exalted Lorillards, the son of Catherine the Great herself. I had to hear about it from Dotty Merryweather. Apparently Trip and that hideous Lydia were invited. She told me they want your father to leave the carriage house at Sage Hill because Trip wants to live in it when they are married. I can't understand how Clarence would allow such a match." She rattled her empty glass, "Freshen my drink, will you?"

Margot took the glass and went into the kitchen, violently hacked ice out of the metal ice tray, poured the requisite three fingers of vodka, and sliced a lemon for garnish.

When she came back, her mother had changed channels and found a nature film. Jackals tore at the carcass of a water buffalo. Margot felt equally savage.

"I told them I have no control and less interest in what Harrison does or where he goes. Especially after his lawyer sent me a letter demanding alimony. If you can imagine such a travesty. He's behaving like the hired help with his hand out. Well, he can go whistle. He won't get another red cent from me."

"I'm going to bed," said Margot.

"Go."

Peggy tried to light her cigarette with a plastic lighter but the flint wouldn't catch. Enraged, she threw it across the room, where it hit a porcelain figurine of a girl holding a balloon, knocking it off the shelf. The jackals bounded free and wild across the savannah.

Once Margot would have gone into the kitchen and retrieved the pan and brush and cleaned up the broken shards. But now she just bent over, picked up the lighter, put it back on the table next to the ashtray, and walked slowly out of the living room, into her bedroom, into her bathroom, and ran the bathwater loud and gushing to drown out the howling.

Lowered her naked body slowly into the water, savored the steep as the heat soothed. The water made aquarelle shadows against her skin. She closed her eyes and thought of nothing, and when she opened them she saw a trail of red menstrual blood in the water. It floated away from her and she caught the thread in her fingers and drew it out of the water, viscous, clinging to her fingertips like a jelly creature from the sea. This was life, but a sign of life washed away too. And the thought came to her, in remembering Maddy's contented wisdom, all the Mad healed by love coming, life coming. You just have to have it.

IN THE MORNING, WHEN she brushed her teeth, Margot regarded the white Pill, pushed out of its foil into her palm, as a reproach: for sex, for the negation and for the permission. Small and white, innocuous, it was the last Pill in the pack. Never mind, she would never have sex again! Never-never land—but how wonderful it would be to be Mad, all madness repealed. How wonderful to have a baby—but not a husband! To hold a child and love a child without all the unpleasant business of man and his pushing-in penis. Margot smiled to herself. Shirley would approve: the end of the patriarchy! She washed her face of sleep and dreams, refreshed, a new day: she was sure that in the future it would be possible to genetically arrange such a thing. When she looked in the mirror, she saw that the scar above her eyebrow had faded almost to white.

Leave-taking, Margot looked around at her old teddy bear and her junior microscope and the row of picture books on the shelf, childish things from another age. She packed her leather-bound volumes of *Peter Pan* and *Alice in Wonderland*, her biography of Marie Curie, a few other favorite books, the pearl necklace her father had given her when she was a baby, and the botany diary she had kept one summer at Farnsworth when she had diligently painted a different leaf on each page. She took the things she would miss not to have. She was surprised her bag was so light.

PART

THREE

ADVANCING

32

THE SNOW WALLS ALONG MASS AVE MELTED AND THE DAF-
fodils thrust up their yellow heads, and then a great nor'easter flattened them again with a late snow dump at the end of April. Margot
did not notice. The deadline for senior theses was May 21. Finals
would start the following week. Graduation was June 10. Coretta
Scott King had accepted the invitation from the student body to
give the commencement speech in place of her slain husband.

End of the academic year: everyone was stressed out, strung out
on bennies, wrist scratching. Hellos in hallways were reduced to
brief monosyllables. "Taut as a G-string," said Flashman, strumming an air guitar. The lines outside professors' offices were long.
Dr. Fred was away for a week, apparently writing protocols for practical exams, but Thomas Cleverly told Margot he had in fact flown
to England to meet with the folks at the Cavendish.

"That's where he did his PhD work, and that's where Sanger is.
Right now, for genetics, it's the best place to be."

"What about you?" Margot asked Thomas.

"My thesis work is pretty much done. Maybe I'll follow Dr. Fred
to England's green and pleasant land."

Margot was dismayed. She had kind of assumed that if she stayed
in Cambridge, Cambridge would stay the same too: Adam on her
left, Flashman on her right, Vicky in the corner with her report-

er's pad. But Flashman was waiting to hear from Imperial London, Vicky had decided to study law at Columbia, "nearer home, but not home." Shirley was undecided, "but somewhere in Europe, most definitely Europe." Margot felt like everyone was moving on just as she had found her place.

MARGOT DESCRIBED HER MOTHER'S drinking to Richie, sitting at the Crimson Cup over beers. She asked him what she should do, but really she was asking: What will become of me?

She told Richie about the red IRS letters, the liens and the compound bank interest and all the canceled credit cards. She didn't tell him about the smashed porcelain, the empty fridge, how her father had sold his war medals, the pathos of lost peas hiding under kitchen cupboards.

She wanted Richie to reassure her: Don't worry, I'm here, I'll take care of you. Perhaps she half wanted him, in that moment, to say, Marry me, Margot, and everything will be alright again. But he didn't. He said that it was impossible to help someone who didn't want to be helped.

Margot ventured, "Maybe I need some help—"

Richie shifted in his seat, looked out the window, looked uncomfortable. "The problem is—"

Margot hated it when people began advice in this way.

"The problem is—graduate students are as poor as church mice. And an MA is only halfway to a PhD; it's not worth anything by itself. And if you go whole hog, it's going to be an uphill battle. Colleges will always give men tenure because they have families to support. What you should do—"

Margot hated that phrase too, she covered her ears with her hands. "Lalalalala!"

"I don't want to discourage you—"

"But you are! You are!"

Richie sat back, irritated.

"Well, you could always get married," he said in a tone of restrained reasonableness, "and study on the side, like a hobby."

"Why does everyone think getting married is the answer to everything?"

"Calm down," said Richie.

Margot didn't realize she had raised her voice. Chastened, she shut up.

"Anyway," he continued, oblivious to her affront, "I need to figure out what *I'm* going to do too. I realize now Hal can't stay at Sage Hill. There's too much history, too much—he needs open spaces, a fresh start, countryside. But I don't think he can live alone, and I'm the only one he trusts."

"Maybe you should try the other Cambridge," said Margot tersely. "It seems to be the green and pleasant land everyone is heading to suddenly."

33

EXAM MODE. FOR WEEKS MARGOT SUBSISTED ON WONDER Bread, Kraft Singles, peanut butter, coffee, cigarettes, and an unshakable routine: up at six, work, sleep at midnight.

When the proctor said, "You may now begin," Margot picked up her pen and neatly wrote her name and student ID number at the top of the page, then put the pen down in the pen groove at the top of the desk, took up her pencil and began. Multiple choice was her favorite. Essay questions made her arm ache and rubbed an ink callus into her forefinger. She plotted graphs, drew schematics, labeled diagrams. After an exam, it was her habit to award herself a jelly donut and a half-hour walk to clear her head, before going back to revision. A week into exams, she was so far into the tunnel that she couldn't imagine a light at the end; she existed in a state of numb and blinkered rote.

After the final paper, Molecular and Cell Biology, the professor announced with a happy flourish: "And for the last time! Ladies and gentlemen, you may put your pencils down!" The hall of students erupted into whoops and cheers, but Margot dared not join in. Tomorrow was her thesis defense. Flashman tried to reassure her, "Don't stress out, they're just going to ask you what you know," but Margot's discomfort at public speaking meant that this was the test she had been dreading the most.

She hurried out of the hall and took herself for lunch at a diner a little way down Mass Ave, where she was sure of not bumping into any Harvards. Coke, grilled cheese, *Boston Globe*. The headline read: FIGHTING INTENSE IN KHAM DUC. They were calling up reservists again. A hundred thousand more draftees. There were going to be a lot of master's candidates this year.

DESPITE HER NERVES, HER tendency to wring her hands instead of leaving them quietly in her lap, a hesitant cough from smoking too much, and saying "hapless" instead of "haploid," Margot emerged from her thesis defense reasonably—well, not happy, that was not her way—but satisfied. She took a long walk along the river, watched the sculls slice through the water. It was only ten in the morning, but she was dog tired. She let the sun fall on her face, lit a cigarette.

And ran into her cousin Phyllis.

"Did you hear?"

"What?"

"Robert Kennedy is dead!" There was a note of triumph in her voice.

"That's terrible," said Margot.

"Of course it's terrible," said Phyllis in a tone suggesting otherwise. "It's yet another indication of how the country is falling apart at the seams, how radical violence is threatening the law and order of the Republic." It was a neatly worded sentence, delivered without hesitation, as if it had been repeated many times.

Margot said, "Yes, I suppose so."

"I mean you can weep and light candles as much as you want, but someone's got to get on with running the country. Don't you think?"

"I don't know what to think," said Margot. "It's shocking."

"Shocking," repeated Phyllis without feeling. "I expect everyone will get out their black armbands again."

Margot went up to her room. She lay on her bed listening to the radio. Stentorian voices intoned poignancy between the jingle-jangle of car dealership commercials. Something had changed, they said, nothing would ever be the same again and no one knew where it would all end.

34

"MARGOT, ARE YOU LISTENING TO ME?"

"Yes."

"Did you book the taxi to take me back after the ceremonies this evening?"

"Yes."

Her mother cast her opprobrium over the joyous throng in the Quad.

"Because I can already see this is going to be an absolute zoo."

Peggy had driven up for graduation with the Geralds. They were all staying with some friends of the Geralds in Back Bay. Larry had taken his parents to lunch; Harvard's graduation was tomorrow. On the Radcliffe campus Peggy was doing a good impression of being unimpressed. She complained about the line for the ladies' rooms— "as if they never expected so many people!"; about Margot's outfit— "Are you wearing trousers to deliberately provoke me?"; about the posters for the antiwar march: "'Make love, not war'! I don't know why everything has to be about sex these days."

Whitman Hall was full of expectant parents, fathers in suits, mothers in Sunday church hats, one or two older brothers in uniform. Everyone politely clapped as President Bunting shook each student's hand and presented them with a rolled diploma tied up with a ribbon. Margot was not the only girl in Radcliffe's Class of

'68 who walked up to the stage wearing trousers under her black academic gown. Shirley had tied a wreath of daisies around her mortarboard. When she got up on the stage, she put both her arms high in the air and flashed the V sign for peace. The spell of formality was broken and the students in the hall all whooped and cheered and the noise rolled and grew so that by the end, when the band started up, the trombones could hardly drown out an impromptu chorus of "Stop the war!" that a group of sophomore peaceniks had started.

Margot spotted her mother sitting at the back, close to the exit, her pearl broach pinned to the lapel of her gray suit, and holding, on her lap, her patent leather pocketbook with two hands. But then Margot lost her in the exuberance of the melee. All sorts of girls she hardly knew were hugging her and high-fiving as they flowed towards the exits in a hollering mass. Shirley caught her by the elbow, "Smoke?" Margot nodded and they ducked down the alley beside the college admin office. Shirley lit the end of a fat doobie, and the paper flared with an orange flame.

"You wore the trouser suit!"

"Yes I did!" Margot took the joint from Shirley and dragged a burning lungful of weed.

"I can't believe it's really happening."

"What's happening?" asked Margot, blinking, smoke in her eyes.

"The end . . . the beginning . . . the end of the beginning," said Shirley, twirling her fingers airily.

"I've got no idea what's happening," said Margot.

Shirley let a mouthful of smoke escape and re-inhaled it through her nose.

"Just go with the flow."

There was a great confusion as students tried to find their parents. Margot went into the dining room and found Table 26. Her mother was already there.

"Margot, there has been some mistake"—her mother flicked her eyes towards the Jeffersons.

Margot advanced with her best smile forward.

"Hello! You must be Vicky's parents!"

Just then, Vicky arrived with Cordelia, and Shirley with her parents. Everyone began to introduce themselves, and Peggy's discomfort was subsumed by the general friendliness.

"It is all very impressive," said Mrs. Jefferson, looking up at the oak beams of the vaulted roof.

"All the more impressive," said Cordelia, "when you consider it almost didn't happen."

"Yes, the proposed boycott," said Mrs. Jefferson. Her hair was styled in the same dome as Margot's mother's.

"Well, protests are all the rage, I hear," said Peggy, and everyone allowed themselves to laugh, but not too loudly. "But will someone please tell me what is being protested?"

"Just about the whole world order, it seems to me," said Mr. Jefferson. "I worry how much division it brings. I don't know how much the country can stand."

"The center cannot hold: that's what Mr. Robert Kennedy said," said Mrs. Jefferson, echoing her husband.

"I find it all very alarming," said Peggy, and everyone—to Margot's mild astonishment—nodded in agreement. She let her shoulders drop; the marijuana spread its glow.

Shirley had always derided her parents as stolid midwesterners, but Margot was sitting next to her father and found him funny and warm. He teased his daughter, "Well, I sure am impressed you managed to find time to graduate in between all your shindigs and diggin' it." He passed the peas to Peggy as graciously as a French waiter and cut through Cordelia's ice with a deft backhanded compliment, "Being British, you'll know all about class."

None of the parents had gone to college, and in this they discovered a commonality.

Shirley's father raised his glass and proposed a toast, "To such fine daughters, of whom, I am sure, we are all very proud."

Mr. Jefferson added, kindly, "And for you, Cordelia, because

I'm certain your parents are heartbroken to miss your graduation, England is so far."

"My parents have never been heartbroken about anything except the death of Walpole the Labrador," said Cordelia. The joke didn't translate; she compensated with rancor. "They simply had a better invitation." Shirley's mother's mouth made an O. "They went to stay with Graham Greene in the south of France." To which there was no response, and so Cordelia added, "The writer."

Peggy said, "I always thought his books were rather poor."

The Jeffersons and Shirley's parents started to talk about the differences of raising girls versus boys. Margot watched Peggy's mood sour as the conversation ebbed away from her. She thought about asking her if she would like some dessert, but she knew that once her mother's mood was set, nothing could sweeten it. There was a kind of freedom, Margot realized, in not being able to do anything about it. Shirley caught her eye and tilted her head towards the exit. During a gap in the speeches, Margot made a ladies' room excuse and followed her.

"What a nightmare," said Margot in the alley.

"Cordelia is a bitch on wheels," agreed Shirley.

Margot let the dope linger in her lungs. When she blew the smoke from her nostrils, something was expelled that had been clenched inside her. She felt a simultaneous lightening and a heavy breathiness.

"Better?" asked Shirley, looking at her slantwise.

Margot stretched her arms up towards the sky, trying to catch a cloud.

"Yeah."

When they got back to the dining room, the tables had broken up. Margot saw her mother marching towards the throng at Phyllis's table.

"Peggy, how very gracious of you to come and say hello." David Stern had filled out since Margot had last seen him, and was wearing a navy blue blazer and a silk tie. He made a small continental bow.

"Aren't we the proud parents?" he said, waving towards Phyllis and Margot, who were standing at arm's length.

Peggy took a step back and drew a long breath. Margot watched as the violence gathered. She touched her mother's elbow to try to guide her away but was shrugged off.

"Proud?" Peggy spat. A glob of saliva landed on David Stern's lapel, sparkling as brilliantly as the diamond on Phyllis's engagement ring. "Pride is not something to be given away to other people! Pride is something to be kept for yourself, when there is nothing else left!"

She turned to the door, the crowd parted and made way. Margot followed. Outside on the curb, Peggy took a cigarette from her cigarette case and held it up. Margot dug her Zippo out of her bag and lit it for her.

"I was right," Peggy said, blowing the smoke in Margot's face. "Four years of college and you have no husband to show for it. Even that guttersnipe cousin of yours has managed to plan her future better than you. Maybe that's a lesson she learned from her mother after all."

Margot felt a shadow of sadness and loss; she wanted to say something to commemorate the moment, something about family and coming together, about how sad it was that Sarah was not here to see her daughter graduate—

The taxi arrived. Peggy got in and Margot watched her bouffant coiffure grow smaller and smaller in the rear window as she drove away. Tomorrow was the Harvard commencement and a lunch party with the Geralds. Margot prayed for rain, for a failure that was not her own.

JAGGED ON THE PAVING stones, almost twisted her ankle crossing the street, Margot made her way back to the Quad. People were beginning to disperse from the dining room. She could hear a band playing Beatles covers; an after-party in the senior common room.

The room was smoky, fuggy, dimly lit with red and purple spotlights borrowed from the theater department, and the dance floor was already packed. Margot tripped over the lintel, drawn to the thump of the speakers that hammered in her own anger. She reached up her arms, pounding her fists in the air to the beat of "Sgt. Pepper," shouted the lyrics into the void.

The music filled her with its boom and bounce, the bass thumped in her chest.. The cadence of the minor F burred against a longing inside, the loss and emptiness she kept on the topmost shelf, high and far out of reach. As the music surged, she hugged herself by the shoulders, swaying to the despair of the chorus.

For a moment she stayed like that, arrested, gently listing to one side and then the other, almost still, almost crying. Then the lead guitarist stepped forward announcing, *a-one-two a-one-two* and the drummer crashed through a bridge to a new beat and the pure chime of a piano. Margot's toes tapped, but the idea of getting help from her friends brought the tears tumbling down. She made her way through the sea of bodies, pushing, gulping, into the corridor, stopped for a moment to catch her breath.

"There you are!" Shirley was with her friend from Lowell House.

"I put my mother in a cab."

"So you're free!"

"Come with us!"

"Where?"

Margot followed them across the Quad into the music school. A bunch of seniors had commandeered one of the soundproofed practice rooms and stuffed it with cushions and beanbags. A couple of guys were strumming guitars, a lit major Margot only knew by sight shook her tambourine. Vicky, sitting cross-legged with a bottle of beer, waved hi! There was no window and the air was thick with marijuana smoke. Margot hesitated, Shirley took her by one hand and the Lowell guy by the other.

"Hey girl, it's mellow," said the Lowell guy.

Vicky held out a bottle of beer. "You want one?"

"Yeah," said Margot, sitting down beside her, "thanks."

"Wow," said Vicky, "your mother is a piece of work."

"I know," said Margot. But in an odd way, until Vicky said it, she didn't. "I don't think anyone has ever said that to me. It's actually kind of cool, it's like a confirmation."

"I bet you always thought it was your fault. That she was angry because you did something wrong."

"Yeah."

"When someone is mean to you, it's usually because they hate themselves."

"Did you get that in sociology class?"

Vicky laughed. "I think I might have."

Margot drank the beer, downed a shot of tequila and then another, took the proffered roach, hot and friable, between her thumb and her index finger, drew down to inhale, held the smoke in her lungs for a whole swilling minute, passed the joint to the left. A couple of people danced in a corner, the Lowell guy borrowed a guitar and started singing silly lyrics over old Bing Crosby tunes. "I'm dreaming of a ham sandwich—"

Flashman showed up after midnight. "Margot! Vicky! There you are! I've been looking for you everywhere! I'm under orders to bring you back to the Zoo for a last blast."

"I'm down for the count," said Vicky, signaling surrender. "My parents want to get on the road at some crazy-early hour."

"I'm sleepy. I want to sleep," said Margot, even as she let Flashman pull her up from the floor. After all, it was graduation, a night to say yes, not no—

The DPhils had invited some of the Meselson group, Dr. Fred had sprung for a keg, and Adam had tacked up rainbow party decorations. The Doors were playing spaced-out doom on a record player. A girl wearing an orange dress was slumped on the floor in the corner by the narwhal tusk.

"Is she OK?" Margot asked.

"Ludes and Jack," said Flashman, rolling his eyes.

"OK, what do we need here?" Dr. Fred asked Margot.

"Cup of coffee, please," said Margot.

Dr. Fred took her by the hand and led her to a Perspex sample divider box and lifted the lid. "We got shrooms, we got weed, some very interesting medical-grade speed . . ."

Her whole life Margot had been sensible. *Fuck it.*

"I want to go up," she told him, miming an airplane taking off. "And away!"

"Aha! You want to go on a trip?"

Margot did not quite understand, but his hand felt warm on the small of her back and it had been such a long haul of weeks of working and worrying and tonight was unfolding like a strange adventure. Margot thought she might as well follow the yellow brick road. *Go with the flow.*

"Yes, I want to go somewhere different."

"Delysid," prescribed Dr. Fred, "just a tiny tad," and he unwrapped a brown paper twist of powder and tapped a few grains into her palm. "Lick it," he told her.

Margot heard Flashman say, "Hey man, are you sure?" but by the time she started to wonder what he was talking about, the powder had already dissolved on her tongue.

At first nothing happened and Margot, insulated by the warm buzz of alcohol and dope, felt quietly gratified that she was handling her first real drugs so well. The Meselson guys were dancing with a couple of student nurses, their arms made wavy tendrils like seaweed in the tide. Thomas Cleverly introduced her to his girlfriend, who had candy floss lipstick and wide black pupils that seemed to grow wider and wider.

"Y'all talk in code," she said with a southern drawl.

"The code of life, man, the code of life."

"Ew, what the heck are those!"—she pointed to an aquarium strewn with twigs and leaves.

"Those are Adam's guests," said Dr. Fred.

"Having no humanoid friends," explained Thomas Cleverly, "he has brought his stick insects."

"They're nocturnal," explained Adam.

They all peered into the aquarium.

"How many can you see?"

"One!"

"No, there's another one!"

"Is the same one!"

"Not that one!"

"Look, there's one behind the curtain!" said Margot.

"No, that's a hallucination."

"It's winking at me."

Thomas Cleverly kept pointing to the same twig insisting that it had moved a back leg.

Adam kept trying to tell him, "No, that's Esmeralda!"

"Which one?"

"You can tell by her eyes."

"I found another one!"

"Oh yes, that's de Gaulle."

"Of course! I can tell by his kepi."

"He likes to hang out with Princess Margaret."

"With me! That's me!"

"Yes, the Princess Margot of the Chromosomes, that's you!"

Margot lay on the floor laughing, looked up at the ceiling cracks swirling into a map of the universe that showed everything blissfully and obviously connected. We me Esmeralda and every eukaryote. The floor was floppy and her body was nothing but gauze. Time sloped off somewhere. Margot held out her arms into the great and mystifying void, comforted by the absence of past and future; all was perfect just here, where the candy floss blossomed into a beautiful peony.

When she looked up, everything was awash in hues of green and blue, striped with paintbrush strokes into horizontal planes; horizons intersected and ran into parallel lines—or was it perpendicular?—and fell down stairs, against tessellations of brick and into the sideways beams of headlights. Stars skidded above. He held her hand and they flowed along with the flow. Everything was tangled and simultaneously everything was resolved. There is no single origin or a single answer, we must multiply into myriad. Margot opened her arms to embrace the rushing possible, opened the door that was not her fault, into a space of Mad-ness and shamelessness, crawled back to the origins of life and catapulted forward into the lightning ecstasy to make a new beginning.

35

Woke to a red world and a throbbing head. Her brain ticked very slow. It took several extendable moments for Margot to realize that she was in her own bed in her own room, but also, disconcertingly, that the weight on her chest was a man's arm. Her eyelids were stuck fast with sleepy dust, she had to rub them to open them and it was quite complicated to send a message to her hand to move upwards to her face to do this. Her mouth was dry and could not talk and her head raged and could not think. When she opened her eyes, the sun shone directly into them like a laser beam. Which didn't make any sense, because mornings on this side of the Quad were usually dark—

Her eyes opened blearily and she saw by the dial of the alarm clock on her bedside table that it was already past noon. Saw that the arm belonged to Dr. Fred, who was lying there naked, hair spread out on the pillow in a halo, perfectly asleep.

Margot levered his heavy arm away. Dr. Fred shuffled his hand under his cherub chin, mumbled, did not wake. She knew—by the cold, sticky patch on the sheet, by the razor burn on her top lip and the achiness between her legs, but she did not exactly remember. And there were several more pressing concerns: her heaving head, her heaving stomach, and the fact that Harvard commencement had already commenced—she looked at her watch—an hour ago. If she hurried, she might make it in time for the speeches.

She showered, brushed her teeth, washed her face. When she looked in the mirror, her face looked jagged and she couldn't connect the kohl pencil to her eyelid. Margot realized she was still tripping. Her vision was sparkly and her thoughts traveled in lightning strikes of panic above a waiting lake of powerful dread. There were purple circles under her eyes. Her fingers felt inside the pocket of her vanity case for a stick of concealer, and found instead the empty packet of Pills she had stopped taking when they had run out and had been too exam-busy to ask Richie for more. Beside them was the little brown bottle of Valium, left over from when she had stitches in her forehead. She felt the ragged edge of panic; the Valium would bring her down. She swallowed the blue tablet with a gulp of water.

Margot dressed in her plain navy dress and put on her good pumps. Ran down the stairs. Outside it was pouring rain. She had to run back upstairs to fetch a raincoat and an umbrella. The gutters were streams and there was a great pond at the intersection by the church; passing cars threw up sheets of water. By the time she got to Harvard Yard, her feet were sopping wet and rivulets that ran from her umbrella had drenched through the shoulders of her raincoat.

There was no one in the Yard. It was the wrong day. It was Tuesday. It was Wednesday. Her watch had stopped. It was not afternoon, it was morning—

"You looking for the Class Day speeches?" an old porter asked.

"Yes!"

"They've moved them to Sanders Theatre on account of the rain."

Margot turned in the direction of Sanders. She was late, but as she jogged across the muddy verges, she heard the clock strike the quarter hour, maybe not too late, these things never began on time. As she approached the imposing redbrick building, she saw a large mass of people sheltering under the colonnaded entrance, evidently there wasn't enough space inside. Margot realized she would never find her mother and the Geralds in the crush. Better to make up some excuse about the rain and confusion of venue and catch up with them afterwards.

The zoology department was just across the road and she ducked into the entrance hall to get out of the rain. Nausea sloshed in the pit of her stomach. She ran upstairs to the bathroom and knelt in front of the toilet bowl.

Her stomach retched a thin foam. There was a crack in the porcelain and she looked at it for a long while trying to find meaning in it, was bending her neck to follow the thin line upwards when it moved slightly. Margot thought she was still hallucinating, but no, it was a spider, sheltering under the rim. The obvious thing to do was to flush it away, but she felt too tender to harm a living thing. A tear spilled over and splashed into the white hole. She scrunched up toilet tissue to fashion a bridge for the spider to climb out of his cave and unlocked the stall. Maybe she could hide under the toilet rim too.

Who was she to deny the imperative of sex, of drugs, of rock-a-bye-baby, production, reproduction? Syllables caught on her sobs. Some voice deep inside, not hers, not her mother's, not anyone's she recognized, said: *This is life*. All this time she had been peering at its molecular constructions instead of living it. *It hurts*, said the voice, *this living business*. The body, Margot reflected, knew very well how to regulate these tribulations. It cried tears to salve, deployed leukocytes to fight infection; when skin was torn, it copied skin cells to rebuild it; once a month her womb thickened and waited for an embryo, and then flushed itself clean and began another cycle. And as she realized this, panic seized her again and she began to count, climbing backwards through the days—to remember when she had had her last period—

Without really meaning to, muscle memory, her feet walked towards the Zoo. The door was ajar and inside Flashman was picking up empty bottles and putting them in a black garbage bag.

"Hey there." The bottles clinked loudly in the sack.

"Hey."

"You OK?"

"My head feels weird."

"I should have stopped him—"

"I'm sorry."

"Don't apologize, Margot, you're always doing that."

"I know."

"I mean, it's your business who you go to bed with."

"What are you doing?"

"Cleaning up."

"Do you want some help?"

"Aren't you supposed to be at the graduation thing?"

"I was late, I couldn't get in."

Margot sat down and looked at the detritus around her, by day-light the pink smear on the bench was not a blooming peony but an icky piece of bubblegum.

"I'm a bit freaked out," she said.

"We've just graduated, I'd say that's a pretty normal reaction."

Flashman wiped down the bench and took up the garbage sack in one hand and his book bag in the other. "Do you want to grab a bite?"

"I have to find my mother—"

"Blow her off." Flashman looked up at her from under his curly bangs.

"I can't. I—"

"Well, this is it then. I'm off day after tomorrow."

"You too?"

"Imperial College London."

"Congratulations."

"Thanks."

Flashman stood for a moment, encumbered by a bag in each hand, looking as if he might put them down and hug her, but Margot walked out ahead of him.

"Oh by the way, in case you forget," he said as she turned towards the stairwell, "there's still that personal sample of yours in the deep freeze in the cryo room. Everything not claimed by next Wednesday is going to get tossed."

She watched Flashman disappear down the stairs, and she would have liked to go with him but she didn't. Trust herself.

She recalled with a stab of acuity that for a moment when Trip was inside her, she had shifted to accommodate him. He had smiled down at her then and said, "That's my girl," and she had almost wanted to believe that she *was* his girl, and everything had turned out happily ever after after all.

The linoleum on the floor of the corridor was blue. Margot sat down all at sea, her thoughts churning a foaming wake. *O still, small voice of calm*, a line from her favorite hymn, came to her, even as another pharmaceutical bout of nausea swept over her. Oh God. She tried to pray but it felt absurd. If anything, she should be punished from on high, not redeemed. The linoleum was soft and cool under her bare legs. The only thing she could think to do was to try to stop thinking.

Margot rose from the floor suspended by the merest filament of consciousness, went to the cryo room and pulled out three drawers before she found the small plastic vial with her name written in white chinagraph pencil along the side. She used tongs to remove it from the frigid sleeve. Wrapped it in a handkerchief and put it in her pocket. The vial froze the fabric of her dress stiff and burned her thigh. The cold radiated a searing spot of guilt, of revenge, of penitence and contrition, of exoneration too and maybe even absolution.

Outside it had stopped raining but fat wet drops dripped from the trees. The crowd under the portico of Sanders Theatre were standing around a small speaker set up on a table, listening to the broadcast hopes and fears expressed in Coretta Scott King's determined and articulate address. Presently came the rushing noise of applause and the mass egress of a large body of parents, faculty, and graduates, the hand-in-hand promise of the well-to-do and the to-do-well.

Sanders Theatre had two exits, neither in view of each other, and Margot knew she was sure to choose the wrong one and miss her mother and the Geralds. They had planned to have lunch at the house of one of Larry Gerald's ancient Greek professors, who was hosting a small barbecue for his favorite students. Margot and her mother had been invited as extras.

She turned into Franklin Avenue and up ahead, standing on the sidewalk, waiting—she would know that toe-tapping impatience anywhere—was her mother, wearing a pale blue suit, and Mrs. Gerald. Peggy caught sight of Margot and thrust her arm in the air as if she were hailing a cab.

MARGOT MANAGED TO BALANCE her out-of-bodyness with her out-of-her-mindness, a paper picnic plate sloping dangerously under the weight of a slippery hamburger, a lake of relish, a plastic glass of punch, and not just Larry—"Hey Marg, heavy night, huh?"—who was boring but perfectly affable, but also the surprise of being confronted with Chip Reid and his wife and, inevitably, the chronic Cordelia Chatsworth, who was dressed in a military jacket over a pink Biba skirt and looked like she'd stepped off the cover of *Vogue*.

"Oh hullo," she said to Margot.

"Oh hullo," Margot echoed. A hand appeared from behind Cordelia's back and a small man emerged.

"I'm Magnus," said the man, friendly. "I think we've met."

Margot did not remember, made an awkward smile and raised her elbows in apology to show her hands were occupied with food and drink.

"Here, let me take that for you," said Magnus, relieving her of her punch cup.

She was glad to shake his hand and keep hold of it for an extra second or two for stability. Her heels tottered on the flagstone patio.

"That hamburger seems to be rather heavy for you," he said kindly. "Would you like to sit down?"

There were a couple of tables set up in the clearing under a big Douglas fir at the edge of the garden. Margot walked, watching her feet step over the uneven ground, didn't want to trip on a pinecone. Sat down, Magnus opposite her, and saw, walking across the lawn, a familiar figure. His hair was shorter, he was dressed in a suit, with one arm pinned, but there he was. Sandyful.

"I heard you were going to be here," he said.

"Well," said Magnus, magnanimously, politely backing away, "I'll leave you two."

Margot marveled. "Ours is not to reason why."

"Tennyson," said Sandy.

"You're a poet, I know."

Sandy launched into a complicated explanation of logistics—from Providence, through a rainstorm, a delayed meeting with Coretta King, waiting for the big march tomorrow, a hotel room at the Charles and bumping into his uncle in the bar—Margot nodded dumbly.

"I'm boring you."

"No you're not. I'm tired, that's all. It's been—"

She looked into his face. The light under the trees was green, the thunderheads above glowered against the rosy blush along his cheekbones. His blue eyes looked so directly at her that it made her dizzy and she had to look away.

"Are you OK?"

She told him she had been up late, drunk too much, overslept, the stress of exams, of course the whole awful Bobby Kennedy thing, she felt just terrible she had missed Mrs. King speak, how was it?

"Everyone seems to be depending on my generation," she said, "as if we're supposed to right the wrongs of every age. It's probably all written on our chromosomes in any case, everything neatly plotted out, traits and illnesses and death foretold just like ancient Greek oracles. Are we like our parents? Or are we completely different, I mean isn't rebelling just the opposite of the same thing, it's not creating, it's just reacting. And what next? What next? I am every graduate cliché!"

Sandyful smiled, stilled her trembling hand, took the lighter from it and lit her cigarette.

"Am I foaming at the mouth?" Margot put her hand to her face to cover it.

"A bit."

"I don't know why you're smiling," said Margot, drawing the smoke into her lungs like a breath of fresh air.

"Maybe I am just happy to see you."

It began to rain in earnest. Sandy took off his jacket and held it above her head. The hired chef labored on, smoke rising from his grill. Everyone hurried inside, carrying their plates.

Sandy and Margot turned into the library. Sandy stood in front of the wall of books, angling his head to read the spines.

"Ah, here we are," he said, pulling out a thin blue volume of Sappho, opening it and running his finger through the index to find what he was looking for. *"You asked me what I suffered, who was the cause of my anguish, what would ease the pain of my frantic mind."*

"You once told me that there was nothing in our lives or our world that the ancient Greeks had not already contemplated."

"Did I?"

"Yes, the night we first met, at that New Year's party."

"Yes, you up and left with your childhood sweetheart."

"He's not my—he's nothing."

"Really? Because the way you were dancing with him at the lobster place at this New Year's certainly looked like something."

"I drank too much that night, I shouldn't have let him—" Margot stopped herself. "He was only trying to make Lydia jealous."

"Well, it made me jealous," Sandy said.

"I know. I saw. I'm sorry. I regret. I mean—"

"What do you mean?" Sandy looked at her squarely.

Margot took a deep breath, she was too tired to dissemble.

"I didn't want to dance with him. I wanted to dance with you. I wanted to kiss you—ever since we kissed in the library I wanted to kiss you again. But you disappeared, you keep disappearing—"

He might have kissed her then; he wanted to. But the door creaked and Peggy appeared on the threshold.

"I've got a terrible headache. I'm going back, I need to lie down with two Bufferin."

"Mama, this is Sandy Full, Larry Gerald's cousin."

Peggy ignored Sandy's extended hand. "Margot, you'll have to drive me in the Geralds' car and then return with it."

"Maybe I can call you a taxi," said Sandy helpfully.

"It's graduation day, there won't be a cab for love or money."

"Let me drive you then," said Sandy.

Peggy nodded her assent. "Let's go through the garden. I don't want to deal with the theatrics of goodbye."

By the curb, Sandy opened the passenger door.

"Isn't your mother the one that ran off with the chauffeur's son?" said Peggy, getting in.

"My father," said Sandy.

"I always wondered what became of her."

"They're still happily married."

"Well, it just goes to show: parents don't always know best."

In the backseat Margot rolled her eyes; Sandy winked at her in the rearview mirror.

"I should have ignored my father and married Clarence. Then none of this would have happened."

"But you wouldn't have had me," said Margot.

"That's true; clearly that man only produces sons," said Peggy. "All of them, in my opinion, second-raters."

"I always thought you liked Trip," said Margot.

There was a long pause, akin to a sigh. "Trip Merryweather," said Peggy, "is not his father."

Sandy found the address in Back Bay without difficulty. He got out and went around to the passenger side, where Peggy was waiting for him to open the door for her. Margot stood on the sidewalk, arms by her sides.

"Goodbye, Mama."

"People keep telling me I should be very proud of you," said Peggy, then walked up the steps and rang the bell for the maid to let her in.

Sandy came up behind Margot and put his one arm around her waist.

"Let's get out of here."

IN A DREAM SANDY drove them back to Cambridge. In a dream, they sat together in the bar of the Charles Hotel sipping whiskey sours. When Margot announced she was suddenly ravenous, Sandy miraculously found a table at the fancy booked-for-months-on-graduation-weekend restaurant. Margot felt very grown-up. Sandy ordered a bottle of red wine. It tasted like velvet. They ate steak and baked potatoes. Chocolate ice cream for dessert. Brandy on the ter-race, Mr. and Mrs. Full?

"Yes we are," said Sandy.

"Very full," said Margot.

They talked about everything and nothing and the spaces in between. Mad and Shirley, Miss Wall, the Berlin Wall, divid-ing cells, VC cells, the beauty and treachery of the jungle. Sandy described long night marches numb and exhausted, seeing crazy things in the darkness. There wasn't anything he couldn't do with only one arm, he told her, "except hold a rifle, ironically."

He made a small laugh, more relief than regret. "But at the same time it feels like everything I have done since is the result of—*it*."

Something in Margot unlocked to hear Sandy had an unname-able "it" too.

"I went into army intelligence because I thought it would be interesting. But you soon realize you know things you never wanted to know. Training drills obedience into you. But your real self, the part of you that gets scared on patrol, that wants to stop and help some poor Viet family struggling on the road—"

"The part of you your father told you to keep," said Margot, "by looking up at the stars—"

"For a while I kept shuffling files, pretending it was normal—South Vietnamese intel reports, rubber-stamped detentions, death sentences, Jesus, the photographs—"

Sandy stopped, didn't let go of Margot's hand, started again. "There's the physical side of the before and after my injury. I am still adapting, I think, I'm trying to—but it's hard to sleep sometimes, I have weird two-armed dreams and then I wake up with an aching phantom limb."

"It's trauma," said Margot. "An injury is sometimes visible, sometimes not."

Time would heal, but there would always be a scar. Mad, Hal, Richie trying to help Hal. She thought of her mother, battling the world all alone, trying to be a good daughter for a dead father. She thought of her own burrowing withdrawal, the pain that was too painful to think about, that lingered like the sharpness of a bruise. The things that happened to people made people who they were as much as they were written in genetic code.

"Yes," said Sandy. "There was a doctor in the VA hospital who had some fancy military-grade acronym for it—he told me my flesh wound would heal fine, but that my brain would take a little longer. I didn't really understand what he meant."

Sandy looked into her eyes. Midnight behind the light. "It feels good to talk to you," he said.

Margot reached up and brushed a strand of his hair at his temple, pressed her palm against his forehead, and Sandy pressed his forehead back into the cup of her hand.

He kissed her in the elevator. In his room Margot stood in front of him, unzipped her dress and let it fall to the floor. She stepped forward and took off his jacket, unbuttoned his shirt, roamed her hands across the scarred nub of his shoulder.

They made love slowly, then faster, finding the slippy rhythm easily. Margot gave herself up to flashing flushes of heat and sensation. She lay beneath him, feeling the heft of his body, inhaling his tannic funk, and squirmed like a cat in the closeness.

"You OK?" Sandy asked.

"Yeah," said Margot, and then pulled him over so that she was on top, rocking, looking down on him. Sandy smiled at her and put his hand behind his head, gently kidding, as if he was lying back on a beach enjoying the sun. Then he sat up, so they were even, level. The new angle pushed him further inside her, and Margot had no idea how loud she cried, as deep and wondrous as oceans.

DAWNING, PEWTER LIGHT, STILL cloudy. Margot was not yet awake, but she could hear Sandy up and moving around the room and felt him sit on the mattress beside her. She fluttered her eyelids, loosely unfocused. His face looked somber in the gray daylight. She heard him say, ". . . that girl I told you about—I'm supposed to marry her . . ." Bliss turned to static hiss. Margot watched him put on his overcoat. She didn't say anything because it was still a dream and in dreams anything could happen next. Perhaps he would not go.

He went. She had not heard the second half of his sentence: "I'm going to call it off. Stay here. I'll come back." Maybe Margot heard it and thought she had dreamed it. Maybe she heard it but didn't believe it. Maybe it was easier to accept that Sandy had vanished again, as he had before, because it was easier to believe that he would leave than to believe he would come back, that he loved her, that she was lovable. Hoping was only a kind of imagining. She was only Margot after all, underserving, not-allowed, not-good-enough. She had felt it inside herself from the moment of her fall. The fall was her fate; she would never quite get what she reached for. There would always be a snag, a trip, an unlucky gust of wind. She would always be the girl who missed the egg, the point, the ball; her princes would turn into frogs.

Margot heard the heavy click of the door, fell back into the reddish space behind her closed eyes, into oblivion.

When she woke up properly, it was still too early and already too late. She felt heavy and spaced out, her head crunched from the wine, her mouth was an alkaline desert, and between her probing fingers she was swollen and sore. His going canceled his coming and the being and the being held in his arms. Her mind raced to the passion and braked sharply, too late to stop it from going over the cliff.

It was as if Sandy had never been there and this banal beige room was the continuation of a drug fugue that seemed to have been dragging down her right mind for days. Hungover, appalled: she knelt before the altar of the toilet in a different bathroom flushing shame just the same. White tile daggered light. She closed her eyes. Ran the shower. Washed herself thoroughly with soap and water. Brushed her teeth and watched her blood mingle in the sink with the white spat-out paste. Held his toothbrush up to the mirror as an evidentiary article of self-disgust.

She said the word "slut" out loud, unafraid to take its punishment.

Dressed mechanically. Pulled the collar of her raincoat up. Stood stock-still for a moment, an ice cube. Put her hands in her pockets and found the small plastic vial there.

Funny how you can freeze something and thaw it out and it is still alive. Germline cells, spiraled links in a chain that never forgot . . . the humiliation of Marvin, the Trip thing, her own complicity in the Trip thing, hadn't she always wanted . . . the mortification of Dr. Fred. It was all unfair and wrong and stupid, and yet she had repeated the same mistake over and over. She shivered with a premonition. Because if it was the right time of the month for Dr. Fred, then it could just as easily be Sandy's. An evil inkling occurred to her. Recombinant DNA.

Turkey baster.

Cunt.

Slut.

And in an instant of scientifically calibrated contempt, she swiped her forefinger through the opaque jelly in the vial and inside herself.

36

MARGOT WENT BACK TO HER ROOM AND LOCKED THE door and slept dead. Woke the next day, got dressed and presented herself in front of the master's panel for her interview. Seven professors sat behind the dais, their faces dark moons shadowed by the windows behind them. Margot sat on a narrow chair with a black vinyl seat. She looked down at her fingernails and answered their questions about the future of microbiology and her work on triple X chromosomes as best she could, which was mechanically, in a state of almost catatonic self-loathing.

That evening she heard Richie calling her name outside her door, stuffed her head under the pillow, couldn't face his pity. She crumpled up the note he put under the door and threw it in the trash without reading it.

Afterwards she went to the 7-Eleven and bought enough potato chips, Kraft Singles, and peanut butter for a siege. She locked her door, sat on her bed with her headphones, read and read and read. She ignored the knocking and the banging and the hollering in the corridor, everyone packing up and leaving for the summer. After two days, when it was quieter, she went out to the Coop and bought *Jules et Jim* and read it in one long night. The next day she went back and bought *Anna Karenina*, hoping it would hold her for a long time. She finished it in two days, driven on by foreboding. She remembered Cordelia's parents visiting Graham Greene and read *The End of the Affair*; love blown up by a bomb. *For Whom the Bell Tolls*, another bomb. Carson McCullers, Colette. She skipped over the shelves of Jane Austen, couldn't bear the happy ending. *Bonjour Tristesse*. She wanted to pile on the pain so thick that it would form a crust that would crack and break the fever.

SHE KNEW SHE HAD failed to get into the master's program even before she saw the list.

Margot had fully absorbed not-good-enough as her mantra, burring burning intimate, no voice in her head dared contradict it. She dug the trench of her failures deep enough that she could not see the sky. All her A's were dismissed as mere regurgitations of fact; studying hard was nothing to be proud of. College was supposed to be the best time of your life and she had wasted it. She now remembered the triumph of the XXX twins as a fluke.

One night she dreamed that she had failed to graduate because she had forgotten to complete an auxiliary requirement. Her subconscious was so convincing that when she woke it took Margot several minutes to remember that she had indeed submitted the paper and that her dream was a lie.

She took her diploma out of its leatherette case and held it up to the light. Yes, that was her name next to the date and the official stamp of RADCLIFFE. She was not fooled by her achievement, but still, there it was: irrefutable in black and white. Flotsam from the wreck. Somewhere in the world there would be a lab that needed an assistant. Margot bent her neck over the document in the same leaning-over-arc gesture she used to look down a microscope. Something of the swan. Did she smile?

The next day she went to the Pan Am booking office downtown. She thought of Mad staring at the departures board and choosing Marrakech. Morocco, she dismissed as too exotic, too hot. Toronto? Too close. Paris? Too French.

London. Green parks, gray skies, black railings. An image of Rosalind Franklin at work in a basement lab at King's College came to her mind. Her shoulders were a little hunched as if she was concentrating her whole energy, her whole being, looking down into the lens. There was something inward in her posture that comforted Margot, and yet there was something futuristic about the picture too (where had she seen it? *Life* magazine?), as if the microscope were a bionic extension of herself.

London was far enough that she could not afford a return ticket. "One way," she affirmed to the man who copied out her name and a series of very long numbers onto a triplicate carbon copy ticket. She somehow imagined that the shock of the unknown would provide the balm of a new beginning. She wanted to arrive incredulous on a new shore. Sandy had taught her that knowledge was pain, and the pain made her want to unknow everything and everyone she'd ever known. She did not know that Sandy had been turned away from the Quad entrance by the porter; or that he had tried to call a dozen times and never got through to the switchboard, which had switched to summer hours. She did not know he gave a note to Larry Gerald, who forgot to deliver it, and sent letters that piled up in the admin office for several months afterwards in a basket marked "no forwarding address."

When she boarded the plane to London, Margot did not know that she was three weeks pregnant.

ACKNOWLEDGMENTS

THANK YOU FIRSTLY TO BILL CLEGG, WHO PUSHED ME through six, seven, eight or more drafts with kindness, patience, and perfectly pitched comments; a better reader no writer ever had. Thank you to Matt Weiland, champion, friend. Thank you, Mum, backstop, cheerleader, archivist. Thank you to my friends, of whom I am lucky enough to have many, for hugs and phone calls and bottles of wine, for listening and encouraging and reading and being there: Julia Hobsbawn, Anna Seassau, Nina Planck, Merryn Somerset Webb, Hedgecoes plural, Dominique Fell-Clarke, Toby and Caroline Young, Vaughn Smith and everyone at the Frontline Club, Sean Langan, Helena Boas, Michael Goldfarb, Justin Davies, Janine di Giovanni, Nina Burleigh, Kim Ghattas, Deb Amos, Eugene Linden, Euan Rellie, Thomas Dworzak, Adrien Jaulmes, Guillaume Bonn, Jon Lee Anderson, Steve Coll, Alison McAdam and Simon Rodberg, Stephen Hargreaves, Lucas and Laurence and Clea Menget, Rupert Shrive, Peter and Kristin Becker, Rett Wallace, Stephanie Saldaña, Natalie Azoulai, Rachel Donadio. Et merci aussi à la communauté si accueillante de Locquirec: Gaëlle et Yann Cholet, Kat et Thibault et Axel, Corio et Elo, Edith Le Brun, Harold van Lier, Virginie et Thierry, Jeff et Cristel, Patrick Tellec, Nicholas Kahn and Sarah Faulkner, Clothilde et Joachim et les Bonnets Rouges. I would also like to say a special thank-you to the baristas who have let me write (at some length) in their café-sanctuaries: Fred at Café Tabac in Montmartre, Yvan et Catherine at Chez Tilly in Locquirec, and the Café Veronika in Lviv, which continued to serve the greatest croissants in the world through the air raid sirens and the war.

ABOUT THE AUTHOR

Wendell Steavenson is a novelist and reporter who has lived in and reported from post-Soviet Georgia, Iran, Iraq, Lebanon, Egypt, and Ukraine. The recipient of a 2021 Guggenheim fellowship and a 2014 Nieman fellowship, she is the author of *Paris Metro*, a novel, as well as three books of reporting: *Stories I Stole*, about post-Soviet Georgia; *The Weight of the Mustard Seed*, about life in Saddam Hussein's Iraq; and *Circling the Square*, about the Egyptian Revolution. Her writing has appeared in *The New Yorker*, the *Guardian*, *Granta*, the *Economist*, the *Financial Times*, and other publications. Born in New York and raised in London, she now lives in Brittany, France.